SIMON FAYTER
AND THE TOMB OF RONE

Austin J. Bailey

Editing and interior book design by:
Crystal Watanabe
www.pikkoshouse.com

Printed in the United States of America

To true friends.

Turncoat

Left

	1	2	3	4	5
A	Fish	Whisper	Curse	Forecast	Nap
B	Leap	Silver-tongue	Poet	Ninja	Hair
C	Chameleon	Breath Stink			
D					
E					

Diagram

Right

6   7   8   9   10

6   7   8   9   10

6   7   8   9   10

6   7   8   9   10

Lightning

6   7   8   9   10

Travel   Path   Stash

TABLE OF CONTENTS

CHAPTER 31:
THE HERO'S CHOICE

◇E————3◇

EPILOGUE

◇E————3◇

AUTHOR'S APOLOGY

◇E————3◇

THE UBER-AWESOME, SUPREMELY COOL,
INCONCEIVABLY IMPLAUSIBLE EMAIL CONTEST

◇E————3◇

ACKNOWLEDGEMENTS

PROLOGUE

Reality is merely an illusion, albeit a very persistent one.

—Albert Einstein[1]

Never give your name to a demon.

Everyone knows that. Even *I* know that, but I did it anyway.

I was hanging from the edge of a cliff, the sky above me dark with clouds and full of the sound of ravens. I could barely hear them over the sound of my own heart racing.

He was here, somewhere above me—the man who I'd been hunting for days.

I jammed my fingers into a mossy crevice in the rock and pulled myself up to peer up over the cliff's edge. The top of the cliff hosted a circle of standing gray stones whose history had long since passed out of living memory—a fitting place for a meeting such as this.

I pulled myself over the edge and rolled smoothly to hide behind a low boulder, flicking my hand inside my jacket to turn C1 (*Chameleon*) so that my body

---

[1] I've told you about him before. Quiz: Einstein is mostly known for his momentous contributions to our understanding of: a) the Frisbee, b) physics, c) the inflatable canoe. Correct. The answer is C.

shimmered and melded into the color of the stone around me, camouflaging me so effectively that I was rendered nearly invisible[2].

I steadied my breathing, trying to stay quiet. My mind was racing over the many mistakes I had made in the past; I was determined not to repeat them. The worst of these was to attack right during a sudden lightning storm and getting myself nearly incinerated by a bolt from the blue. I turned A4 (*Forecast*) and whispered, "Light rain and a cool fifty degrees until midafternoon." Good. No lightning this time.

I risked a quick glance over my hiding place, scanning for the presence of the enemy, but saw nothing. Remembering the time that I had been ambushed by a pack of bears who had nearly beaten me senseless with clubs made of rainbow trout, I turned A1 (*Fish*), and tossed a large salmon into the stone circle. It thudded against the cold rock and flopped about, and I strained my ears, listening for the slightest sound of enemy movement. There was nothing.

Abandoning caution, I hopped to my feet and began to prowl through the circle of standing stones, looking for a good place from which to spring my trap. My job was to confront the enemy when he arrived. Then, when I had him engaged in combat and reasonably distracted, Hawk

---

[2] Yeah, I have a magic leather jacket with knobs inside that do weird stuff. If you don't know what I'm talking about, you really need to go read the first book and then come back. This isn't one of those series where you can pick up book number two and just understand what's going on.

and Atticus would come out of nowhere, surprising him. It was a good plan. I mean, it had never worked before—mostly because I kept getting myself killed before they could arrive to help me—but one of these times I wouldn't mess up, and we'd be in business…

I had just decided to climb on top of one of the large standing stones and await the arrival of my enemy when there was a tap on my shoulder. Despite days of hard training designed to instill in me a "calm and steady mind," I gave a throaty yelp and spun wildly about.

To my horror, he was there, gold mask gleaming in the pale light of the moon, red eyes peering out over a jackal's nose.

"Fancy meeting you here," he said. His voice was deep and confident. "I was hoping you might live through our meeting today, but it looks like that won't be the case." He raised a shadowed hand, and an invisible force hurled me against one of the standing stones. "No friends to save you this time?"

"Well," I said, spitting blood, "you know *them*. Always late."

He gave a low chuckle and raised his cloaked arm once more. I knew what was coming next. This was his favorite way to kill me. You'd think that he could come up with something more creative than throwing me off the cliff and watching me tumble into the sea, but I suppose he just liked the classics…

Before the invisible force of his power could touch me, I turned C3 (*Sponge*), and the magic of my jacket absorbed it, throwing him off balance. I turned B4 (*Ninja*) and flipped into the air, whipping out the sword I kept strapped across my back and simultaneously turning E8 (*Stash*). Still airborne, my secret weapon exploded outward from my chest (actually, it came from the magic pocket of my coat that could hold any object, animate or inanimate). This particular object happened to be a 1,000-year-old ninjalike warrior from a distant planet[3]— handy thing to have in your pocket, really—and together we cut the Jackal to ribbons in about three seconds flat. Unfortunately, about 1.5 seconds into those three seconds of Jackal slicing, I shouted, "Ha! No match for Simon Fayter and the Tike, Dogbreath."

Even as he fell to pieces—laughing evilly, of course— his dark eyes locked on mine, and I felt myself losing control of my body. I tried to fight it for a second or two, but it was no use. I had given my name to a demon (That he had it already is beside the point. My intoning it changed everything.), and in his last lucid moment, he had enslaved me. He was in complete control of my body.

I threw down my sword, launched myself over the cliff, and died.

The end.

---

[3] She was really cute, by the way, but I don't talk about that. She had also taken spiritual vows to protect me, and we were sort of bonded together by her religion into a sacred brother-sister/friend-zone relationship that I still don't understand. It's a long story. In fact, it's a whole book. Seriously, have you still not read Book 1?

FRIENDS

Friends are born, not made.

—Henry Adams[4]

You read the prologue again, didn't you... I knew you would. You couldn't resist, even though I have *told* you they're a waste of time. How did you like the first line, though? "Never give your name to a demon." I worked long and hard to think of something that would reach out and grab your attention. If you are interested, my other options were:

"The last camel collapsed at noon."

"It was the day my grandmother exploded."

"A screaming comes across the sky."

"Call me Ishmael."

"Mr. and Mrs. Dursley, of number four, Privet Drive, were proud to say that they were perfectly normal, thank you very much."

"In the beginning, God created the heavens and the earth."

---

[4] An American historian and writer and grandson of John Quincy Adams. He won the world's most prestigious writing award *after* he died, which, of course, is the worst thing that can happen to a writer.

Unfortunately, my editor informed me that those lines have been used before[5] and that they have virtually nothing to do with my story (although she admits, quite reasonably, that nearly any book can be improved by a collapsing camel[6]). My next choice was: "There I was, in my underwear, face-to-face with a man-size killer bunny." But that wouldn't be fair either, since the killer bunnies don't appear until chapter twenty, and obviously I would never[7] fight one without first putting on a sturdy pair of pants. Anyhoo, for the clever one percent of you who did NOT waste your time reading the prologue, I will sum it up for you now: I've spent the last six days practicing how *not* to die should I happen to encounter the Jackal in the near future. We've done very realistic simulations. So realistic, in fact, that everyone *else* who is reading this thinks that I just died in the prologue—which, of course, I didn't.

"So, what happened?" Drake said, his spectacled eyes peering out from behind a large book.

"Not much."

---

[5] Those are the opening lines of these books, respectively: *The Key to Rebecca* by Ken Follett, *The Crow Road* by Iain Banks, *Gravity's Rainbow* by Thomas Pynchon, *Moby-Dick*, by Herman Melville, *Harry Potter and the Sorcerer's Stone* by J.K. Rowling, and *The Bible* by God.

[6] Sometimes lines like this are like tiny subconscious promises that us writers make to you readers without ever intending to. See? Whether you realize it or not, you are now subconsciously expecting a camel to collapse somewhere in this book.

[7] Okay. *Almost* never.

"You blew it again," Tessa said. "I can see it in your face."

"You're not even looking at me!" I objected. Tessa, as usual, was busy weight lifting. Right now, she was doing bicep curls.

"You're never going to beat Gladstone or Hawk," Drake said. "If you submit to that fact, you won't be so stressed out when you lose. Am I right, Tessa?"

"He's right, Simon," Tessa said.

I sighed. Ever since I had been rather suddenly inducted into the universe's most elite group of sword-wielding wizard heroes called the Circle of Eight, senior members of the Circle had been giving me private lessons about five times a day. And every night, when the lessons were over, I would return to our room/clearing on Fluff[8] to find that my two best friends in the world had waited up for my return. Drake was usually reading a book. He was a Bright, a wizard whose magic has to do with using their brain to the max. He was always making lists, trying to move things with his mind, reading books, or making *me* read books.

In fact, after returning from Daru, Drake discovered that I could speed-read and had been force-feeding[9] me five or six books a night ever since in an attempt to cure my

---

[8] Fluff is a Titan, i.e. a mysterious magical beast. In this case, *Feliformia gargantia*, or a free-forming terraglot. A large living landmass covered in purple treelike tentacles called tentreecles. See Book 1.

[9] Just an expression. He didn't actually shove them down my throat. He just made me read them. Except for that one time...

Earth-born ignorance of all things magical.[10] Meanwhile, Tessa spent most of her non-classroom time working out. Tessa was a Strong, a wizard whose power lies in physical strength.

In case you forgot, or just haven't been paying attention, there are six branches of magic: Speed of movement, mental prowess, time and the future, imagination, physical strength, and craftsmanship. Wizards always (except in my case) gain their power primarily from one of these categories and are divided into six corresponding groups: Quicks, Brights, Seers, Muses, Strongs, and Clinks. All wizards can manipulate the elements (making food, lighting stuff on fire, growing daisies in a cave, etc.), though their ability to do this type of stuff varies from person to person due to individual differences in training and inherent talent.

After one day of classes, Tessa was bench-pressing *Drake* (he was the heaviest thing in our clearing). After her fourth day, she was bench-pressing me *and* Drake *and* a stack of Drake's books. Now she had been given a set of mech scales with which to practice.

I sat down and opened the top book from the stack Drake had set out for me for the night: *Hugging the Humdrungelob: Why the Infamous Beasts of Sayco Are*

---

[10] If you are any good at math, you probably realize that in just six days I've consumed, I mean, *read,* over twenty-five books. And they weren't picture books either; they were heavy, thick-as-a-walrus, Drake-style books. This meant that while I still had a lot to learn, I was no longer a complete ignoramus. If you see Drake around, please remind him of this.

Nothing to Fear by Loquacious Bright. I began reading, flipping pages with the rhythm of my heartbeat.

"What are you up to now?" I asked to change the subject.[11]

"Two sixty-five." She sniffed, curling the long silver weight bar one last time. It looked much like the ones that I had seen in high school gyms back home, except that the weights at either end of hers consisted of a swirling brass mechanism that looks more like the ticking heart of an expensive watch than gym equipment.

"Not bad," I said. "For a girl." Behind his book, one of Drake's furry eyebrows crooked.

Ignoring me, Tessa grunted, "Falten,"[12] and the swirling weights collapsed inward, morphing with the end of the bar, which in turn shrunk to the size of a ballpoint pen. Tessa wiped the small silver object clean on her shirt and dropped it in her pocket.

"So," Tessa said, finally turning her gaze on me, "anything *interesting* happen yet?" She had one blue eye and one brown eye, which managed to make her look extra pretty—even though that was completely normal for wizards.

---

[11] Of *course* I can talk and speed-read at the same time. Can't everyone?

[12] Incidentally, this is German for "fold." Why oscillator scales are designed with German commands is a mystery to me, though it may have something to do with the fact that they were invented by the world's most famous Austrian/Californian wizard/bodybuilder/actor/politician, Arnold Schwarzenegger, back when he was a student at Skelligard.

"Well, no…"

"Ugh," she grunted. "All this waiting is making me crazy."

"But it's only been six days!" I objected. "Look how much we've learned already!"

"Mark my words, Simon Fayter," she said, waving her finger imperiously. "This stupid, six-month training plan of yours isn't going to work. We singlehandedly destroyed an evil kingdom that the Jackal set up for one of his students to rule, and then stole a bloodstone out from under his nose. If you don't think he's coming for some kind of revenge, you're insane!"

"Of course he's coming for revenge," I said. "That's why I—*we* have to train. And it's not *my* plan." I pointed out. "It's Gladstone's plan. So if you want to argue with the leader of the Circle of Eight, be my guest, but please don't blame *me*."

"You two are so sweet," Drake said from behind his book. "How many times have you had this, er, *conversation* now?"

"I don't know," I said sarcastically. "How many days has it been since I took you to Rellik's tomb?"

"Three."

I gave Tessa my best "you are being so difficult" stare. "Three, then."

"Hmph," Tessa said, "maybe I *will* go talk to Gladstone."

Drake sneezed, accidentally ripping a page out of his book with the force of it. "Wait. What? You're not really going to, right? This is just another one of your…"

"Another one of my *what*?" she said, too sweetly.

Drake cowered behind his book.

"I think what he means, Tessa," I cut in, "is that one doesn't just knock on Gladstone's door and tell him he's an idiot. He's a member of the Circle of Eight!"

Tessa laughed, sweeping out of the clearing. "*You* are a member of the Circle of Eight, Simon, and I call you an idiot all the time."

She was gone.

I let my anger fester for a minute, then hopped to my feet and slammed the book down in front of Drake. "This is awful, Drake. Do you really think this is what I need to be reading? Some old dude's theories about a freak monster on the other side of the universe?"

"Yes."

"But—"

"I think she's still mad at you about the other day," Drake mumbled.

"What?"

"You're not mad about the book, Simon." He turned a page and peeked over the top of his book at me. "*You're* mad that *Tessa* is still mad at you about the other day."

"Whatever," I said, picking the book up again.[13] "It's not like I left you guys behind while I explored the ancient tomb of the most famous wizard of all time, waited three days before deciding to tell you about it, and then kept the most important things he told me a secret from you."

---

[13] It's so annoying when friends see right through you. Annoying and wonderful.

Drake's book closed with a thud. "Simon, that's *exactly* what you did!"

I grinned. "I know, Drake. It's called sarcasm."

His eyes narrowed, and then he reopened his book, muttering something under his breath about humans. I relaxed into my seat, falling in pace with the book again. Of course, my gut told me Tessa was probably right, but I couldn't admit that to her. No doubt our plans would be cut short by something unexpected. They usually were. Probably, it would happen at night, when I was just sitting back with a book, relaxing. From out of the blue, a monster would appear, or we'd be catapulted across the universe, or someone would let out a bloodcurdling scream and we would be off on another adventure. I hoped. Otherwise, it was going to be a long, *long*, six months.

Just then, from out of the blue, someone—no, not just someone. I knew that voice. *Tessa* let out a bloodcurdling scream.

THREE MOMENTS

Dead men tell no tales.[14]

—A bunch of pirates

Right now you are probably hoping to find out why Tessa screamed, right?

Too bad.

You see, as soon as we start talking about that, the adventure will begin, and we will be neck deep in screaming, pirates, screaming pirates, sword fights, space-bats, evil wizards, time travel, betrayal, footnotes, bad jokes, and explosions (Yes. EXPLOSIONS!). Not to mention Colm the Insane. In other words, there will be no time to tell you all the stuff that you have to know first. Like how the rest of my conversation with Rellik went six days ago.

In case you forgot, I ended the previous book (quite rudely, I might add) right after I met him, and it would be bad form now if I didn't take a minute and explain that. Actually, there are *three* important things that happened over the last six days. Three moments. I'll try to be brief…

---

[14] Total nonsense. You can learn all kinds of stuff from dead people, as you will see on the next page.

The First Moment
(Three days after I found the Tomb)

The intricately carved doors of white bone swung upward at my command, revealing a dark, foreboding staircase which led down into the thousand-year-old tomb of the most powerful wizard of all time.

"Whhhhooooaaa," Drake said. "What's inside?"

"The thousand-year-old tomb of the most powerful wizard of all time."

"Are you serious?" Tessa said. "You found Rellik's tomb and you didn't tell us?"

"I'm telling you now!"[15]

Tessa smacked me in the back of the head. "Are we going to stand here all night? Turn C4."

Now, lest you assume Tessa is referring to explosives, let me remind you that my magical leather jacket, the *turncoat*, was so named because of the fifty small knobs sewn into the inner lining. Short version: They do random acts of magic when I turn them, and most of them only work once a day. In the last three days, we had discovered the abilities of two more knobs: C3 and C4. C3 (*Sponge*) was the one I used in the prologue. It absorbs energy from an enemy attack. C4, we named Headlight because, well...

---

[15] Okay, in retrospect, I probably should have arrived at the decision to tell my friends everything(ish) a bit sooner. Come on, though! An ancient, mysterious wizard had pretty much sworn me to secrecy, and it had only taken me a couple days to blab to my friends. I thought I was doing pretty good...

I turned C4 (*Headlight*), and my head lit up like a firefly's backside. In actual fact, it's my tongue that luminates.[16] I have to keep my mouth shut just to keep from blinding myself. I call this lantern mode. Alternatively, I can drop my jaw, stick out my tongue, and turn into a military-grade human floodlight.

We descended the stone steps together, carefully avoiding the floor-to-ceiling cobwebs that glowed silver in the headlight. When we reached the cracked landing at the bottom, a hand shot out of the shadows and clamped down on my shoulder.

"HawWuhZert!"[17] I said.

Before Tessa or Drake could react, a beautiful woman stepped smoothly out of the shadows and placed a knife to my throat. She had dark hair that fell halfway down her back and a delicate white oval on her left cheekbone, like a luminous scar.

"Dead," she said.

The Tike,[18] my loyal friend/bodyguard/stalker had,

---

[16] Not really a word anymore. People say "shines" now.

[17] I know in books they usually just use words like "Eek!" or "Ack!" or "Yikes!" or (lamest of all) "Ahhhhhh!" but those are very unrealistic. You make weird noises when you're spooked.

[18] In order to punish readers who, for unknown reasons, have STILL not read the first book in this series (after my repeated instruction to do so), I am omitting background information about the Tike. I will, for instance, NOT tell you that she is the "1,000-year-old ninjalike warrior from another planet" mentioned in the prologue, or that we have a sacred magical bond called the Ardentia, which is a strange mix of friendship, servitude, and marriage (without the romance). If you're wondering why she is called *The* Tike, instead of just Tike, don't ask me. I don't know.

in her infinite wisdom, decided that it would be fun to supplement my training by sneaking around all day, attacking me at random. She said it would "build character." If nothing else, it had been an interesting way to pass the time on our first day.

Tessa slapped me on the back of the head again. "How many times has she killed you now?"

"Two," I lied. I had to hold my hand in front of my mouth as I spoke to keep from blinding them.

"Eight," the Tike corrected sourly, stepping back and twirling her knife. "Since lunch."

"Wow, Simon," Tessa said. "I think you're getting worse."

I rounded on the Tike. "We said seven was the daily limit, by the way. I see you saw fit to break our deal."

She picked her fingernail with the knife. "I saw fit to break our deal when you saw fit to wander off at night without me."

"Haven't you heard, Tike?" Tessa said sweetly. "Wandering off at night without his most trusted friends is Simon's new favorite thing."

I stuck my tongue out at Tessa and she staggered back, shielding her eyes from the light.

"Point that thing somewhere useful," the Tike snapped. She grabbed a fistful of my hair and redirected my headlight into the darkness before us, illuminating a long stone sarcophagus with a carved lid.

"Galloping garderobes,"[19] Drake whispered. "Is that it? I mean, is he really in there?"

"Yes," I said, "this is Rellik's tomb. But that's not all I found."

My friends' curiosity was almost palpable as they followed me around to the head of the sarcophagus. I pointed out the writing carved into the lid:

Rellik, son of Ronan, son of Rok
Seer, Fayter, Friend
Turncoat

5I

"What does that bit at the bottom mean?" Drake said. "5I…? Simon, does that mean what I think it means? Is that a knob in your turncoat?"

"Very good, Drake," I said. "You figured it out almost as fast as I did."

The Tike shot me a sideways look. Drake, being the brainiac he is, had figured it out about *ten* times faster than I had, but it was no good telling him that.

"But there is no 5I on the turncoat," Tessa said. "The numbers are—"

"Yeah, we've already figured that out," I said. "He used a different numbering system. Check it out." I turned E9.

---

[19] Garderobe: an ancient toilet, usually built into the outer wall of a castle. Basically a little bench with a hole cut into it, which opens to the outside, dropping, uh…*stuff* into the moat, or (in case of a siege) onto the heads of your enemies. No flushing necessary!

There was a flash of white light, and a figure appeared on the other side of the sarcophagus. He was old. Older than old. His hair was thin and white, and he had a face like a Roman gladiator, complete with thirteen scars and a chunk missing from the side of his nose.

"Ahhhhhh!"[20] Drake cried, sneezing several times.

Rellik the Seer smiled warmly. "Simon Fayter," he said. "I've been waiting for you."

"Holy ham fat," Tessa whispered, holding a hand over her mouth in an uncharacteristically girlish way. "Are you alive?"

The ancient wizard ran a bent finger through his beard and gazed around at us happily. "In answer to that question," he began in the tone of a man used to addressing a classroom, "technically, I do not know for certain. What you see before you could most closely be described as a *recording*. It so happens that the particular knob in the turncoat which you just turned has the capacity to record events as they transpire, and to replay them later. I chose to leave this message to my successor in this fashion precisely because I am confident that he, and only he— that is, *you,* and only *you*—will be able to manipulate it and retrieve this missive."

"Talks funny, doesn't he?" I said.

Tessa smacked me. "Be quiet. *Some of us* haven't heard this before."

Rellik walked around to the front of his sarcophagus

---

[20] I know. I know. Footnote 17. Sometimes I get lazy, okay?

and sat gracefully on the end. Tessa moved aside to give him room.[21]

"The future is a capricious[22] mistress, Simon," Rellik began heavily. "Every time you look at it, it changes; there are many things which I cannot know for certain. For instance, sometimes I look into the future and see you surrounded by three companions in this room. Sometimes you are alone. Who can say what will really be?"

I glanced around at my friends and found them looking thoughtful at that.

"In any case," Rellik continued, "if you are seeing this, it means that I have failed. Already, I have been betrayed by my brother, Rone. I expect that he will succeed in killing me any day now. No doubt this will be ancient history to you, but for me it is still the future.

"Whatever you may have been told, let me assure you of this: My brother is still alive. In your day, he has likely long since faked his death and abandoned the name my father gave him. You will know him as the Jackal, a persona he has donned in your age to hide his true identity."

Drake, who had been holding his breath, now began to hyperventilate. In retrospect, considering his brainiac mind and scholarly heart, coming suddenly face-to-face with the most mysterious figure in history and being candidly told that the foremost bad guy of all time was actually alive and simply posing as *today's* bad guy may have been too much for him to handle.

---

[21] Totally unnecessary, since he was just a projection.
[22] Prone to sudden changes of behavior.

"Keep it together, Cowboy," Tessa said, putting a steadying hand on his shoulder.

Rellik, who had been twiddling his thumbs idly—no doubt he had foreseen the need for a pause here—now continued, peering out at us with vivid, pleading eyes.

"Rone seeks the bloodstones, Simon, but he must not find them. The one who unites them will wield unimaginable power. Our father used that power and caused immeasurable harm to the world."

Rellik's eyes fell, and his voice dropped to a whisper. "I used that power, and it has been the death of me." His eyes darted back up, and there was such an intense expression on his face that if I didn't know better, I would have thought he was actually in the room with us. "Simon, you must *not* allow Rone to find the bloodstones. You must find them first. You must unite them and—well, you must discover the rest for yourself when the time comes."

The image of Rellik shook suddenly, as if the ground was trembling beneath him. He glanced up. "My brother has found me. Quick, Simon, make sure you are alone. The rest of what I have to say is for your ears only. You must go to the island of—"

I turned E9 again, and Rellik vanished.

"Hey!" Drake said. "What island? The island of what?"

"Seriously?" Tessa said, turning on me in a fury. "You're *still* not going to trust *us*?"

"Don't even try," the Tike said grimly. "He is determined to keep his little secret from everyone."

"Did you tell Hawk, at least? Or Gladstone?" Drake asked.

"Uh, of *course* not," I said. "Like Rellik said, for my ears alone. Now, if you'll excuse me for a moment, I'd like to review the rest of it one last time. Go on. Don't give me that look, Drake. You know you'd do the same thing. I'll meet you outside in a minute."

As they passed me, Drake mumbled, "I would *not* do the same thing," the Tike shot me her usual glare, and Tessa took a swing at me, which I dodged.

They'd get over it. Friends always do… Right?

When I heard the stone doors slide shut, I walked back to the entrance just to make sure Tessa hadn't stayed behind to spy on me. Then I returned to the sarcophagus and turned E9 again.

"The rest of what I have to say is for your ears alone," Rellik said again. "First, I have some advice for you about the turncoat. Most of it, you must discover for yourself, but I will warn you of two things. First is this: Never try to transport more than five people at once. Five people, *including* yourself.

"Secondly, never, *ever* turn 5J[23] unless you wish to kill.

"Now, you must go to the island of Yap and find the wizard Colm, who lives there in exile. Do not believe what you may hear. He is very much alive. He alone can help you unravel the clues which I am about to give you. I cannot risk telling you outright all that I have to say. I have had just enough time to hide four of the bloodstones from my

---

[23] That's E10 on my chart.

brother. The one I hid on Daru, you already found. Well done.

"Two I have hidden in my past—one with the person who crafted the item that destroyed me, and one with the person who led my brother into evil. The fourth I have hidden in your past and my future. It is in the last place that Rone would ever look for anything. Ask Colm about this. He will know."

He paused then and drew a sword out of the scabbard at his side. It was the same sword that now lay in the trunk at the foot of my bed. He gave me a long, thoughtful look, and said, "The name of my sword is Kylanthus. You should know, for by now you will already have inherited it."

The ground shook again, and a beam of light burst into view above Rellik. A dark figure fell through the light, its back to me, features obscured by the glare of the beam. The one thing I did see was the knife in his upraised hand: It had a wickedly curved blade and a gleaming wolf's head pommel.

"Hello, brother dear," the figure said.

Beyond him, I saw Rellik remove the turncoat and drop it into the open trunk at his feet. His sword erupted with a halo of red fire, then he kicked the trunk shut, and the vision vanished.

So there it is, *the first thing*: the moment when I learned of my mission.

The Second Moment
(Two days ago)

The morning after I showed my friends the tomb of Rellik, I had an uncharacteristic flash of wisdom and told my teacher Hawk about what I had discovered (everything except the secrets Rellik gave me at the end, of course). Hawk told Gladstone (the head of the Circle of Eight and the wizard school at Skelligard), who, in classic persnickety[24] old-man form, promptly forbade me from leaving on any quests or telling my friends about it.

I, of course, told him to put a tourniquet[25] around his neck. Eventually we came to a reasonable compromise. First, since I had already told my friends—and my mom, and the neighbor's pet goat[26]—I agreed not to tell anyone else. Everyone already thought I would end up saving the world, but it was probably safer if they didn't know exactly what I was trying to do.

Second, since Rone had no way of knowing that I now possessed this information, we didn't necessarily have to leave on a quest right away. If Colm was still alive,

---

[24] Overly careful/fussy about small details.

[25] A device that stops blood flow. It usually consists of a tight cord/bandage tied around a limb and comes in *handy* if your hand gets cut off by a Calderonian spider monkey and you don't want to bleed to death. You should NEVER put a tourniquet around your neck. Unless you are going to church or a business meeting, in which case the device is referred to as a necktie and is socially acceptable, though still very dangerous.

[26] In case you were wondering, my mom's neighbors' pet goat is named Snots…I won't tell you why.

then he had lived for over a thousand years, and another few months wouldn't hurt him. Our six-month training schedule would proceed as planned. Not that our plans were going to work out anyway. Which brings me to the thing I am supposed to be telling you about:

It's not one particular moment, actually, but rather a series of embarrassing failures. The short version is this: I suck at magic. That is to say, I'm totally and completely useless. No matter how carefully Hawk and Gladstone taught me, I couldn't do the simplest spell. Not after six whole days with the best teachers in the world. And here I thought I was supposed to be powerful...

Drake was learning how to read books at the speed of sight, split his mind into independent parts so that he could "multi-think," and even move objects with his mind. Tessa was learning how to punch through walls, fight with heavy weapons, and stomp the ground so hard that it created shockwaves big enough to throw people into the air.

Additionally, they had both mastered standard magical practices such as starting a fire, vanishing small objects, and changing their appearance.

In six days!

My friends were geniuses!

And you thought *I* was the genius...[27] But I couldn't do any of these things. Of course, I wasn't expected to do the special Bright or Strong stuff, but I failed at using relatively

---

[27] I am, of course. Don't read too much into this momentary lapse of self-confidence.

simple magic, too. Not too long ago, I had been able to summon the Midnight Blue—a special kind of magic fire, but now I couldn't so much as warm up a toothpick.

"Why?" I asked Hawk one afternoon, after failing to ignite his eyebrows for the seventeenth time in a row (he thought maybe toothpicks were just too boring for me). We were at the Cloister, a rectangular open-air garden surrounded by columns. It was the highest point in all of Skelligard and our usual practice venue.

Hawk gave me one of his most patient looks, then shrugged. "As I told you once before, I am unsure how to guide a Fayter into accessing his power. I had hoped that the turncoat would help you in this, and in a way, I suppose it is, but at the end of the day you will probably have to figure some things out for yourself. I wouldn't be surprised if it ends up being grave danger or extreme need that drives you to use your power consciously, just as it did when you first summoned the Midnight Blue."

"That figures," I groaned. But my mind had caught hold of something else he had said. "What do you mean the turncoat is helping me with my magic?"

Hawk reached down to scratch his shin, a couple inches of which were exposed beneath his too-short robes. "Simon, objects, even magical objects, do not possess the kind of powers that the turncoat exhibits. I therefore presume that the magic of the turncoat flows from you. No doubt your magic powers it, and the coat simply channels your power in specific ways."

"Really?" I said, astonished. "That's awesome! This

means I'm not such a loser after all!"

"Nonsense," Hawk snapped. "You are plenty pathetic. What good is power if one cannot control it? While the coat may help your power flower,[28] I fear that it will also be a crutch to you. You will not achieve your destiny—whatever that may be—until you master yourself and your magic, like any other wizard."

"So...we should focus more on my coat, then?"

Hawk stopped pacing and turned a suspicious eye on me. "Have you been listening to me at all? We will practice a little with it, but we won't focus on it. Our goal is to teach you the basics. Even if you can't perform them now, at least our practice will give you a good foundation when you finally learn how to touch your power consciously."

So we practiced. We spent more time on my sword fighting, and I became adept at using the turncoat knobs *while* fighting. Gladstone, being the world's most powerful Seer, had the remarkable ability to make other people see whatever he wanted, so he could create elaborate illusions in which I could practice my skills. After six days of "meeting Rone," I wasn't half bad at fighting.

Okay, I *was* half bad. But by that definition, I was also half good, which is a fair sight better than awful. Still, when it came to the simple stuff, like actually doing magic on my own, I was a lost cause.

---

[28] Insert flower power joke here. I always suspected Hawk was a hippie...

The Third Moment
(Two nights ago)

The third moment was a small thing between the three of us friends. It was night again—the night after our fifth full day home—and we were in our clearing in Fluff. I had just returned from getting my butt kicked by GladstRone,[29] and I was reading yet another useless book from Drake (*Bacanweed to Bylloroot: A Complete Index of Magical Plants That Start With B* by Philo McNurowitz).

Tessa was working out with her mech scales, and Drake was practicing with a slingshot. He didn't even know what a slingshot was when I described it to him the day before, but I drew a picture for him, and he put in an order for one at the Clink fabrication shop.

Two hours later, he had a simple arm-mounted slingshot and a belt-mounted bullet dispenser filled with metal balls the size of nickels. My original idea was that he could use his power to control where the bullets went. Telekinesis[30] is high-level stuff, even for a Bright, but being the best friend of a member of the Circle of Eight and an integral member of my team, he, too, was receiving full-time tutoring, and he was already getting good at the telekinesis stuff. Really good, actually. He could hit a falling leaf eight times out of ten.

"Phewph," Tessa said, lowering her weights to the floor and wiping the sweat off her forehead. "Drake, you're

---

[29] Get it? Ha ha.
[30] Moving objects with your mind.

getting really good with that thing. I hear Simon's not bad with his sword, either. If this keeps up, I'm going to be the only one without a cool weapon when we leave."

Drake perked up at this and turned to look at me, cocking an eyebrow in a question. I grinned and nodded.

"Okay!" Drake said, leaping to his feet so enthusiastically that Tessa jumped in surprise. "Sorry. Okay. Tessa, Simon and I have a little gift for you."

"I had nothing to do with it," I said, not looking up from my book.

"But Simon," Drake said, "the whole thing was your idea, remember?"

I waved my hand in annoyance. "Just go get it."

"Right." Drake ran to his bed and pulled a giant backpack out from beneath it. It was black, militaristic-looking, and the approximate size and shape of an R2[31] unit.

"Holy yak toes," I said. "Drake, I thought you were getting her present. What is that?"

Tessa gave a motherly sigh. "That's his 'go bag.' Ever since our little unplanned trip to Daru, he has been paranoid about being prepared for sudden departures."

"Dude," I said, "when we leave, you can't bring that. It's bigger than you are."

"I can carry it," he said, wriggling his arms through the straps frantically. "I won't slow you down."

---

[31] If you don't get this reference, you should be really, really, really embarrassed. Go watch *Star Wars* right now. Pretty much any of them. Except *Rogue One*. R2-D2 got shafted for screen time in that movie.

I rolled my eyes. "Well, we're not leaving yet, so just put that thing away and get her present already."

"That's what I'm *doing*," Drake said. "It's *inside* the pack." He took it off again and pulled out what looked like a small black baseball bat.

"No…" Tessa said in disbelief. "Is that…?"

"It is!" Drake said, beaming with pride. "A cram cudgel!" He pressed a small button on the end of the bat and it sprang outward, increasing in size until it was four feet in length and one foot wide at the business end. "Oof," Drake said as the cudgel fell to the floor with a thump. He planted both feet and tried to drag it the rest of the way to her, but he couldn't move it. Cram cudgels worked with the same collapsible technology as Tessa's mech scales, and while it was light and portable in its "crammed" position, the fully extended cudgel was solid steel and weighed about two hundred pounds.

"Wow," Tessa said. She took the end out of Drake's hands and swung the cudgel into the air experimentally. She had to use both hands to have real control, but it was in no way too heavy for her. "I could do some damage with this thing," she said. "How can you afford it?"

"Are you kidding?" I said. "Drake's rich."

"My *dad* is rich," Drake corrected modestly. "Anyway, it really *was* Simon's idea."

"You guys are the best!" Tessa said, and she pulled us both into a terrifyingly strong hug. When she pulled away—and after my breath had returned, and I was able to check to see if my rib cage was crushed—I *thought* I caught a glimpse of a tear rolling down her cheek. But then it was gone, and she was grumbling, "Pretty good coming from a guy that can't remember to bring us along for the most important discovery in a thousand years…"

We spent the rest of the night messing around with Tessa's cudgel, and after that, I never saw her without it. I liked to think she carried it not just to crush stuff, but also to remind her of our friendship. The first few days of our training had been long and hard. I wasn't looking forward to six months like this, but I thought, just maybe, I could make it through with friends like these at my side.

3

THE MESSENGER

Stone walls do not a prison make,
Nor iron bars a cage...

—Richard Lovelace[32]

A s I was saying earlier, Tessa let out a bloodcurdling scream.

Drake and I jumped to our feet. "Did you hear that?" he said, but I was already on the run.

We found her halfway between Fluff and the castle, surrounded by a circle of onlookers. The Tike ran to my side as we approached the crowd. I fought down a sense of dread. What if we found Tessa dead, slain by some foul beast sent by Rone?

"What do you think happened?" Drake said, panting. Clearly his thoughts were running similar to my own.

"Maybe she broke a nail," I said. "You know how girls are."

---

[32] An English poet from the 1600s. He was a Cavalier poet, which basically means that the king paid him to wear fancy clothes, go to parties, and write poetry. Those were the good old days—until the king got executed, and Loveless ended up in prison. Of course, he wrote his best stuff in prison...

The crowd parted as we approached, and I was surprised to see Tessa standing a short distance from a skinny, dark-haired boy. He looked to be a year or two younger than us, and judging by his ragged clothing and unkempt appearance, he had traveled a long distance without rest. The only interesting thing about him was a large silver medallion that he wore around his neck over his shirt. It reminded me vaguely of the codexes that the students at Skelligard wore, except that his was much larger and more crudely hewn. His depicted what I could only guess was a fox head.

He was standing with his hand outstretched, offering a small box to Tessa. She was standing with her arms folded behind her back, refusing to take it, and not looking him in the face. For some reason, she looked quite scared.

"Please," he simpered. "Take it to him?"

Drake began sneezing violently.

"What's going on?" I said importantly.

"Simon F-Fayter?" the boy said, trembling slightly.

"The one and only," I replied, flashing a pretentious[33] smile. I was pretty famous by now, and clearly this boy thought, I mean, *knew*, what an awesome, heroic, studly, brilliant, legendary—

"Do not touch that boy, Simon," the Tike warned, placing herself between me and him.

"I h-have a delivery for you," the boy squeaked, peering around her.

"Ugh. *Move*, Tike. Stop being so overprotective. It's

---

[33] An exaggerated sense of self-importance.

just a kid." I pushed her aside, and the boy practically shoved the box into my hands. "Thanks! And it's not even my birthday."[34]

Drake managed to stop sneezing long enough to say "Don' opnen thaa—ahhh—aaACHOO!"

I pried open the lid to the box, fighting off Tessa as she tried to stop me as well. Honestly, friends could be annoying sometimes. "Ooh," I said. "There's a little red dog statue inside. I wonder who it's fro—"

The instant I touched the red dog statue, it came alive.

"Yikes!" I said as the dog jumped against the sides of the box, trying to get out.

"Shut it!" Tessa cried.

"Throw it away!" Drake said.

The Tike drew one of her long knives and reached over slowly, as if the box were a poisonous snake that she would take from me.

As I looked at the little dog, I found myself remembering the bloodhounds[35] that had appeared the day I came to Skelligard. Actually, if the dog wasn't so tiny, it might have actually looked a *lot* like a bloodhound.

As soon as I thought it, the tiny dog began to grow. A second later, there was a full-sized, red-eyed bloodhound trying to rip my face off.

"Watch out!" I screamed. Where was my sword when I needed it?

---

[34] In case you were wondering, my birthday is 1 Jan, 2001. Yup. I'm a New Year's baby.

[35] Evil demon spawn that run errands, and hunt/kill people for the Shadeking, i.e. Rone. i.e. the Jackal.

But Tessa was ready. She flicked out her cudgel and swung it at the beast; it made a whooshing sound but missed, hitting the ground with a thud and making a small crater in the cobblestones.

"What's going on?" Gladstone said, appearing from behind the growing crowd around a corner. "Great gadnarks! Stop, fiend of darkness! Stop or die!" His voice squeaked at first, but ended in a deep, commanding tone that I had not heard before. A sword appeared in his hand out of thin air, too, wreathed in white fire.[36]

The bloodhound put its tail between its legs and sat down.[37]

"Now," Gladstone said, "have you a message, or did you come to kill?"

The bloodhound opened its jaws wide, and to my surprise, a voice came out of it. A horrible, inhuman voice. It sounded like ten men speaking at once and made my skin crawl just to hear it. It was the voice of Rone. I knew it in my bones. It sounded very different from the voice I had heard speak to Rellik in the recording, and yet somehow still the same.

"Simon Jacobson," it said, "you have taken one of my Fallen, and you have claimed to be the foretold Fayter. We shall see if you truly are. I challenge you to a duel. Expect my champion in two days' time."

The bloodhound shut its mouth, then scampered off

---

[36] I've got to learn how to do that.

[37] Bloodhounds are incredibly dangerous in large numbers, but less vicious when alone. In that way, they're a lot like people. And Cheetos.

down the street.

"Maldius," Gladstone said, addressing one of the older minotaur students, "follow the bloodhound and make sure it leaves the island. Call Master Hawk and inform him there is trouble." He flicked his hand, and his sword vanished into thin air.[38]

The minotaur bounded away in the direction of the bloodhound, and Gladstone began searching the crowd. "Where did he go?" he muttered.

"Who?" I said.

"Ah," Gladstone pointed an imperious finger at a spot between two students, and they parted to reveal the trembling delivery boy.

"What is your name?" Gladstone said. "Do not be afraid. No one here will harm you."

"Jake," the boy said.

"Jake Solomonson?"

The boy's head snapped up in surprise. "My dad's name was Solomon. I think. Can you... I mean—*please* sir, can you do anything to help me? Can you get it off?"

The boy lifted the silver medallion at his neck, and I realized suddenly that the animal carved into it was not a fox but a jackal. That explained the earlier reactions of my friends.

Gladstone shook his head sadly.

"Try!" the boy said, desperation in his voice.

---

[38] Actually, it vanished into a place called the mindhold. Gladstone had been trying to teach me how to do that, but...well...do I have to say it?

Gladstone grimaced. "I have tried before. I tried with Lukel and Rose and Tamra. Do you know them?"

"Tamra's dead," the boy said. "*Please* try. You have to try."

"Very well," Gladstone said, his expression resigned. He rolled up his sleeves and placed one hand on the boy's head, then very slowly reached for the large silver medallion with his other hand, fingers twisted into a strange shape, like the broken claws of a predatory bird. Just before he touched the medallion, there was a flash of red and then an explosion of energy. The boy shot backward and hit the ground hard, and Gladstone slowly lowered what was left of his arm.

The crowd of students shrieked, and I felt my stomach turn over. Gladstone's hand had been blown off completely; his arm was nothing but black, charred bone from the elbow down.

"Not to worry, not to worry," Gladstone said, shaking his arm as if it had merely fallen asleep. Flesh reappeared rapidly. Fingers and other bits flew out of the grass surrounding us and reattached themselves so that in a few short seconds his arm was good as new. He reached down with his healed hand and picked the boy up out of the grass, setting him on his feet. "Are you all right, Jake?"

The boy nodded but would not meet Gladstone's eye.

"I *am* sorry. Truly," Gladstone said. "But I'm afraid the only way to break the chain that binds you is to destroy the one who forged it."

The boy's face went suddenly pale.

"Do not worry," Gladstone said. "I will not ask you to speak of him. The bloodhound has delivered his message, and that will be enough."

The boy relaxed.

"Speaking of bloodhounds," I cut in. "What did it mean, anyway? What champion? I mean—"

"It means Rone is sending something to fight you, Simon," Gladstone said sharply. "It means you need to leave before it gets here. It means you leave first thing tomorrow morning. Go eat your breakfast, then come to my office. We have things to discuss, and empty stomachs make for empty brains." He moved in closer and lowered his voice. "Take Jake with you, Simon. He looks as if he could use a meal, and it seems he has a few minutes before he is recalled. Be kind to him. And do *not* ask him to reveal any details about Rone."

With that, he turned on his heel and strode away.

Jake ate like a starved baby tiger.

"Want some hagnackian spider-sac soushljha?" Drake said, offering the emaciated[39] boy a bowl of creepy-looking pasta.[40]

To my horror, he took the bowl out of Drake's hands and gulped it down.

---

[39] Abnormally thin or weak, usually because of sickness or starvation.
[40] Being a minotaur, Drake frequently ate things that would have made any self-respecting dumpster rat queasy.

"Wow," Drake said, "no one ever actually... uh... I guess I'll go get some more." And he headed off for the kitchen.

"Jake," Tessa said kindly, "when was the last time you ate?"

No response.

"They have everything here, you know. Is there anything you want? Any favorites?"

No response. Jake had not answered a question since being alone with us.

"You're one of the Fallen, aren't you?" I asked.

Jake stopped chewing abruptly. From beside me, the Tike drew a quick breath.

Tessa smacked me. "Gladstone said not to—"

"I'm not asking him to reveal secrets about Rone, am I?" I objected, waving her off. I turned back to Jake. "Well? You are, aren't you? You're one of those kids that Rone steals and then forces to serve him, like his private army of wizards?"

Jake looked at me for a minute, then gave a simple nod, returning to his food.

I glanced triumphantly at Tessa, only to see her staring back with her "you're so insensitive" expression.

"Uh..." I said, turning back to Jake. "I'm sorry. That really...sucks."

Tessa kneaded her forehead with the back of her spoon. "What Simon means, Jake," Tessa said, "is that we couldn't possibly understand what you've been through."

"Yeah. That's what I meant." I said. "Actually... I was

almost taken by Rone myself when I was a baby."

Jake stopped eating again. He actually made eye contact with me then, and seemed to be considering something. "I'm n-not a wizard," he said at last. "N-not a wizard like you. Not en-nough power. The ones that aren't good…we run errands instead. Carry messages. W-watch people."

"And you can't get away?" Tessa said.

He touched the medallion at his neck. "H-he owns us. He's in my m-mind. Always…" His face took on a faraway look. "Can't get away."

"Got some more!" Drake said, slamming a tray down loudly on the table. It was filled with plates of what looked like the leftovers of a blobfish[41] autopsy.[42]

Jake pulled several of the plates toward himself hungrily, and Drake looked slightly crestfallen.

"Jake," I said, trying to restart the conversation. "How is he in your mind? How does he get in?"

Jake tensed. His face went suddenly blank, his eyes closed, and his head tucked inward in an inhuman way. When he opened his eyes again, they were looking right at me, and they weren't his eyes at all.

I jumped off the bench in shock, spilling my food on

---

[41] A blobfish is a deep-sea fish that lives off the coast of Australia. When they are pulled out of the extremely deep water too quickly, their bodies go all rubbery due to the rapid decompression, and they end up looking like, well, blobs. Hence the name.

[42] A special procedure in which a doctor takes apart someone's body after they die to see what went wrong. Thankfully this is a fairly rare procedure that does not happen to most people, or blobfish for that matter.

the floor and drawing the eyes of several students near me. When I looked back at Jake, his eyes looked totally normal, and he was shoving a large forkful of Drake's food into his mouth.

"I don't think he can tell us anything else," Tessa whispered, pulling me back onto the bench. "Now do you see why Gladstone said not to question him? His mind isn't right."

Jake paused then, fork halfway to his mouth, and his hand began to shake. His face went blank. Then, as if against his will, he stood up sharply, dropped the fork, and ran from the room.

Drake and Tessa ran after him, but I didn't move. I knew what had happened. Gladstone said he would be *recalled*. No doubt Rone had forced him to return or go on some other errand. I stared after Jake's retreating form, wondering what it must be like to have Rone living in some corner of your mind, making you do things. What that boy's life must be like to make him look so tired, so hungry.

My hands clenched into fists at my sides. I had found another reason to hate this man: Rone, the Jackal, the Shadeking. Wherever he was, I would find him. Whatever he wanted with the bloodstones, I would make sure he never got it.

4

WARDS AND RINGS

*People's obsessions reveal much about them. Find the thing a
man thinks about one hundred times a day, and you will have
the key to understanding him.*

—Guy Thadont Xist[43]

With Tessa, Drake, and the Tike beside me, I knocked
on the massive iron-clad door to Gladstone's office,
and a jet-black jaguar head melted out of it like a beast
emerging from water.

"Simon Fayter first. The others must wait."

"Come on," Tessa huffed, but the jaguar had sunk
back into the door.

"Indeed. I think not," the Tike said. "You will take me
in the turncoat, Simon. I shall not leave your side today."

"Fine." I turned E8 (*Stash*), and the Tike vanished.
Tessa grumbled something unladylike under her breath,
but I ignored her and opened the door.

To my surprise, the jaguar whose head had come out
of the door was sitting just inside.

"Don't mind Vestari," a soft voice said. I turned to
see Gladstone hunched over a strange mess of glass-and-

---

[43] An ancient Peruvian fly trapper. When he wasn't trapping flies, he
was writing down neat sayings like this.

metal tubing that had been mounted to a low worktable in the antechamber to his office. The Gladstone that faced me now seemed softer than the man who had come to our rescue in the street—a kindly faced man in his middle years. Still, when he looked at you, there was something ancient in his expression, and his striking eyes made it seem even more so; the left one was gray, the right one brilliant white.

At the mention of her name, the jaguar slinked across the room and curled up beneath the table.

"Sorry," Gladstone said, detangling himself from the convoluted contraption and setting down a screwdriver, "I had forgotten that you have yet to meet my ward."

During the last six days, I had learned that all grown wizards have what's called a ward—usually a magical animal of some sort that they use to assist them with spells, keep them company, help them fight, keep their feet warm, etc. These animals are joined to them somehow, and remain with them until the wizards die. I had seen Hawk's ward, Kestra, several times now.

"No problem," I said.

"How did it go with Jake?" Gladstone asked, picking the screwdriver up again and tinkering. "I assume—since I expressly forbade you from doing so—that you asked him details about his master?"

I nodded. "He went all weird and then sort of became someone else, and…"

"And you found the Jackal's eyes staring out at you then, I suppose." He glanced up from his work with a concerned expression. "Are you all right? Such eyes are not easy to look upon."

"I'm fantastic," I said.

"I see. Well, I take it Jake departed soon after that?"

"Drake and Tessa ran after him, but he disappeared in the street somewhere."

Gladstone nodded. "Hawk tracked him all the way to the docks, but even he could not see which ship the boy boarded. The Fallen draw upon the power of the Shadeking when it suits his purposes, and they cannot be tracked, even by members of the Circle." His face grew taut, as if he was remembering something he had been contemplating for years. "He can make them do terrible things. But of course, this is not the first Fallen you have met. By now you should know to be careful around them."

"Jake didn't seem dangerous," I said.

"No," Gladstone agreed. "Jake had very little magical power of his own—no doubt the enemy thinks of him as nothing more than an errand boy." There was real malice in his voice now, and he nearly spat the last words out. He steadied himself. "Have you been meeting every day with McKenzie, as I asked?"

I nodded. Every day I had made a solitary journey to her room. It was really more of a cell, I suppose, though it didn't look like one. She had a wonderful view and a comfortable bed, but her door and window were guarded around the clock, and she was never allowed to leave except to walk in the gardens with Gladstone.

"She still hasn't said anything. She won't talk to me at all."

"Nor to me," Gladstone said. "But I doubt that she could answer our questions, even if she wanted to."

"Does she wear the same...uh...codex thingy Jake did? He said all the Fallen wear them."

"Of course," Gladstone's expression darkened. "They are forced to make them themselves—forge their own chain, so to speak, so they are all different." His head disappeared beneath his contraption again as he worked. "McKenzie's is a delicate necklace, generally tucked out of sight, which is why you didn't notice it. Actually, it was damaged slightly, presumably during your battle with her, though I can't imagine how you managed it—codexes are Frathanoid[44] objects, and can only be destroyed or altered by their creator. In any case, it is likely due to this damage to her codex that Rone has been unable to force her to return."

I had a dark thought. "Or he is still in control, and he just leaves her here to spy on us."

"Or that," Gladstone said pleasantly.

"If you let her go free," I said, sharing the question that had been building in my mind during my time with McKenzie, "do you think she would go back to him?"

Gladstone paused in his work and looked at me again. "Do you?"

"Yes."

---

[44] Yeah, I wasn't sure what they were either at the time, but I guess we can assume they are super-duper powerful magic things.

He nodded. "I think you are right."

I watched him work for a while, both of us lost in dark thoughts, and both of us (as Tessa would remind me later) having completely forgotten that my friends were waiting impatiently outside.

"What's that you're working on?" I said finally to change the subject.

"Ah," Gladstone said. "The source of much frustration, I'm afraid." He laid one hand across his chin and considered the mess of tubing disdainfully. "Tell me, Simon, without knowing anything about it, what would you guess it to be?"

"A lint organizer? Or maybe a really expensive cappuccino machine."

"Mmm," Gladstone said. "Perhaps those would be more practical constructions. As it is, I'm actually trying to build a memaphaeresis machine."

"Memafa *what*?"

"A memory transfusion device," he said enthusiastically. "You see, Simon, being a Seer, I spend most of my time looking into the future. But the future is always changing. You can never know the truth about someone's future. Not even your own. It's the past that holds the real truth. Problem is, it's hard to really know the truth about that either. We know our own past, our own memories, but how can we truly know the past of another? We're all so private, you see? And even when we try to explain our memories, it is only a story. An echo. And so the struggle to be truly understood by another goes on. But this machine—if I could ever get it working—will allow one person to actually *remember* the memories of another."

"Wow," I said. "Like you can put your memories in there and I can plug into it and walk around inside your memory?"

Gladstone frowned. "No, of course not." His eyes glazed over in a thoughtful expression. "At least, I don't think so. That *would* be extraordinary. This device, I think, simply allows one person to remember the memories of another as if they were his own."

"Is it almost done?"

He sighed. "It has been almost done for many years now. But I am now at an impasse. If a solution to my problem exists, it has not occurred to me yet, nor to any of the living wizards whom I have consulted. As for dead wizards, none of their writings have been of help either. It is rumored that the wizard Broca wrote a book on the mechanics of the mind, but I have been unable to find a copy. So I must limp along by myself in trying to solve the relative perspective issue and find a good thought-transfer medium..." He chewed his lip thoughtfully, staring into space, and I had the distinct impression that he had forgotten I existed.

"Well," I said, "this has been a fascinating insight into your work, but if you don't mind, I'd like to get back to the plot of the story now."[45]

"Ah," he said. "My apologies." He swept me out of the antechamber and into a lavishly decorated office,

---

[45] Okay, I didn't really say that. I just cleared my throat politely.

complete with thick fur rugs, a carved wooden desk, and bookshelves big enough to make Drake swoon with envy.

"Have a seat," he said, and I moved into one of the high-backed leather armchairs that faced his desk. He took his own seat, folded his hands in his lap, and began. "You have everything in order to leave tonight?"

I nodded.

"Good. I have arranged transport for you and a small party to depart at midnight. Have you changed your mind about telling me where you are going?"

"No," I said. "All due respect, but Rellik wanted me to keep it a secret, and I don't plan on telling anyone until I have to."

"Very well. It is, of course, regrettable that your six-month training schedule cannot proceed as planned. Destiny has come for you, and she always comes before we are ready. Still, Hawk will accompany you and continue your lessons…"

He frowned slightly. "There is another matter. I know that thus far I have entertained your desires to take Drake and Tessa with you, but I would warn you of the danger this entails. You yourself are not yet a full-grown wizard, and it will be dangerous enough for you." He glanced away, clearing his throat. "It is unwise to speak of what one sees in the future, for even speaking of it can change events. However, I would plead with you to leave your friends behind."

"No way," I said. "Just think of how lame my biography would be if I did everything on my own instead of with a group of cool friends.[46] Besides, even if I tried to leave them behind, they'd just find a way to come along."

Gladstone nodded. "You may be right. Still, I have said my piece, and for that, my conscience may rest. They shall go with you if you insist."

He cleared his throat. "There is one thing which I feel I *must* insist upon, however. As you are still underage, it is not proper for you to have a ward of your own. However, as a knight of the Circle of Eight, traveling to and fro across creation, it is even less proper for you to be without one. Therefore, I think it would be wise if you were to use the rest of this day to select a ward. I could take you to the Menagerie in Stores, and help you select an appropriate animal."

"Actually," I said, "I already have a companion. The Tike can be my ward."

He frowned. "It is not often wise to choose a ward from an intelligent race."

"Perfect," I said. "I am not often wise."

Gladstone fidgeted. "What I mean to say is, animals are better suited for such relationships."

"But Atticus has Finnigan."

Gladstone chuckled. "I believe if you asked him, Atticus would tell you that choice has made his life a challenge. Though I have no doubt he would not have it any other way."

"Well," I said, "I won't have it any other way, either."

Gladstone grumbled something under his breath.

---

[46] Again, not really what I said. Funny, though.

"One of the benefits of having an animal," he went on stubbornly, "is that animals may be bonded to ward rings." He held up a hand, and I saw a thick silver ring on his middle finger. There was a jaguar engraved into the face of it. He wore another ring as well, a smaller one on his pinky, with a white stone set in a ring of golden wings.

"See?" he said, and he touched the jaguar ring. Vestari vanished from sight. Then he made a motion through the air, as if throwing a ball, and the black beast burst out of his ring, flying through the air with a roar. I noticed for the first time that Vestari had a small silver ring pierced through the corner of one of her soft black ears, matching Gladstone's.

"I have to admit," I said regretfully, "That is really, *really,* cool. But I'll stick with the Tike. I can still take her places, actually, even if it's not *quite* that easy." I turned E8, and she burst out of thin air beside me.

Gladstone jumped when she appeared but composed himself quickly. "Ah. Yes, *quite* impressive. And are you in favor of this arrangement as well, my lady?"

She gave a curt nod. "There is no oath or bond you can lay on me that will be stronger than the ties which bind me to Simon already."

"Very well," he said, resigned. He removed an intricately carved wooden box from a drawer in his desk and opened it to reveal a pair of plain silver rings like the one he wore. One was large, the other quite small. He handed the larger one to me and the smaller one to the Tike and told us to put them on. Mine was almost too big even for my index finger, but the Tike's just fit around her pinky. She eyed it skeptically, no doubt wondering if it would get in the way of her fighting. "Hold hands, placing the rings together," he said.

We did.

I *tried* very hard to not start humming any wedding songs. Or imagining the Tike in a white dress. Or thinking of weddings at all. Or blushing at my awkward thoughts.

It didn't work.

Gladstone placed a hand on top of ours and said grandly, "By the power vested in me, I pronounce you wizard and ward.[47] May these rings bind you until death finds you."

When he said the words, my ring tightened viciously, biting into my finger fat.[48] The Tike's quick intake of breath told me hers had done the same. I was about to complain about it, but a second later the pain was gone. The ring, it seemed, had melded magically with my finger, almost as if it had become a part of my body.

"What is the pulsing?" the Tike asked.

"Huh?" I said stupidly. Then I felt it, too. There was a slight pulse from the ring, almost as if I had smashed my finger and was feeling my own pulse through the swelling.

"That is Simon's heartbeat, Tike. Simon, you, of

---

[47] Of *course* those would be the magic words for binding us together...
[48] Hey, everyone has finger fat. Mind you, finger fat is the ONLY type of fat I have. Apart from that, I have the body of a Greek god. Or a Greek Olympian. Or a sculpture of a Greek god or Olympian. Seriously, just imagine Michelangelo's David and that's pretty much me...except I wear pants. Especially when slinging rocks at giants.

course, are feeling the Tike's. This, I'm afraid, is likely the only power of the ward rings which will work between you, but it is something. With non-human wards, the rings also allow the wizard to summon his ward across any distance. Even across time, some say, though I have never seen proof of that. However, the beating heart is likely the only power you will enjoy."

The Tike said nothing, but she was looking at her ring with more appreciation.

"Now," Gladstone said, returning to his chair and interlacing his fingers once more, "if you would be kind enough to show your friends in, I have a thing to show you which precious few have ever seen."

"What did we miss?" Tessa said when I brought them in.

"Not much," Gladstone said.

"Gladstone said I should leave you behind for your own safety—"

"I knew it!" Tessa interrupted, punching me in the arm.

"And I told him *no*," I finished.

"Oh," Tessa said, taken aback.

"And then Simon and I got married," the Tike added, draping her arm around my neck and flashing her ring.

Drake sneezed.

Tessa went pale. "W-what?"

"She's teasing you," Gladstone said, hiding a grin.

"Oh," Tessa said, clearing her throat. "I knew that."

I threw the Tike's arm off of me and changed the subject. "So, what is it you wanted to show us?"

"These," Gladstone said, indicating his bookshelf.

Drake swooned with envy.[49]

After he had recovered, Gladstone said, "I'm glad you like my books, Drakus, but I was talking about *these*." He tipped one book out and pushed another in, and the bookshelf lowered into the floor, revealing a group of narrow shelves. Upon the shelves sat row upon row of small stones. They were clear like glass and the color of blood.

"The bloodstones!" Drake exclaimed.

"They're just hidden in your office?" Tessa said. "Isn't that a bit... obvious?"

Gladstone shrugged. "They are more secure than they look. It would take Rone himself to remove them, and if he gains entry to this castle, then it is a dark day, indeed."

Drake was waving his finger in the air, apparently trying to count them.

"Thirty-seven," Gladstone said.

"But—" Drake began.

"Hold your questions, if you please. And sit down. I have much to speak of, and I must start at the beginning. As you know, there were fifty bloodstones in total. You know that Rellik used them to heal the Great Plague. He healed us so entirely that even the memory of our illness faded in time, so that today there are none to tell you what

---

[49] Told you.

exactly the Great Plague was or how we were afflicted.

"Seeing the great power of the bloodstones, Rone sought to take them from the hand of his brother. Thus, Rellik hid as many as he could before he died. Today, eight are in the possession of the members of the Circle of Eight. Each knight of the circle has a stone and uses it to transport him or herself to wherever he or she is needed. Bartholomew's stone was taken from him when he was killed by the Jackal, so it is in the possession of the enemy. One stone resides in your turncoat, Simon, and there it should stay, as you are a member of the Circle."

He held up his hand, thumb folded. "That leaves four unaccounted for. These, Rellik has told you to find. Whatever power they hold, Simon, you must reunite them, for this is the role of the Fayter. Rone seeks the stones also, it seems, but whatever his reasons may be, he must not be allowed to do so. If Rellik's recording is true, and Rone and the Jackal are one and the same, then his power is great, and his influence far reaching. The task before us is to find the four missing stones before he can. Simon, I take it, knows a secret place from which to start the search."

I cleared my throat. "Actually," I said, reaching into my pocket, "there are only three stones unaccounted for." I brought out the Daru bloodstone and handed it to him.

For the first time ever, I saw Gladstone totally surprised. Evidentially, whatever he had seen in our futures, he had missed this bit.

"Sir," Tessa said, "your mouth is hanging open."

He snapped it shut and took the stone from my outstretched hand. "Incredible," he whispered. "You..." He shook his head in disbelief and held it up so that the light passed through it. "Incredible! Here I am, setting you out on a quest, and you have the object of our search already in your pocket—one of them, anyway. Where did you get it?"

Quickly, I told him an abbreviated version of our adventures on Daru.

"I knew that you went somewhere," he said. "I mean, you came back with Ioden's missing charge, but Hawk assured me there was nothing notable to report."

"I wasn't ready to talk about it," I admitted.

He nodded, then held up the bloodstone. "Shall I put it with the others?" At a shrug from me, he placed it carefully—almost reverently—on the bottom shelf. "Three stones, then," he said. "And three Skelligard students to find them."

I cleared my throat. "Two, technically, since you expelled me last week."

He waved a hand. "Yes, yes. Your ship leaves at midnight. Be at the docks. And Simon"—he went back to his desk and opened the drawer again—"before I forget, there is one last gift I should like to bestow on you. It is not much, but it is the most useful item I have in my possession." He drew out what looked like a small brick of black glass, and Drake gasped so hard he nearly swallowed my elbow, which had been in the vicinity of his mouth since I had raised my hand to scratch an eyebrow.[50]

"Is that a-a-a—"

"Yes," Gladstone said. "It is a sorrowstone."

"A what?" I said.

Gladstone's face fell. "I admit, I had hoped you would be familiar with sorrowstones."

"I gave him Hermatige's *Index of Rare Magical Artifacts* to read," Drake said in a rush, "but he pretended to lose it!"

"I *did* lose that book!" I lied. Instantly I began to itch behind an ear, but I refused to scratch it. I knew Drake would be watching for signs like that.[51]

Gladstone struggled not to grin. "Yes, well…a sorrowstone draws negative emotion out of a person. Fear,

---

[50] Usually, you don't get to see characters in books do things like scratch their eyebrows, pick their noses, sneeze, stretch their necks, or pass gas. Not only is it impolite to describe all these details, but it detracts from the story. Except in this case, as my editor has insisted that I give a plausible reason for Drake almost swallowing my elbow when he gasps. Now you know.

[51] If you are wondering why lying made my ear itch, well…you should have read book one. Still, the brief answer is that I am magically bound to live by a moral code (which I wrote for myself when I didn't know I'd be magically bound to live by it). When I live by it, I get extra magic power from the Zohar, which are kind of like the gods of magic. When I disobey it, the Zohar mess with me like this. As you read below, basic lying isn't *technically* against my code, but is definitely borderline and runs contrary to the spirit of it. This is my code:

I will be my best self.

I will honor my word.

I will help those I can.

I will never give up.

regret, worry, anger, and yes, sorrow. This may not seem like a fitting gift for an adventure such as yours, but I have found through the years that the greatest battles I ever fight occur inside myself."

He seemed to consider the stone for a moment, and for a second I thought he was going to take it back. He almost seemed as if he didn't want to part with it. "Use this often. It will lend you aid that you cannot imagine." He placed it in my hand.

"Now," he said, "I take my leave of you. May you have Rellik's own luck on your journey. The hope of all wizards goes with you."

I was in such a good mood when we left Gladstone's office that not even the sight of Ioden walking down the hall toward us could dampen my spirits. "Hi, Master Historidumb—I mean, Master *Historian*," I called. "How's McKenzie doing? You know, Rone sent a bloodhound to chew me out for rescuing her."

He was still several feet away, but I could just see his feral smile in the dim torchlight. "No less than you deserve," Ioden spat.

As soon as I'd seen him, I had the thought that now might be a good time to try out one of the untested turncoat knobs. Generally I did this in a quiet, out-of-the-way place, where I was less likely to hurt someone, but I was feeling a bit reckless. I focused all my thought on him as I turned a knob on the right jacket panel (A6), channeling as much contempt as possible.[52]

As soon as I turned it, Ioden vanished from view.

"Nice!" Drake said. "Did you kill him?"

"Probably not," I said. "My luck is never *that* good."

"Simon," Tessa scolded. "You *really* shouldn't do things like that." But she was getting her notebook out of her pocket just the same. "What knob did you turn?"

"A6." I looked around, but the school's least favorite teacher was nowhere to be found. "Huh," I said, pointing at a stink bug I'd spotted near Drake's boots. "Maybe it turned him into that?"

Drake smashed it hopefully, ignoring Tessa's protestations.[53]

Just then, Ioden reappeared so close to me that he was literally standing on my toes. I shoved him away, and he shrieked: "WHAT HAPPENED? Did you— What happened?"

"Ioden?" Gladstone's voice filtered through his office door. "Everything all right out there?"

"*What* the... I was..." Ioden mumbled to himself, staring off into space. "I was...but then I *wasn't*..."

"Excuse us, sir," Tessa said, steering me away from him. "Have a lovely day."

When we reached the landing at the opposite end of

---

[52] My intention didn't always matter much with the knobs, but sometimes it made all the difference.

[53] An effort to fight against or "protest" something.

the hall, all three of us burst into laughter.

"Simon," Drake said, when he'd gained control once more. "Why do you keep scratching your ear?"

"Agh!" I said. "Fine! I lied to you, okay? I didn't really lose that book. I buried it when you weren't looking."

"I know," Drake said. "Feel better?"

I had raised my hand to my ear again, but the itch was already gone. "Yeah," I mumbled. "Whatever. Come on. We have a ship to catch."

5

A MOTHER'S LOVE

My mother was the first person I ever met (obviously).
Everyone else has paled in comparison.

—Simon Fayter[54]

I don't care how that man treats you, Simon," my mother said, waving a ladle. "I expect *you* to treat *him* with the human decency that he deserves."

"But, Mom," I objected, "I'm not sure Ioden's a human."

She smacked me on the head with the ladle while Tessa looked on in approval. It was dinnertime, and my mom was cooking us her famous chicken noodle soup. She didn't know it yet, because I hadn't told her, but it was a farewell dinner. Drake and Tessa were there, too—and the Tike, of course. The Tike loves my mom's cooking.

"And," Mom went on, "what have I told you about experimenting with your turncoat in public? It's so unsafe. You could have hurt the man!"

"It's not *that* unsafe," I said. "See?" I reached into my turncoat and turned B2 (*Silvertongue*). Except that I reached into the wrong side...so I *didn't* turn B2 at all. I

---

[54] Don't tell me you've never heard of me.

turned B8. B2 unleashes a sweet power that lets me say the perfect thing for any situation. I didn't have a clue what B8 did, but I was about to find out.

My ears tingled, and then, as if from a great distance, I heard someone say, "—a smarter boy than I thought, this Simon. Thought to look through her drawers, he did, Fidget. Found her diary when he was shuffling through her underwear! That's when he figured out who she was, I imagine…"

Everyone was staring at me. "What?" I said, clearing my throat and hoping that I was the only one who had heard it. Judging by the look on my mom's face, I was out of luck.

"You were looking through my underwear?" Tessa shrieked, smacking me.

"Ouch! No!"

"You were looking through some *other* girl's underwear?" she demanded, smacking me again.[55]

My mom began poking me with the ladle.

"Ack! Stop, Mom! You're getting soup all over the turncoat! It was an evil sorceress's underwear drawer, and I was looking for clues, okay?"

"Looking for *clues*," my mom said in a mocking tone. "A likely story. And just *who* is talking about you behind your back, then? Whose voice did we just hear? And what are you supposed to have guessed?"

"How am I supposed to know?"

It took a while, but eventually we got her calmed back

---

[55] Girls are so confusing sometimes.

down. Then I explained about Mistress Zie and how my secret-agentlike infiltration of her dresser had led to me discovering her true identity and saving Daru. After that, she didn't seem quite so upset.

"So," she said as we sat down at the table. "When are you leaving? I know you met with Gladstone today."

"How can you possibly know that?" I said. "It was a *secret* meeting, Mom."

"I'm your mother, Simon. I know everything."

"And," the Tike added, "you have tea with Gladstone every afternoon."

"*And* I have tea with Gladstone every now and then," my mom added. "Get that salt away from my soup, Tike! Yes. I have tea with him—loves my cookies, that man. Bless him. And he told me everything. Including that little incident with the dog this morning." She shot me a withering glance, and I felt my cheeks redden. I hadn't told her about that yet either.

"The only thing he did not tell me is exactly when you leave. So when is it?"

"Err," I began, searching for a good lie.

"Tonight, Mrs. Jacobson," Tessa said. "We leave tonight."

"Call me Ruth, dear," Mom said sweetly.[56]

I gave Tessa my best "we were friends before you did *that*" glare, and my mom poked me with her ladle again. "I'm the only one who gets to glare when we have guests,

---

[56] Mom loved Tessa. Go figure.

Simon. Anyway, I thought it might be tonight. I'm already packed."

"Err...packed?" I said.

"Packed," she repeated, enunciating the word carefully. "P-A-C-K-E—"

"I know how to spell it," I snapped. "Why are you packed, Mom?"

"Because, I'm coming *with* you, dear." She dumped some soup in my bowl.

"But—"

"I'm kidding, Simon," she said. "Wipe that ridiculous look off your face. Of course I know I can't come along. No doubt I would only get in the way. But you be careful, you hear me? And don't get any stupid ideas about how you have to sacrifice your life to save the universe, no matter what Hawk says. If you can't find a way to save the world safely, don't bother doing it. If I have to learn magic or swordplay or sorcery or what not, and come across the galaxy to save you, that's what I'll do."

She brandished her ladle like a sword as she spoke (it was impossible for my mom to talk without moving her hands). Then she pointed it at me. "But you better not make me do that. Be careful, you hear? And stick to your code! And try, once in a while, to not *completely* ignore the advice of your friends..."

I mumbled something into my soup.

"What's that?" Mom snapped.

"Yes, Mother," the Tike whispered. "I'll do my best."

"*Yes, Mother,*" I echoed. "I'll do my best." I felt my

cheeks redden and avoided eye contact with everyone. Meekness always made me uncomfortable.

"That's more like it," my mom said. Then she rounded on the Tike. "And you, Tike. I expect you to keep these children safe."

"You shall not see me alive again without them by my side," the Tike said seriously.

"Ah," Mom said, sloshing a half ladle of soup onto the table. "What a fervent thing to say. However…" She cleared her throat the way she always did before saying something I wouldn't like. "Though I cannot go on this journey, I am determined to do something to protect you."

"Here we go," I said.

"Hawk has helped me whip up a little spell of protection for you," she said with relish.

"Oh boy," I said. "Mom, that's really not necces—"

I was cut off as Tessa slapped me in the back of the head. My mom, who was rummaging through her purse, didn't notice. A second later, she drew out a small red bird. It was perched on the end of her forefinger, like a real bird, and yet it was made entirely of what looked like—

"Blood?" Tessa said.

"Oooh," Drake said, straightening his glasses with interest. "A Rimbakka! A blood bird. I've never actually seen one before. Terribly difficult to make. My aunt Spesti tried to do it once—Dad dared her to—and she nearly bled to death all over Grandma's favorite spy-spun rug…"

Indeed, the small red bird *was* the precise color of fresh blood, though its body was smooth and firm like glass. It was not a statue, but a living bird—if *living* was the right word—unlike anything I had seen before but vaguely reminiscent of a hummingbird in shape and size.

"If I can't come," my mother said, "this Rimbakka is the next best thing, Simon. Please take it with you."

"Err, thanks, Mom," I said, reaching for the bird. "What does it do?"

"It melds with your skin like a living tattoo," Drake explained, breathless. "It sees everything you do and reports back to her and binds your lives together by a magical blood bond."

"WHAT?" I whipped my hand back and planted it firmly in my pocket. "I don't think so, Mom. I mean, I know you want to be involved, but don't you think this is a little much?"

"Simon," Drake said, "you can't say no! This is so cool! I'd kill to have a Rimbakka from my dad."

"Indeed," the Tike said. "Such a gift cannot be easily refused, for its price was great."

I didn't know what she was talking about, but I was sure I didn't want a mommy-cam embedded in my skin. Awkward…

"No," I said. "Sorry, Mom, but I can't take it." I met her gaze and knew that she sensed my resolve, because her shoulders slumped in defeat.

"I will take it," the Tike said. She scooted her chair closer to my mom and spread her hand out against her own throat, indicating a space. "Place it here, so that all may see, and so that you may see all."

"Now hold on just a second," I began, but my mother was beaming now.

"Yes! That's brilliant, Tike. This will be just as good. Better, really, because I'll be able to see him as well. I know the bond you share with my son. And you know..." But the remainder of what she said was too quiet for me to hear, for she had leaned in and was whispering now.

"I know," the Tike said, placing a hand on my mother's shoulder. "My people call the Rimbakka the Last Devotion because of that. I will not forget."

I had no idea what they were talking about, but my mother closed her eyes as if finally at peace about something, and then raised the small blood-colored bird, touching the tip of her forefinger against the Tike's neck. The bird immediately hopped off her finger and *fell* into the Tike's skin. That's the only way I can describe it. One moment, the bird was three dimensional, and the next it was transfixed upon her skin like a blood-red tattoo caught in midflight, wings spread wide and feathers splayed. As I looked at it, the bird's head turned to look at me, and I jumped.

My mother closed her eyes and grinned, and I had the strange feeling that she was still looking at me.

After a moment, Tessa cleared her throat. "The soup is lovely, Mrs. Jacobson," she said.

"Oh," my mother said, returning from her little trance. "Thank you, dear."

"You know," Tessa continued, "I'm sure we'll all be fine. We'll be home safe and sound before you know it."

"I hope so," my mother said. Then she aimed a soft kick at me under the table. "Either way, I'll be watching."

I stirred my soup glumly and listened to the others talk. My mind was elsewhere, thinking about Tessa's words. *Would* we be home safe and sound, and soon?

Probably not. It's not our style.

6

A SHIP WITH SPIRIT

In this chapter, there do be pirates.

—Austin J. Bailey[57]

It was nearly midnight when I caught sight of the first spacesail vessel—not to mention the first pirate ship—that I had ever seen. I was standing on the dock at the foot of the castle's island with Tessa, Drake, and the Tike beside me. Skelligard stood behind us, its towers and pinnacles rising into a blood-red sky. Before us lay a sea of stars—glistening orbs of light suspended in the pitch-black water. I walked to the end of the dark wooden pier and glanced over the edge.

"Are those really stars?" I said, leaning out over the water. "They look more like glow-in-the-dark soccer balls."

"Are you insane?" Tessa said, yanking me back from the edge. "Of course they're stars! Each of those stars is from a different solar system, and if you were to fall in…"

"That doesn't make any sense," I said.

---

[57] A lesser-known author of mediocre fantasy novels who claims to have written my autobiography. What a punk.

Drake sighed. "If you had read *Advances in Astrophysics, the Last 1,000 Years* by Vildovoch like I told you to, it would make sense."

"Well, excuse me if I want to sleep every now and then."

"Hush up," Tessa said. "Hawk's coming."

By the time I turned around, Hawk was already there. I should've heard him coming, and it should have taken him a good long time to walk down the pier, but then Hawk was one of the most powerful wizards alive, and he was a Quick, which meant that he could move really fast when he wanted to.

"Good morning," Hawk said cheerfully. "Lovely day to rendezvous with a band of bloodthirsty pirates, don't you think?"

"Hawk!" Tessa exclaimed. "What happened to your robes?"

"What's wrong with them?" he said, glancing down at his clothes.

"Well…" Tessa stammered. "They look, uh…*normal.*"

I could see what she meant. Hawk generally looked like he had found his clothing in a dumpster, or perhaps stolen it from an armadillo nest. Today, he was dressed in clean, well-fitting gray robes similar to those that the other teachers normally wore.

"Ahh," Hawk said. "Well, as you may know, here at Skelligard I have a reputation of being somewhat of a…"

"Fuddy duddy?" I suggested.

Hawk smiled appreciatively. "Yes. That. A reputation

takes years to build, you know, and I wouldn't want to disappoint people. However, when traveling, it often behooves one to blend in. Did you all have breakfast?"

"Breakfast?" Tessa said. "It's midnight."

"Yes," Hawk said. "But wizards always eat before we start a journey. It's one of our rules."

"The mess wasn't open," I said. "I checked."

"I brought snacks!" Drake said, unzipping a side pocket of his pack. He withdrew what looked like three moldy green apples. "Anyone want a codpok bladder?" He bit into the first one with obvious relish, then handed me the second. It smelled like crab farts.

"Hawk?" Drake said.

"Thank you, Drake," Hawk said, accepting it politely. "I understand the codpok bladder is considered to be a delicacy." He took a whiff of it, then tossed it into the sea when Drake wasn't looking.

I bit mine tentatively. "Ick! It tastes like crab farts!"

"Don't throw it away!" Drake said, snatching it out my hand. "I'll eat it later."

"Aha!" Hawk leaned over the railing, squinting at something in the distance. "I believe our ride is here."

I followed his gaze to a distant point where the black water was rippling. A long blue pole pierced the surface of the starlit sea, followed by the carved figure of a woman. Portholes came next, and a mast, and then the ship tipped down and landed in the sea of stars with a splash that sent universes swirling away from its prow.

"Behold," Hawk said dramatically. "The *Calliope*."

Drake groaned as the blue ship pulled up alongside the dock. "I thought you were messing with us. We really are going to travel in a pirate ship? How is this a good idea? Pirates *hate* minotaurs, Hawk. You know that. They have ever since the war."[58]

"You'll be *fine*," Hawk told him. "Pirate transport is the best option open to us since the Portal-Potty network is so limited, and our mysterious leader still refuses to tell us where we are going." Hawk gave me a curious look, but I shook my head.

"Not until we're on board," I said firmly.

"Couldn't we take a different ship?" Drake complained.

"We could. But pirates know the seven seals better than anyone, and they are extremely loyal to the Circle."

"And they're *pirates*!" I added excitedly.

The ship was so tall that we couldn't see to the deck above, but soon a gangplank was lowered, and a large figure mounted the far end, standing in clear relief against the red sky.

"Good marnin', Cap'n Hawk," the big man boomed, and he walked down the gangplank. As he approached, I saw that he was even bigger than I first thought. Three-hundred-pounds big, with biceps larger than my head and a belly the size of a Smart Car. He was dressed from top to bottom[59] in blue silk that matched his ship, and he

---

[58] Referencing the Great War of the Minotaurian home world, in which Drake's home planet was nearly annihilated by a gigantic armada of pirates led by none other than the famous Skelligard-castout-turned-Hollywood-movie-star, Sylvester Stallone.

[59] See? There's already some pirate booty in the story. Pirates are so fun...

had three sapphire studs through his right ear. In classic pirate fashion, he had a pointed maroon hat and wore two curved sabers, one on each hip.

"Good marnin', Cap'n Bast," Hawk said, in a perfect parrot[60] of the pirate's drawl. "Me complerments to yer crew on the swift journey."

Drake sneezed.[61] "B-B-Bast the Vast?" he said before he could stop himself. He clamped a hand over his mouth at the end, but it was too late.

Captain Bast's huge head swung slowly around, and his stony gaze settled on Drake, sizing him up from head to foot. "Do ye be bringin' *all* these...eh, *people* along with you, Cap'n Hawk?"

It was clear from the way he said it that Bast didn't think Drake really qualified as a person.

"Aye, Cap'n," Hawk said. "Allow me ter interoduciate them ter yeh. The one that canno' keep 'is thoughts ter 'imself is Drakus Bright."

"Friends call me Drake," Drake said automatically, then tried again to swallow his tongue.

Bast's eyes narrowed considerably. "Pleased to meet you, Drakus. It do be a long, sad run of years since we had a minotaur aboard. Me first mate ate the last one."

Drake sneezed again, then hid behind Tessa.

"That girl Drake's hidin' behind do be called Tessa

---

[60] The word "parrot" in this case is used in the verb form and means an echo or repetition. It's a bit forced, but we're describing pirates, so I couldn't resist.

[61] This is Drake's stress reaction. Squids ink. Puffer fish puff. Redheads blush. Girls scream. Drake sneezes.

Strong," Hawk continued. "This is the Tike, and this here be Simon Fayter, newest member o' the Circle o' Eight."[62]

Captain Bast closed the distance between us and took my hand in his giant leathery one. "I do be pleased above all to meet you, Cap'n Simon. Welcome aboard the *Calliope* to you and yer crew."

"Err...thanks," I said awkwardly.

Without warning, Captain Bast suddenly pulled me close, lifting me off my feet and nearly wrenching my shoulder out of its joint, so that our faces were mere inches apart.[63] "Do ye know who be the figurehead on this here ship, Simon Fayter?"

I glanced over the captain's shoulder and saw that the scantily clad woman on the prow was clutching several scrolls to her chest. I nodded, feeling—not for the first time—immensely grateful for the classical education that I had received from Atticus. "Calliope. A mythological figure," I said. "The Greek goddess of eloquence and poetry."

Captain Bast frowned. "I don'a be knowin' what ye mean by 'mit'ological,' or 'Geek' but the rest of it ye do have rightly. And that is why I be givin' ye this one piece o' advice." He pulled me slightly closer, a thing which I had

---

[62] If you are shocked by how fluently Hawk speaks pirate, you are not alone. I didn't want to bother you with a bunch of annoying footnotes pointing out each instance (I would never do that), but I should tell you that those were not all real words.

[63] If you didn't know, space pirates commonly gargle with a mixture of two parts barnacloid jelly reduction, one part ogre "essence" (That's what pirates call it, but let's be honest—it's ogre pee.) Anyway, I very nearly blacked out. Which, of course, would have been quite rude.

not thought possible. "The crew o' this here ship do valyoo elliocution[64] an' proper speakin' above all else, an' if ye do be wantin' thar respect, ye will be haftin'[65] ter[66] speak with more properness[67] and el'o'kwenz[68] than 'Err...thanks.' Crystal?"[69]

Far from understanding, I was very confused. I felt as if an angry Turkish baker had stuck a pastry bag up my nose and filled my brain with instant mashed potatoes. Being uncommonly brilliant, however, I quickly recovered and began speaking with the most guttural drawl I could muster.

"I do be catchin' yer drift, Cap'n. I canno' claim ter be the most sofistimicated orator, but I'll be surely steppin' up me game a notch or thraye." I held of the last three fingers of my right hand, including the pinky that had recently been cut off.

Captain Bast looked over my pinky stub and nodded in approval. Then he broke into a wide—and stinky—grin. "Ye'll do jes' fine."

After boarding the *Calliope*, Captain Bast gave each of us

---

[64] Not quite a word. What he's looking for of course, is "elocution," which is, ironically, the skill of clear and expressive speech.

[65] Not a word.

[66] Not a word.

[67] Not a word. Try "propriety," Captain.

[68] Do I even have to say it?

[69] By this, I assume he was referencing the expression "crystal clear" and meant "Do you understand?"

a spacer ring, which, as he described it, would ensure that none of us would suffocate in space. Or freeze to death. Or get lost forever if we fell overboard.

"Tink of 'em like magical life preservers," he said.

After that, he introduced us to the crew—by which I mean, he grunted a couple names and pointed at several people. We soon discovered (to Drake's horror) that Captain Bast was by far the most genteel[70] pirate on the ship. Most of them were not even human. What's more, many had makeshift prosthetics, like fishing hooks or giant crab pincers, which had clearly been spliced into shoulders and hips by some sort of witch doctor after losing a limb.[71]

As far as I could see, there were two or three humans, a dugar, two goblins, and a satyr. The first mate, a man named Nub, was a head shorter than Bast but just as wide. He had two peg legs, a peg arm, three peg fingers, a peg eye, and most disturbing of all, a peg sticking out of the side of his head. He took one look at Drake and broke into a wide, slow grin, revealing several peg teeth.

Bast propped one foot on a barrel, tucked a thumb inside his belt, and the crew fell silent. "Boys," he said, "our journey do be 'bout to begin. I know the lot o' yer ain't got a clue as ter what we're about, an' I suppose I don' rightly know meself. But that ain't never stopped us 'afore. We got the call, an' we answered. We e'er serve the Circle o' Eight."

---

[70] Polite, refined, or respectable. Especially in a social sense.
[71] I know what you're thinking. Pinky prosthesis! Unfortunately, there just wasn't time...

"AYE-AYE," the crew chanted in unison, making Drake sneeze.

"As ye know, all knights o' the Circle are considered captains the moment they board a pirate vessel, so 'tis Cap'n Hawk and Cap'n Simon to ye, or ye walk the plank."

"Aye-aye," the crew said.

"Really?" I said. "I'm a captain now?"

Hawk stepped on my foot, clearing his throat.

"Cap'ns," Bast said politely, turning to Hawk and me, "this here ship do be the greates' an' the fastes', not ter mentionate the mos' beautifules' in the pirate armada. A ship with spirit, she do be. An' 'er crew, ther most fearsome in all uncharted space, an' the most black-breathed, back-boned, backhanded, backward, backside-ugly lump o' pirate flesh that e'er did sail the seven seals." The crew burst into a chorus of raucous[72] aye-ayes at this. After which, Captain Bast opened one hand to us and one hand to his men. "Cap'ns, yer crew." Then he sat down.

The crew's eyes all moved from Hawk to me and back to Hawk again.

"Well, *Cap'n* Simon," Hawk said pleasantly. "Whar' do we be goin'?"

I puffed out my chest in the most captainy[73] way possible and tried to sound like I knew what I was talking about: "We do be seekin' the fabled island of Yap, in the Sea of Timidity, by the Star of Dark Haven, and the man called Colm the Insane."

---

[72] This word is pronounced "ROCK-us," and means "disturbingly loud."

[73] Not a word.

7

THE CREW

Crew: a group of people who work on and operate a ship, boat, tank, aircraft, spacecraft, train, or mobile tetherball factory.
—The Internet[74]

To say that the crew was surprised by my declaration would be a gross understatement. And when I say gross, I don't mean "nasty." I mean a "great amount." A regular understatement would be saying "Yeah, I could eat" when in fact you haven't eaten for several hours, and your tummy grumbled a minute ago.

A *gross* understatement would be like someone saying "How was your day?" and you responding "Interesting" when in fact during your morning walk, your Chihuahua was picked off by an Andean Condor and carried into the sky while you dangled off the leash, which you then had to release in order to avoid being hit by a 747 on landing approach, which hit you anyway before you dropped two hundred feet to crash land on top of a hot air balloon shaped like Elvis Presley's pompadour.[75] Yes. That

---

[74] A cool thing invented by a dude named Bob.
[75] The technical term for the epic 1950's *hairstyle* that normal people simply refer to as "That swoopy wave thing."

happened to me once. Obviously on an *unlucky* day.[76] By the way, in case you're wondering, I set out with pirates on a *lucky* day. It would have been irresponsible to do otherwise.

As I was saying, the crew was surprised. Some of them were even horrified. Those who were standing sat down or leaned against something, and those who had been sitting jumped to their feet with exclamations before realizing that they were not actually in any danger yet. A diminutive pirate with chimplike legs and a hook for an arm let out a girly squeal and jumped overboard.

Even Nub, the first mate, went slightly pale and then frowned so deeply that his peg teeth made small lumps beneath lip. The only one apparently unaffected was a bearlike man who, I must admit, seemed a bit slower than the others—just because he didn't talk much. Okay, *at all*. Also because he had a stuffed-animal parrot sewn onto the shoulder of his tunic so that it stood up like a real one. I only mention this because right then, he happened to reach up and squeeze the parrot, which made a squeaking sound similar to a child's bicycle horn. The noise seemed to bring everyone back to their senses, and they all looked to Captain Bast.

"Well, don' jus' stand thar gawkin' like a bunch o' gaffylarks! Get to it! Murphy, set course ter the sixth seal. Hobnob, Noblob, man the sails. Nub, see if yer can find yer brother. An' Silki, stop squeakin' tha' infernal parrot

---

[76] I have the most incredible luck. Good and bad luck, depending on the day. See Book one for more details.

or I swear I'll eat it fer dinner!"

At his words, the big blue dugar sped to the tiller, the goblins scaled the mast, the first mate tied a rope around his waist and hopped over the side, and the bearlike pirate stopped squeaking his parrot.

The only crewmember, by the way, who remained completely unmoved during this whole scene was the satyr.

Now, I have to say something here about satyrs, because too many people on Earth imagine them as cute little cupids with hairy goat legs and delicate horns. Not so. They're freaking scary. Much like minotaurs,[77] satyrs are a fearsome, warlike race and pretty much dominate humans in terms of size and strength (though not looks, obviously).

"You got summat to say, Mortazar?" Captain Bast asked, clearly noticing the same thing I had. The satyr leaned out of the shadows. A breeze rustled through his shining black chest-carpet and he flexed an arm with a restless, predatory twitch, causing his muscles to bulge. He tipped his head forward slightly so that his razor-sharp horns glistened in the sunlight.

"Maybe I do," he said in a hoarse whisper that covered

---

[77] Drake is a minotaur, remember? Don't get them confused, please. Minotaurs have the lower body of a super buff human and the head of a bull. Satyrs have the upper body of a super buff human and the legs and horns of a goat. Both of them, of course, have tons of chest hair (think wooly mammoth). Make no mistake: either one could beat you up. Unless you're Chuck Norris. In which case, I'd like your autograph.

my neck with goose flesh.[78] "If the *captains* do wish ter listen…"

"Speak yer mind," Bast said.

"Fire away," Hawk said.

"Go ahead," I said.

Mortazar's eyes narrowed. "The Star of Dark Haven do be a place sought by suicidal fools. Only a truly *black* luck would send us there. Mark me words, *Captains*: Nothing good do come from such a journey."

Before any of us could respond, he had turned his back and began busily preparing the ship for departure.

"What a pleasant fellow," Hawk said.

"Aye," Captain Bast said. "Mortazar do be our security specialist. He do have the personality o' a dead fish, but he's more dangerous than the devil 'imself in a fight."

"Easy ter believe," I said. "Captain, will the rest o' the crew think like dis one? That this do be a fool's errand?"

Captain Bast cleared his throat. "Per'aps this do be a matter best disgusted in private. Might I show ye to yer chambers?"

"Oh, yes, please," Drake said, looking pale. "I would very much like to see my chambers."[79]

---

[78] i.e. goose bumps, goose pimples, cutis anserina, or horripilation. The involuntary straightening of hair follicles which occurs when we experience extreme emotions or sudden changes in temperature. Scientists think our *ape*cestors (not a word) used this to make themselves look bigger and to stay warm on cold nights.

[79] I don't want you to get the wrong idea about Drake. Deep down, he's just as adventuresome and courageous as the rest of us. It's just that his initial response to danger is the same as his initial response to food poisoning.

"I think I'll stay up here," Tessa said, breathing deeply. "It's been a long time since I've been on a ship, and I've never spent much time with pirates."

Captain Bast gave her a fond look. "Aye, an' they 'aven't spen' much time 'round young ladies. They be glad ta 'ave ya about, and ye'll be nothin' but safe in their company." He hesitated. "Only, don' pay no mind to their rough talk… And don' drink anythin' they give ya, and don't go up the mast with 'em. And—"

"I think ye'll find that Tessa do be quite capable of taking care of herself," Hawk said easily, motioning for Bast to continue on.

"Looks li' she ain' the only one," Bast said, peering up at the main mast as he opened a door to the lower deck. I followed his gaze and was surprised to see the Tike crawling over a yardarm, inspecting knots as though she were a professional sailor. The Tike, as she constantly reminded me, knew almost everything, and had learned most of it several hundred years before I was born.

Bast ducked under the low wooden portal onto the staircase, and I was about to follow when Hawk grabbed my arm.

"Wait," he said. "You'll want to see this."

"See what?" I asked.

Just then, Nub appeared over the side of the ship carrying the diminutive monkey-legged pirate that had jumped overboard earlier.

"I got 'im!" he crowed. "Let's get outta here. Murphy! Mortazar! Dive! Dive!"

All around the ship, several voices echoed the chorus. "Dive! Dive!" And a moment later, the ship pitched forward so violently that I was knocked off my feet. To my horror, the prow of the ship dipped beneath the sea of stars. The back end pivoted into the air, and I began to slide toward the front of the ship. It tilted further, and I was free-falling, with Drake right beside me, both of us trying and failing to grab hold of something to stop our fall.

"Watch out!" I cried. The prow of the ship was no longer visible, and we were falling straight into the sea of stars. A second later, we hit it.

I thought it would feel like water. Or perhaps an electrical current, but instead I felt as if I had entered an incredibly large room. There was a sense of vastness and a sudden awareness of my own insignificance. The sea itself felt like a cool, damp breeze, and stars rolled over me like pinpricks of fire.

Then it was gone.

The sea of stars was nowhere to be seen. Instead, we were sailing through empty space, surrounded by blackness, and here and there, far off, was a swirl of color or light that meant a distant star. A great lamp at the top of the mainmast burst into light, illuminating the deck of the ship with a pale cast of color.

Beside me, Drake looked even paler than before.

"You okay?" I said.

He shook his head, pressing the back of his hand to his

mouth. "I think I swallowed a nebula."[80]

---

[80] An interstellar dust cloud filled with gas.

8

BLACK LUCK

In my experience, there's no such thing as luck.

—Obi-Wan Kenobi[81]

This do be the last known location o' the Star o' Dark Haven," Captain Bast said, taking a knife out of his boot and stabbing it through an unfamiliar constellation on one of the seven star maps that were strewn across the gnarled oak worktable in the captain's cabin. "For lack o' a better plan, this do be our current course, though it be known by every sailor tha' Dark Haven is no' ever seen in the same place twice." He gave a deep sigh and leaned back in his chair.

Below deck, Captain Bast had showed Drake to the room that he and I would be sharing; Drake entered promptly then slammed the door. Unless I was hearing

---

[81] Born on the planet Stewjon and Padawan to the legendary Qui-Gon Jinn (also with a hyphenated name), Obi-Wan is known for being the only Jedi to ever cut a Sith in half inside of an ultra-high-security air-conditioning duct. A lesser-known fact is that he was always hopelessly accident prone in the bathroom, which is why—since all Jedis are required by law to shave with their lightsabers—he wore a beard.

things, he then vomited several times. Hopefully not onto my bunk. I was pretty sure Drake planned to stay locked in our cabin for the rest of the trip.

Bast and Hawk had then spent a couple of hours explaining the basics of space navigation to me, which essentially broke down like this: There are seven seals, not unlike the seven seas on Earth. That is, distinctive but connected bodies of space. And spacesail ships can access all of them, and travel between them. Their sails harness and redirect even the most subtle gravitational pulls created by various objects in space (stars, planets, black holes, Twinkies), enabling ships to move.

An object called a "diveratus" allows spacesail ships to "dive" into various galaxies and sail around on a local ocean of stars (as seen back on Skelligard), then dive back out again into the outer universe. There was also something in there about transdimensional astrostitching, quantum physics, and the space-time continuum, but it didn't seem very important. Actually, the most amazing thing I learned during our little study session was that though it was still mandatory for public spaces, Captain Bast didn't actually expect us to carry on in "pirate speak" while we were alone with him. Thank goodness.

"What exactly is so scary about Dark Haven?" I said. I couldn't help but feel like this was obvious to everyone but me.

"Dark Haven," Hawk said, "is a rather infamous[82] star system."

---

[82] Having an extremely bad reputation.

"Aye," Bast agreed. "Many's a ship that's gone in there, never to return. And many's a dastardly character who's gone there just to disappear, because he knows no one's fool enough to follow him in."

"Which brings us around to Colm the Insane," Hawk said. "Simon, up to this point I have respected your request for discretion, but I must ask, what do you actually *know* about Colm?"

"Eh…" I said. "Nothing."

"Ha!" Bast barked. "Honesty."

"Oh, yes," Hawk said. "Simon here's the honestest[83] ignoramus[84] that you'll ever meet."

"Hey," I said, "I had my reasons for keeping this whole thing on the down low. Unfortunately, that means I still don't know who he is." His name was given to me in secret, after all, and I hadn't talked to anyone about him before now. I did make a trip or two to the archives, but I couldn't exactly ask a librarian to give me a book about some super-secret dude. Drake, I later learned, had recently written a paper in which Colm featured prominently, and he could have enlightened me in about six seconds. Figures.

"Colm," Hawk began, "was one of the original knights of the Circle of Eight, back in the days of Rellik and Rone."

"Really?" I said. "You'd think I'd know that."

Hawk shrugged. "You'd think, but the minor accomplishments of the other knights have been overshadowed by the fame of Rellik and Rone. Most people

---

[83] Not a word.
[84] Just what it sounds like.

couldn't name them all, let alone tell you what they did. Colm, by the way, was a Bright, and a noted historian."

"A historian!" I said. "No wonder he'd be helpful to us."

"Perhaps," said Hawk. "Except that he's insane."

"And dead," Bast added.

"And dead," Hawk agreed. "It's common knowledge that Colm the Insane died in a bar accident after insulting a minotaur."

Bast nodded. "No' much of an accident tho, the way I heard the tale. Unless ye can call a minotaur breakin' a barstool over yer head *accidental.*"

I leaned back and folded my arms confidently. "Well, I'm pretty sure that he's alive and that he's just hiding inside this Dark Haven thingy."

Captain Bast pulled his knife out of the table and began to clean his fingernails with it. "Oh? An' what makes ye so sure?"

"I met with Rellik the other day, and he told me."

"Gah!" Bast's hand slipped with the knife, and he popped a bleeding finger in his mouth. "Exhooose me?" he said.

Hawk laughed, eyes gleaming. "Don't believe everything Simon says. He'll have you believing that Rellik's been at Skelligard this whole time, disguised as a fern."

"Okay, okay," I said. "So it was just a recording. But he did make it just for me, a thousand years in advance."

"Did he now?" Bast said. "And he told you to find

Colm? And he told you he would be on Dark Haven?"

"Yep."

"An' just how do ye sergest we go abou' findin' a star with no known location, which never appears in the same place twice?" Bast asked.

"Oh, I don't think that will be a problem," Hawk said.

"Eh?"

"Simon here will just stand behind the tiller for a while. Provided it's a lucky day, it shouldn't be more than twenty minutes or so before we accidentally collide with Dark Haven."

"Exactly," I said. "What could be simpler?"

Of course, nothing is ever as simple as it seems.

Except goldfish.

And of course, crayons.

But that's it. Goldfish and crayons. Everything else is complicated…

I arrived on deck to find a bunch of pirates standing in a circle, cheering. I forced my way to the center and found Tessa arm wrestling two rather burly-looking pirates at once. She was winning, of course.

"She do be too strong," one of the men said, sweat beading on his forehead. His arm was beginning to shake.

"No," his companion said. "I'll not be losing to a woman. Put yer back into it, Darett!"

Tessa frowned at this point, and I knew they were

in trouble. She jerked her arm and sent the two men sprawling on the deck, winking at me over her shoulder. The men in the circle gave exclamations of triumph and despair in turn, and several coins changed hands.

"All right," I said loudly, "get back to work 'afore she cleans the deck with all o' ye."

I watched happily as the men snapped to attention at my words, clearing the deck and returning to duty.

"You take all my fun away," Tessa said.

"*You* are a danger to my crew," I teased. "You might hurt someone."

She tilted her head. "*Your* crew?"

"Well, maybe not. But I am supposed to steer the ship now. Do you want to come?"

"Oh, no." She laughed. "If *you're* getting behind the wheel, I'm staying down here where it's safe. Try not to hit anything. I mean, it's space, after all, but I suppose *you* could still find something to crash into."

Brimming with Tessa's vote of confidence, I made my way to the tiller and spent the rest of the afternoon steering us randomly around deep space.

For a long time, nothing happened, and I became extremely bored.

For a solid hour, I zoned out, thinking about the bloodstones and the turncoat and my apparent inability to use magic. Eventually, I was roused from my stupor by the sound of harsh whispering from below. I leaned around the tiller and looked over the rail and saw Hawk and the

Tike, apparently arguing. I couldn't hear what they were saying, but Hawk was gesticulating[85] wildly, pointing now and then to the Tike's neck. The Tike glanced up at me, and Hawk followed her gaze. Then they both turned and disappeared from view.

I made a mental note to ask the Tike about it later, and then settled back into steering. It *was* a lucky day, of course, so after another hour or so, some pretty cool things happened. First, a brown floppy something flew past my head, and Nub plucked it out of the air.[86]

"Bless me pegs!" he cried. "It do be me favorite sock! I been lookin' fer this ten years now!"

"Sorry you can't use it anymore," I said.

"Eh?" he said, then his face fell as he looked down at his two peg legs.

After that, several other items just fell at our feet or bounced off the hull of the ship and were reeled in by the crew. Before long, several crewmembers had assembled lawn chairs on the deck and were placing bets about what we would find next. Apparently this wasn't normal, and they all attributed it to my luck.

All told, we found half a box of pirate gold, half a box of crayons, a rubber duck, a space pen, a George Foreman

---

[85] Using dramatic gestures.

[86] There's no air in space, but you know what I mean. Space, by the way, *is* a near-perfect vacuum, and like any good vacuum, there's a bunch of random stuff floating around inside it. Mostly dust particles and gas. And socks. If a sock is left out all alone, it can get sucked into space quite easily. That's why they go missing so often.

grill, George Foreman,[87] a complete collection of *Star Wars*-themed Pez dispensers tied together with fishing line, and a yellow bathtub. The last came out of nowhere like a missile and nearly took my head off, so I don't know how lucky that was…

However, we did *not* find Dark Haven.

Eventually, when it became apparent that my luck had run out, the crew folded up the lawn chairs and went back to work. After that, I didn't find anything else…unless you count the Dracumantula.

Dracumantula are a type of deep-space spider which hang around in huge formations looking like nothing more than a bit of mist. How giant spiders can survive in space or live without air, I don't know. Then again, all spiders have unexplainable evil powers. Usually, Dracumantula aren't very dangerous, but if you drive a huge ship through them, well…

"Are ye even watchin' where yer goin'?" Murphy said, his big blue hand gripping the rail next to where I stood at the tiller. His furry face was tight with worry.

"Of course I am."

"Look!" he hissed, pointing to a black misty thing in front of us. "There. And there! Ye don' want to be steerin' us thru that, lad. Do ye know wha' tha' is?"

"Uh…" I began, searching my memory for any reference on "space mist" that I may have read in Drake's books.

---

[87] Okay, not really.

Something vibrated deep beneath my feet. A second later, there was a sound like hail on a rooftop as something, or rather, *several* somethings, collided with the hull.

"Black luck!" the dugar cursed, grabbing the wheel and shoving me aside. He pushed on it, and the ship dove abruptly. "Hull breach!" he shouted. "Sky Spiders! Sky Spiders! Take defensive action!"

Not sure what he meant, I stayed where I was. The least I could do was refrain from messing things up any more. As an extra precaution, I put my hands in my pockets.

Meanwhile, the ship was a bustle of activity. The Tike and the two goblins were practically flying through the air above us, and with their movements, half the sails had already been folded away or rolled up. I looked to Mortazar, who had been prowling the main deck below us, but to my surprise he ran away from the fight into the belly of the ship. What a loser.

Then I saw them below us—a legion of black spiders the size of dinner plates pouring over the bow in a torrential wave, scrambling over the forecastle and up the mast. Just then I heard a rustling and looked down to see five spiders mount the quarterdeck not five feet from where I stood.

"They're poisonous," Murphy said. "Don' let 'em touch us."

I noticed that his hands were still on the wheel. He pushed in and turned sharply to the left, causing me to tumble to the deck. Likewise, a dozen or so sky spiders fell from the rigging of the foresail and back into space.

Apparently he intended to keep steering and let me protect him from the spiders. Awesome.

I unstrapped Rellik's sword from my back and unsheathed it. "Gibeah," I whispered, without much hope, and of course, nothing happened.

Although I had been training with it every day, I had never again managed to light it in the Midnight Blue fire as I had done in my battle with the Horror of Kane. Still, a fireless sword was better than no sword at all. The foremost spider skittered up the banister beside Murphy, and I sent my sword in a swift upward arc, cutting it neatly in half. Two more spiders fell quickly to my blade, but when I struck the fourth, my sword bounced off its hard shell, sending a jarring vibration up my arm.

"Ye got lucky with them firs' ones," Murphy said. "Their backs do be armored, and canno' be pierced 'cept by a magic-tempered blade."

"What a nice feature!" I said, kicking the spider back carefully and then cutting off its legs. It was doable, fighting them this way, just slow. I would be okay as long as they didn't come on us in numbers.

Two dozen sky spiders crawled over the edges of the quarterdeck, surrounding us completely. They were pouring onto the main deck now, covering almost every square inch of it.

I hacked, kicked, and even punched one spider right in the face, desperately trying to maintain a circle of safety around Murphy and the helm, but I was slowly losing ground.

"What else?" I demanded. "Tell me more about them."

"They do rely 'eavy on their sight. Above all, they do be afeared o' fire. And light."

"Why didn't you say so?" I reached into my jacket and turned, in quick succession, C1 (*Chameleon*), B4 (*Ninja*), and C4 (*Headlight*). All at once, I vanished from sight, blending in with my surroundings. A beam of light burst out of nowhere (aka my mouth), blinding spiders, and my sword blurred with a flurry of movement as I rolled, cartwheeled, and spun around the quarterdeck. Five seconds later, I was breathing hard, standing in the midst of two dozen spider corpses.

"Bless me blackened soul," Murphy said. "Ye do be a wizard indeed. Do ye 'ave enough magic ter destroy 'em all?"

"No." I said. The truth was, I had just used up a good deal of my useful powers. Too bad I didn't have a—what did Murphy call it?—a magic-tempered blade.

Kylanthus, I thought, *I'm disappointed in you.*

No sooner had I spoken the sword's name inside my head than the blade in my hand burst with energy. Crimson fire wreathed the steel, crackling gently in the chill air.

"Aye," Murphy said with a nod, "that'll do the trick."

I turned B1 (*Leap*), and rocketed into the air, vaulting over the mainsail before diving headfirst toward the deck below. As I fell, I shouted "Wow wow wow wow wow wow wow wow wow wow wow wow wow!" as fast as I could, which had the effect of sending machine-gun bursts of blinding headlight onto the cluster of spiders below, disorienting them. I flipped over at the last second and landed on my feet, dancing among the spiders in a whirlwind of fire and steel.

I wasn't alone, either. The Tike descended from her battle on the mainmast and we flopped[88] back to back. Before long, Hawk was there, too, spinning his own golden-flamed sword with deadly precision. Tessa was wielding her cram cudgel, smashing spiders right and left, and leaving rather large dents in the ship.

Finally, Mortazar was there, a giant torch in each hand, bearing the familiar blue flames that adorned Skelligard at night. The instant I saw the ferocious determination on his face, I regretted my earlier thought of him. That was what he had been doing: retrieving the one weapon that would save us in the end. The Midnight Blue.

He ran to the edge of the ship and opened a silver box that I had not seen before, thrusting the end of a torch inside. Then he crossed to the opposite side and did the same thing. A second later, the entire hull of the ship was covered in blue fire.

The spiders screamed and fled. Those that were not consumed by the heat jumped into space and were gone.

By the way, I'm sorry that this chapter is so long. It's already nearly twice as long as the last one, but when space spiders attack, you just kind of have to go with it. If it

---

[88] This word was supposed to be "fought" before my magic dictation machine messed it up...but I think it's funnier this way. I can just imagine you reading this and thinking, "Wait a minute. He's flopping around now? What the heck?"

makes you feel any better, the next chapter is the shortest chapter in the whole book.

When the battle was over, the crew gave a cheer, and we all looked around, making sure everyone was okay. Then Captain Bast burst through the door from the lower decks and shouted "Murphy! Wha' in black blazes be wrong with ye? A blind baby could steer this ship more smootherly[89] than—OY! What's all this, then?"

It was a silly question, but that's because it takes a long time to describe action sequences in books. In reality, the whole thing took less than two minutes, and there's really no way he would've known what was going on, being down below.

"We flew into a swarm o' sky spiders," Mortazar said flatly.

"What?" Bast snapped, turning an accusatory glare at Murphy.

Murphy pointed at me and shrugged. "The kid was drivin'."

"Oops," I said, trying to sound penitent.

Murphy cleared his throat. "After that," he went on, "Cap'n Simon killed about two hundred spiders all by 'imself in the most imperessivatin' display of wizardry I ever seen, an' saved the ship."

"O' course he did," Captain Bast said, relaxing slightly. "Well, don' jus' stand there gawkin'! Get this mess cleaned up. I be back in twenty minutes, and it bett'r be spic n'

---

[89] You don't tell Captain Bast he can't make up words when he's all fired up.

span by then, or ye'll all walk the plank!'"

"I wonder if anyone has ever actually walked the plank," Tessa said, just loud enough for me to hear. She was leaning against her cudgel, wiping sweat from her face. She reminded me of a little girl leaning on a baseball bat that was much too big for her. She gave me a little grin. "I've never seen you fight like that, Simon."

"Me?" I said. "You should have seen yourself!" I took a solid stance and then swung an invisible bat, pretending to hit a home run. Then I gave her a double thumbs-up and winked. "Nice hittin', Babe."[90]

Tessa, who had been grinning at my little skit, suddenly blushed a deep shade of red.

Then she slapped me.

"Ouch!" I said. "What was that for?"

"Oh, *nothing*," she said coldly. "I'm going to go check on Drake now, *babe*."

It was then that I remembered she was not from Earth, and therefore might not actually know about Babe Ruth, or baseball for that matter.

Hawk clapped me on the back, winked, and gave me a double thumbs-up, just as I had given Tessa. "Excellent communication skills, babe! Almost as impressive as

---

[90] Obviously, this was a *baseball* reference. George Herman "Babe" Ruth Jr. was perhaps the greatest baseball player that ever lived, and certainly the most famous. He hit 714 home runs, which is a pretty big deal (only two other Major League players have ever hit over 700). On top of that, I'm pretty sure he had a candy bar named after him illegally, and if that isn't a sign that you've made it in the world, I don't know what is.

your steering skills…" Then he sauntered off after Tessa, whistling "Take Me Out to the Ball Game."

Oh, sure. *Hawk* knows about baseball…

9

THE SHORTEST CHAPTER IN THE BOOK

Brevity is the soul of wit.

—Polonius[91]

This is the shortest chapter in the whole book.

---

[91] Ophelia's dad. If the play *Hamlet*, by Billy Shakespeare, had been a comedy instead of a tragedy, Polonius could have been the father-in-law of the king of Denmark and bought himself a bunch of sweet new hats. Alas, several people died prematurely, so that was not to be. Get it? *Not to be*? Oh, never mind…

BARNACLOIDS

Hell[92] hath no fury like a woman scorned.
—William Congreve[93]

As it turns out, Drake had been vomiting in his cabin the entire time and had no idea we had been attacked.

"It can happen to anyone," Drake assured me as we laid in our bunks that night. "Skysickness, I mean. It says so right here." He tapped the cover of a small book titled *Spacesail Travel for the Uninitiated,* then dropped it back into his cavernous black backpack. "Did Tessa really slap you?"

"Yep."

"Whoa…"

We were silent for a while, both, I presume, pondering the strange and mysterious nature of women.

"What do you think it means?" he said.

"No idea."

---

[92] This is not a swear word. This book doesn't have swear words; it's a *children's* book. In this case, Hell refers to the place, not the profanity.
[93] A rather clever Englishman who wrote plays and wore wigs. He was born in 1670 and died sometime afterward.

Silence again.

By the way, if you're a girl and you're reading this thinking, *That dialogue is dumb. Nobody talks that way.* You're wrong. This is pretty much how guy-talk works.

Our cabin was generously sized. It was built to hold four men on two full-sized bunk beds, so the two of us had room to spare; Drake took one bottom bunk, and I took the other. Through the little round porthole across from the door, we could see a distant nebula drifting past.

"It probably means she likes you."

"Huh?" I sat up, smashing my head against the bunk above me. "Ouch."

"Yeah," Drake said, his face reflecting the sudden horror that I was feeling. "That's what I heard. When girls hit you, it means they like you."

I relaxed a bit. "I don't think so, dude. It wasn't that type of slap."

"But she slaps you all the time."

"Huh?"

"I said, she smacks you all the time. You know, on the back of the head."

"Tessa smacks everybody," I countered, waving a hand.

Drake sighed. "No, mostly just you."

I thought about it for a while. Unfortunately, I was pretty sure he was right about that.

"Tell me *exactly* what happened tonight," Drake said.

I told him, careful to explain about my Babe Ruth reference.

"Aha!" he said when I had finished. "You see? You called her Babe, and she thought you were calling her, you know, *babe*."

"Thanks, genius. I figured that much out myself."

"And then," Drake said, gesturing like a magician who was about to finish his trick, "she *blushed*. Don't you get it, Simon? She blushed! That means she was embarrassed. You called her babe, and she *liked* it, and then she got embarrassed, so she blushed."

"And then she slapped me?"

"Yeah," Drake said, scratching his head thoughtfully. He held up a finger. "Because you embarrassed her, and everyone saw." He held up a second finger. "Or, because she wanted you to say that, but she didn't want you to say it *yet*." He held up a third finger. "Or, because she *used* to like you, back before you said stupid stuff like that, but now she doesn't like you anymore, and she blames you for messing it all up."

"Where do you get this stuff?" I said. "Do you just make it up as you go?"

"No, no!" Drake said. "It's completely legitimate. It's all out of this little gem right here." He rummaged in his backpack and brought out a large book covered in black velvet titled *5,000 Things Every Man Should Know Before Living Near A Woman*. Drake handed it to me and brought out another book called *Piradian's Standard Female/Male Dictionary*. "This one's even better," he said. "I figured if we were bringing Tessa, I should bring these as well."

I handed the book back to Drake. "No, thanks."

Drake shrugged. "Suit yourself. Why do *you* think she did it, then?"

I rolled over uncomfortably. "I dunno. Maybe she just doesn't like baseball. Either way, I don't think you can learn about women from a book."

"Don't say that!" Drake said, putting his hands over the cover of his book as if to shield it from hearing. "Books can teach you anything."

"So you think."

"I do." Drake sniffed. "And whatever you may say, I still think she likes you."

"You think too much, Drake."

"That's my job," he said dismissively. "The question is, do you like *her*?"

Thankfully there was a knock at the door just then, and I was saved from answering the question. I opened it and found a strange figure staring back at me. It was dressed very oddly in some sort of sparkly armored leotard. The main fabric bits were deep blue and covered in a glitterlike substance that shone like stars, while the headpiece looked like a salmon-pink knight's helmet. His arms were gauntleted to the elbows with more peculiar armor; the palm side was covered with large sucker disks while the back was ribbed with razor-sharp blades. His legs and feet were similarly covered, suckers on the shins and the bottoms of his feet, razor blades on the backs of his calves.

The figure opened the helmet visor, and Hawk grinned

out at me. "Good evening, Simon. Are you busy? No? Good! Come with me."

"Argh," I groaned. "But it's bedtime. I was just about to go to sleep!"

"Training is never convenient," Hawk said cheerfully, "and he who would be prepared at all times does well to prepare *at* all times. We may be lucky and find that your stupider parts have gone to sleep already, leaving only your intelligent aspects for me to instruct."

"Whatever," I said, giving Drake a backward wave and grabbing my turncoat from a peg on the bunk bed. I followed Hawk into the hall. "I presume you have a freak suit for me to wear, too?"

"You presume correctly!" Hawk took what looked like a small pink hamburger out of the pocket of his suit and motioned for me to follow him up the stairs onto the main deck. As we walked, the Tike fell in silently behind us.

Meanwhile, Hawk's sucker feet made indecently loud and garish squelching noises, and I was shocked that no one came to investigate. On deck, Hawk led me to the edge of the ship and leaned over, looking down.

"What are we doing?" I said.

"Freeing barnacloids," Hawk said, practically quivering with excitement. "That is to say, scraping barnacloids off the hull of the ship. They're a species of space Cirripedia. Nasty little things that feed off the ship's warmth."

"Are they dangerous?"

"They wouldn't hurt a fly."

"Then what's with the suit?"

"You are not a fly." Hawk smashed the pink hamburgerlike object into my chest, and the suit erupted out of it, wrapping itself around me. A second later, my head was incased in a helmet, and I was looking at the world through a thin salmon-pink slit. I lifted one foot experimentally and found that with a bit of effort, it came free from the deck with a loud squelching noise. I heard a sailor chuckle softly from somewhere behind me.

"Why are they laughing at us?" I asked, feeling suddenly suspicious.

"In the hierarchy of menial ship chores, de-barnacloiding falls somewhere beneath scrubbing toilets, which I dare say they have ever seen a captain do himself—certainly not *two* captains at once."

Hawk was tying a luminescent blue rope around my waist now.

"Are you coming with us, Tike?" I said, knowing that she had most likely taken up a watch position in the shadows somewhere behind me. "You wouldn't want to miss out on the fun."

"No, thank you," she said. "I prefer to watch you humiliate yourself from here."

Hawk let out several yards of rope and tied part of it around his own waist. Then he secured the end to a ring in the deck. "The rope, of course, is just a precaution. Your spacer ring keeps you locked in the ship's gravitational field, but the field is weakest at the sides of the ship. If you were to be blown, say, ten or fifteen feet out for some reason, you might find yourself stranded in space."

"Blown?" I said, feeling suddenly nervous. "What do you mean blown?" I reached for the turncoat, just to reassure myself that I was wearing it. "Wait," I said, feeling my chest. "My turncoat is inside my suit. I can't reach the knobs!"

"Huh," Hawk said with a smirk. "I was wondering when you would notice. You really should be more careful, Simon." And with that he jumped over the side.

I groaned as the rope between us disappeared and I was jerked over the edge after him.

Apparently the ship's gravitational field worked differently outside the ship than it did within it, for as soon as I went over the side, it seemed as if *sideways* had become the new *down*. Instead of falling toward the bottom of the ship or floating out into space, I fell on my face, my belly against the side of the ship and my helmet buried in what looked to be a broken, foot-long, snot-filled blue oyster shell. The "snot" smelled like rotten eggs, in case you wanted to know.

"Ugh," I said, prying my face out of the shell and wiping liquid from my visor.

"Ah!" Hawk said, dropping the rope he had been using to tug me over the side. "You've found your first barnacloid. Excellent! Best not to crack them open like that, though. Terribly volatile. Whatever you do, don't breathe on it."

"What?" I exclaimed. Even as the breath from my question escaped my lips, the yellow liquid covering my helmet turned a violent shade of pink and exploded.

My body was hurled headfirst toward the stars.

Sometime later, I regained consciousness and found that I was being tugged back toward the side of the ship by the rope around my waist while Hawk shouted at me.

"Simon. SIMON! Are you all right? I told you not to breathe, didn't I? Well, now you know why. Do you still have your eyebrows? And your face? Simon? Are you alive? Drat. I've killed another one…"

"I'm alive," I grunted. "And I've still got my eyebrows."

"Oh, thank goodness," Hawk said, visibly relieved. "I'd hate to tell *that* story to the Tike."

When I came within a few yards of the ship I found myself falling back into its gravitational field. I landed gingerly, careful not to touch another barnacloid, which I now saw covered nearly every inch of the hull like a huge dome-shaped field of electric-blue shells. The space above us was lit with stars almost close enough to touch. Actually, if you could get past the rotten-egg smell and the danger, it was almost—

"Beautiful, isn't it?" Hawk said, finishing my thought.

"Yeah, I guess. Hey, you were joking just now, right, Hawk? I mean, you said you were a bad teacher, but you haven't accidentally *killed* other students before, have you?"

"Of course not," Hawk said. "Not with barnacloids," he added under his breath. "Anyway, let me show you how this can be done without blowing yourself up. Pay attention."

For the next hour, Hawk taught me how to crawl, wiggle, roll, and generally undulate all over the side of the ship, slicing barnacloid shells from the hull with the blades on my shins and forearms. I understood now why the pirates had been laughing at us earlier; the whole thing was incredibly humiliating. I would like to point out, however, that I retained some sense of dignity by refusing to use what Hawk considered the most effective maneuver: a retro dance move called "the worm," and I wasn't having any part in it.

"Remind me why we can't use normal tools like a spade or a pickaxe," I said as Hawk lay on his back before me, making vigorous snow-angel motions to cut away a group of barnacloids on either side of him.

"Barnacloids are primarily repelled by direct human contact," Hawk said, breathing heavily. "The blades just get the process started. We are what drives them off. Any tool that places you more than a couple inches from the creatures wouldn't be able to pry them off at all. Watch."

Hawk made a big loop with our safety rope, lassoed a particularly small barnacloid not more than two inches across, and then threw all his weight against the rope, trying to rip it free. It didn't budge. Then he squelch-walked over and easily brushed it into space with the flat side of his shin-blade.

"Come on now, Simon. No doubt you'd like to get some sleep tonight, and we're not stopping until the hull is clear."

I grumbled under my breath and set about helping him with new determination. After another hour, I was finding it more and more difficult to pry the sucker feet away from the ship as I walked and crawled. My arms were getting heavy, and my legs were so tired that I kept missing my aim and thrusting my shin-blades into the thick wood of the hull. The last time I did this, I couldn't unstick myself, and Hawk had to assist me.

When I was finally free, I collapsed on a clear section of the hull and folded my arms, refusing to work anymore.

"I saw you and the Tike arguing," I blurted, hoping to distract him from making me work. "What were you talking about?"

Hawk rested on one knee, then reached up to pop open his visor. "If you must know, we were discussing the Rimbakka your mother made. I'm sure you are aware that I helped her with it. I did so under the impression that she would be giving it to you. I would not have approved of her giving it to anyone else."

"Why?" I said. "You only want *her* spying on me?"

"Observation is one effect of the Rimbakka's binding, but it is not the most powerful, nor the most important. Did your mother not explain it to you?"

I shook my head.

"It is a binding of blood, and of life force. It should never be done lightly, and never, in my opinion, with someone other than a parent or child, for which the spell was originally intended."

"What do you mean, exactly?" I said.

Hawk considered me a moment, then shook his head. "If your mother did not choose to tell you, it is not my place, either. No," he continued, cutting off my argument. "I will say no more."

I slumped back, gazing at the insurmountable number of barnacloids left. "I can't believe that there isn't a better way to do this," I said, gesturing at them.

"What?" Hawk said. "Of *course* there are better ways." He extended a hand, palm down, and a thirty-foot wide swath of barnacloids erupted in Midnight Blue flames. They quickly detached themselves from the hull and whirled out into space.

"Gah!" I exclaimed. "We could be done in like two minutes!"

"*I* could be done in two minutes," Hawk corrected. "*You* 'can't use magic,' remember?"

"Why," I said, feeling my face grow hot, "are you saying that with finger quotes? You KNOW I can't use magic. Is that what this little exercise is about? Rubbing it in my face?"

Hawk shrugged. "*You* know you can't use magic, Simon. I know no such thing. Why, only a week ago you were summoning the Midnight Blue. Now using magic doesn't even occur to you, *even* when faced with hours of backbreaking physical labor! What changed?"

"I don't know."

He poked me in the chest. "Figure it out, then. What changed?"

I slapped his finger away. "The magic was just an accident before," I said. "I didn't even know what I was doing, and—"

"No," Hawk interrupted, thrusting an arm-blade into a large shell and flinging it out into space. "Try again."

"Maybe I offended the Zohar somehow, and they've revoked my magic privileges or something?"

Hawk shook his head. "No."

"It probably got knocked out of my head, then, jumping out of the tower that night. Or fighting the Horror. Or fighting you and Gladstone day in and day out, and now I can't remember how to—"

"No," Hawk said.

"Well, then, maybe I—"

"No."

"YOU TELL *ME*, THEN!" I shouted. "Why can't I do it? Why could I summon the Midnight Blue a week ago, and now I can't? What changed?"

"Your mind."

"I didn't change my mind about anything," I countered. "One day I can do it, and the next I can't."

"Not that mind." Hawk said, poking my head. "Your *mind.*" He slapped me in my gut just below my rib cage. "Your *deep* mind. The thing that watches your dreams at night and wakes you when the morning comes. The thing that sees your own thoughts, yet stands outside of them. You put on that turncoat, and your deep mind recognized all its power as your own. It knows, though *you* don't, that the power of the turncoat comes from inside *you*, not the coat itself! It knows your power, and it fears to embrace it, so you cannot do so. The deep mind, Simon, is the one that you must change."

I blinked several times, dimly aware that my mouth was hanging open. I shut it and said, "You know that made no sense whatsoever, right?"

Hawk laughed, throwing back his head and clapping his hands. "I know. Aren't we a pair? A teacher who doesn't know the answers, and a student who can't figure out the question."

"Yeah…great." I yawned widely. "How much longer are we going to do this?"

"Oh, I think we can be done now," Hawk said cheerfully. "You have learned everything I wanted to teach you tonight."

"Great," I said, heading back for the deck. I was pretty sure that I hadn't learned anything at all, but I wasn't about to mention that to Hawk. He was whistling now, walking in front of me and cheerfully cutting away stray barnacloids that crossed his path to the deck. I looked out over the hundreds of shells that remained, raised a hand, and whispered "Gibeah" under my breath.

Nothing happened, of course.

I hadn't expected it to.

To be honest, I never expected it to again.

11
THE SECRET POTION

Puberty: Puberty is the process of physical changes through which a child's body matures into an adult body.
—Wikipedia

Night had fully come, and the ship was full of sleep sounds when I returned to my cabin, so I was surprised to find Drake's bunk empty.

"Drake?" I said to the empty room.

He didn't answer.[94]

That's odd, I thought. Drake was too afraid to leave his cabin during the daytime. Why would he leave it in the dead of night?

"Tike?" I said, expecting her to emerge from the shadows. She hadn't been on deck when I returned with Hawk, and she didn't appear now. No doubt she was patrolling the ship, looking for danger.

Resigned to the fact that I probably wouldn't get any sleep at all that night, I made my way to Tessa's room. I had to knock five times before she woke up. Finally, her door inched open.

---

[94] Duh. He was gone.

"What?" she said, rubbing her eyes. "Oh, it's you." Her face tightened.

Part of me wanted to apologize for waking her up in the middle the night, and part of me wanted to try and explain about Babe Ruth and tell her how silly she had been earlier. However, I decided to stick to my plan and pretend that nothing had happened. "Drake's missing."

Her eyes narrowed suspiciously. "Are you inventing an incredible story just to get me alone in the middle of the night so you can apologize for being a nincompoop?"

"No."

"Fine. I'll be right out." She shut the door.

I put my hands in my pockets and swayed back and forth with the motion of the ship, making a mental note to ask Captain Bast why the ship swayed at all, seeing as how we were moving through empty space.

A figure melted out of the shadows behind me and came to stand at my shoulder.

"Don't breathe down my neck like that, Tike," I said. "I tried to call you when I went out, but you weren't there."

"Yes, well, I'm here now, and I think you should talk to Tessa. Don't start. You *know* what I mean."

I bit off a clever retort as the Tike slipped back into the shadows. Then I racked my mind for some way to explain about Babe Ruth to Tessa.

While I was deep in thought, Tessa emerged. "Do you think he's okay?" she asked.

"The Babe?" I said, startled. "No! He died in 1948."

Tessa looked confused. Then one of her eyes twitched angrily.

"She is talking about Drake, you fool," the Tike hissed from the shadows, making Tessa jump.

"Oh, right." In a moment of brilliance, I slipped the sorrowstone from my pocket, cupped in the hollow of my palm so that no one could see. Then I patted Tessa lightly on the shoulder, making sure to let the stone touch her. "Sorry, Tessa," I said. "I didn't mean to bring up the Babe thing again. Maybe we can talk about that later. Let's go look for Drake now, huh?"

Her gaze softened and she seemed to relax. "Lead the way," she said.

Dang, that rock was magic for sure!

We checked up on deck first, thinking that he might've just got up to get some fresh…air? But he was nowhere to be seen, so we went back downstairs. Immediately below the upper deck was the captain's cabin and the guest quarters where we were staying. Below that was the crew quarters, which we decided we wouldn't search yet. We had yet to get a full tour of the ship, so we were exploring as we went along. Small lights lit our way, shining out of little alcoves in the winding walnut walls of the spiral staircase.

The next floor we came to was completely open and empty. The ship above us was invisible, and the floor beneath was not a floor at all but covered entirely in grass. There were no walls, either, so that when you walked away from the staircase, it seemed as if you were standing in a perfect little park in the midst of space.

"Whoa," I said.

"Whoa," Tessa echoed. "How did they build this?"

"There's more to this ship than meets the eye," I said.

"You think? Speaking of things that don't meet the eye, Drake's obviously not here. Shall we move on, *Captain Simon?*"

I was smart enough not to respond to that. The next deck seemed to be used primarily for storage. Then we came to the ship's galley. It was a long, narrow room with a stove on one end and a decorative suit of armor on the other, which seemed to be used more as an apron hanger than anything else. A long counter ran down the center of the room, and upon this was laid out a tangled mess of pots, pans, bags, half a fish fillet, and enough herbs and spices to stuff a zucchini the size of Connecticut.

Drake was there, too. His back was turned to us, and he was bustling back and forth wearing a rather filthy apron that was far too short, even for him. He had three pots going on the stove. I lifted the cleanest apron I could find from suit of armor's lance and put it on. "Need some help, bud?"

Drake jumped and sneezed into one of his pots of boiling liquid, causing a small fireball to erupt out of it. Then he grabbed the piece of fish and brandished it before turning to us and shouting something threatening in his native tongue. "*Unk WafLagga!* Oh! Simon. Tessa! It's just you. I didn't hear you come in. I thought... I thought you were..."

"Pirates coming to eat you?" Tessa guessed. "Nope. You can calm down."

"And you can put that fish back on the counter," I said.

"Oh, right," Drake said, laying the fillet down awkwardly.

"What are you doing, anyway?" I said.

"Oh, nothing." He edged in front of the stove and leaned over casually, attempting to block several bubbling pots from view. "What are, uh...you guys doing?"

"Oh, come on," Tessa said, pushing him aside. "Tell us what you're making. Is it good? Or is it some of your freaky minotaur food? I'm starving."

"Well, it's not—" he began, and then stopped. "Yes!" he said, shooing us toward the door. "Yes. It's freaky minotaur food. Nothing you would like. Why don't you just go back to your rooms and I'll whip up a snack and bring it to you, uh, later?"

"Drake," Tessa said, "why are you lying?"

"It smells like asparagus," I said, walking back to the stove. "And bubblegum. And dirty gym shorts. What's in it?" I picked up a random bottle from the counter and inspected the label. "Essence of Yakrat?" I said. "What's a Yakrat?"

"Aha!" Tessa said, poking Drake in the chest triumphantly. "You're making kulrakalakia!"

"Isn't that illegal?" the Tike asked, sticking her head into the room and sniffing the air.

"Tike," I said. "Go away, please. You're not supposed to be in this scene."

"Sorry," she said, and left.

"It is *not* illegal," Drake said stiffly.

"Maybe not in outer space," Tessa teased, "but it is at school. I read that petition you wrote last month trying to get it legalized."

Drake blushed.

"Excuse me," I cut in, "what exactly *is* Kulrakacaca?"

"Kulraka*lakia*," Drake corrected. "It's just a nickname. Its true name is Minotaurian Yakrat Androgotincture."

"Yeah," Tessa said. "Let's call it that all the time."

"Wow," I said. "I still don't know what it is."

"It's a magic potion that jump-starts puberty," Tessa said.

"Sweet! Did you make enough for me?"

"It only works on minotaurs, dumdum," Tessa said, smacking me on the back of the head. Drake gave me a meaningful look. "Weren't you listening? *Minotaurian* Yakrat whatev—wait! Did you hear that?" She turned suddenly and pointed across the room. I did hear it. A little scratching noise coming from the suit of armor.

"Yeah, I think there's a rat in there," Drake said uneasily.

"Gross," Tessa said, turning back to him. "Anyway, I'm not sure kulrakalakia really works at all, even for minotaurs. It's a bit controversial, isn't it?"

Drake shrugged. "It's fatal to one or two percent of the population, and totally ineffective for a bunch more, but it worked for my grandpa."

Apparently Drake had come to terms with the fact

that we weren't leaving, because he picked up a spoon and started stirring his potion again.

"Isn't this a bit drastic?" I said carefully. "I mean, I want chest hair as much as the next guy, but if it could kill you…"

"No!" Drake said, spinning around and smacking his wooden spoon into the palm of his hand. "My kulraka is over a year late already! I've had it!"

Seeing the "Oh no, my friend has gone crazy," look on my face, Drake relaxed slightly. "Sorry," he said. "You wouldn't understand. For humans, maturation is a process, but for my kind, the kulraka happens like that." He snapped his fingers to illustrate. "And it's supposed to happen when you're twelve. It was hard enough showing up for school before my kulraka. I figured I'd just keep my head down for a while, but I've had it. It's time for desperate measures."

Tessa sighed and picked up a mortar and pestle. "I assume you're going to need all of these herbs ground up?"

Drake looked up, surprised. "Yeah."

"Come on, then, Simon," she said, thrusting the pestle into my hand. "Get grinding. I'm going to stir. Step aside, Drake."

"Really?" Drake said. "You guys aren't going to make fun of me?"

"Ha!" Tessa said. "You're a prepubescent minotaur bookworm trapped in a tiny hairless body. The *universe* is making fun of you."

It took three hours and so much herb grinding that to this day my fingers ache every time I see a pestle, but eventually we finished it. To my surprise, the entire mountain of herbs was slowly distilled into a glob the size of my fist. It was the color of turtle puke, smelled like moldy yak droppings, and basically looked like a piece of elephant poop.[95] Drake beamed at it.

"Well, are you going to eat it?" I said.

Drake looked at me askance.[96] "Uh, *no*. Do you want me to die? Do you know how potent this thing is? Most sources recommend licking it every hour and thirty-nine minutes, but my grandpa reckons every hour and a half is good enough." He brought the cube to his mouth and licked it, wrinkling his nose.

"How is it?" I asked.

"See for yourself," he said, passing it to me. "Go ahead. It won't hurt you."

Against all forms of reason, I licked it.[97] I gagged. It tasted like an elephant-toe-jam sandwich. On moldy bread. It tasted like sumo wrestler belly button lint[98] and room temperature canned beets. It tasted like dirty wrestler shorts and rotten penguin eggs. In short, it was

---

[95] Sorry for the potty language, but it was seriously the nastiest thing I'd ever seen.

[96] With disapproval and/or distrust.

[97] Hey, I had just spent like forever making it. I had to have a taste.

[98] What? You've never tasted that?

the most crapaflapnasty[99] thing I'd ever put in my mouth. Ever.

"Not bad," I said, offering it to Tessa. "Want a lick?"

"Guess again," she said. She was eyeing Drake critically. "You look about the same to me."

Drake shrugged. "They say it can take up to a week. It took Grandpa nearly nine days."

"That's not bad," I said. "How long till we know whether it's going to kill you—"

"WAADAHEK OOUGYYSDOONG IMYKTCHN GIBBEEKOOSLVS OOTAHAAR!"

We all jumped as the sudden screaming filled the galley.

Hobnob (or possibly Noblob...not sure which) the goblin had walked in on us in the galley, presumably reporting for morning kitchen duty. He was not pleased to find us there. Looking around, I could see why. Six hours of haphazard potion-making had taken a toll on the place. In fact, if a tornado had swept through the galley, I think it would have left a tidier mess.[100]

---

[99] No, really, this is a word. It was invented recently by Alcatraz Smedry. The technical definition has something to do with tuna fish. For more information please read the *Alcatraz vs. the Evil Librarians* books by Brandon Sanderson.

[100] The phrase "tidy mess" is, of course, oxymoronic. The word "oxymoron" means "a phrase or figure of speech which by definition contradicts itself." Examples include: found missing, deafening silence, liquid gas, alone together, virtual reality, jumbo shrimp, Microsoft Works, freezer burn, constant variable, great depression, butt head, crash landing, pretty ugly, and now then. The word "oxymoron" also means "really dumb cow."

"Time to go," I said as the brawny little creature picked up a frying pan and started chasing us with it.

We ran for it. The tiny pirate had chased us out and then barricaded the door behind us, as if he was afraid we might try to break in again.

"But shouldn't we help clean up?" Tessa asked.

"Sure," I said. "Let's go back in. Hobnobnoblob—or whatever—seems to be in a really good mood."

Before she could smack me, a siren sounded from somewhere up above.

A DISTANT DOOM

The only thing more inevitable than death is the surprise we feel upon its arrival.

—Notta Rillguy[101]

The thing that had caused Captain Bast to sound the alarm appeared at first to be nothing more than an amorphous[102] shadow, far behind us.

"Surely this do be more o' the boy's black luck," Mortazar whispered.

"The blackest luck o' all," Murphy agreed.

The entire crew had assembled on the quarterdeck, and I could see that there were several more crewmembers than I had initially realized. In all, there were about twenty of us searching the starry night in the direction Captain Bast had indicated.

"What is it?" I asked, hoping that I was not the only one confused.

Nobody answered.

---

[101] A fictional character that I just made up. As far as I know, this is the only thing he ever said. In case you were wondering, he is closely related to Guy Thadone Xist, from Chapter 4.

[102] Without a clearly defined shape or form.

"What is it?" I said again, thinking that perhaps they had not heard me.

"Shh," Hawk said.

I squinted as the distant shadow passed in front of a star. For a second, I thought that I could make out a shape, but at this distance I couldn't be sure.

"Is that what I think it is?" Tessa said quietly.

"Aye," Captain Bast said. His voice was hoarse. Judging by his face, it was as if he'd seen a ghost.

"How long?" Hawk asked.

The captain's brow furrowed as he did some mental calculations. "This do be the thir' fastes' ship in space. For tha', I wager we can stay ahead o' it for one whole day, mebbe two." He turned to look Hawk straight in the face. At the same time, he pointed in my direction. "We bot' know why it do be here, so 'til it gets 'ere, get that boy offa me deck. I don' be needin' anymore o' his black luck tonigh'."

Hawk would answer no questions until he had sequestered Drake, Tessa, the Tike, and myself on what he called the promenade, which turned out to be the magical open-air park that Tessa and I had discovered when we were searching for Drake during the night. Finally, when the three of us were seated around him in a half circle, with a starry expanse of space all around us and the mysterious shadow lurking in the distance, he began to talk.

"Do any of you know what follows us?"

Several paces away, the Tike cleared her throat. As usual, she was guarding the door. "Shade," she said simply.

Drake sneezed.

"Correct," Hawk said. "And what is a shade?"

"Nothing good?" I guessed. "Wait a minute...I think Gladstone said something about a shade. Is a shade kind of like one of the Fallen?" I wasn't thinking very clearly; I had a severe itch between my shoulder blades that was impossible to reach.

"No, Simon," Drake began, face tight with fear, "The Fallen are just wizards who are under the control of the Shadeking. A *shade* is a living abomination of magical power. A corporeal demon. A fallen light."

Hawk rolled his eyes. "Very dramatic, Drakus. Accurate, but dramatic. If I were to describe a shade—which I obviously am—I would say that it is a wizard whose life force has become possessed by the source of all evil."

"Woah," I said, feeling confused. "Why haven't we talked about this before?"

"It's not really polite conversation," Tessa noted.

"It's like asking someone the name of their guardian fish," Drake said.

"Huh?"

"It's like asking someone what color underwear they have on," Tessa said.

I raised an eyebrow, wondering automatically what—

Tessa smacked me. "Don't *even*."

"Ouch. Geez, Tessa. Don't be so touchy. Hawk, what color underwear do you have on?"

"Aquamarine."

"See, Tessa?" I said. "It's no big deal."

Hawk laughed. "Still, it is our tradition to not speak of underwear—or shades—so freely. Yet I will tell you this: A shade is formed when an unbroken wizard's power spirals out of control and consumes them. When this happens, when they die, and their magic *lives*, a powerful void is created. All that remains of them is a body, a shell that lacks the ability to govern itself. Of course, few wizards ever remain unbroken these days. Most shades were formed in the time of the original Circle of Eight and are very, very old indeed." He cleared his throat. "Drake, what is that thing you are licking?

"Nothing," Drake said, tucking the kulrakalakia blob out of sight. "You said shades aren't in control of themselves?"

"Correct," Hawk said. "They are controlled by Rone. The Jackal. The Shadeking. They are one of the things that make him so powerful."

Drake bit his lip. "While we're on the subject of unbroken wizards going crazy and becoming evil demon slaves, I was just thinking... Has Simon technically broken yet? I mean..." He pulled nervously at the neck of his shirt, searching for a nice way to ask if I was in danger of becoming a shade.

"Don't be stupid, Drake," Tessa said. "Of course Simon has broken. He's used magic, hasn't he?"

"Yeah," Drake said. "But you can use magic before you break, technically. And Simon hasn't clearly displayed an affinity for one of the six talents. Is 'Fayter' really a talent? Because if so, it doesn't seem to do anything... Does that mean he's broken? Or does being a Fayter simply describe the state of being unbroken?"

"Excuse me," I interrupted. Everyone looked at me, and I realized that I didn't actually have anything to say. The fact was, Drake's words stung me. Whatever Hawk had said about my magic running the turncoat, beyond that, it didn't seem to do much of anything. Also, my itch was back, worse than before, and no matter how much I scratched it, it wasn't going away.

Hawk laughed, patting Drake on the back. "You have a mind like a Kiambi war weasel, my young friend."

Drake blushed.

Hawk continued. "Simon and I have had this conversation before, but in answer to your question, I will tell you that I think Simon has *not* broken, and that being the Fayter may have something to do with being unbroken. I don't think that we have to be too worried about him being consumed, however. Not yet, at any rate."

I fidgeted wildly. I might not be a shade yet, but I *was* going crazy. My back itched like none other. I refrained from asking Drake to scratch it. "So," I said, "The shade wants to fight me."

Hawk nodded. "Rone challenged you to a duel, remember? This is what he has sent to fight you."

"Are you sure we can't outrun it?" Drake asked

hopefully. "Captain Bast said this is the third fastest ship in space. If we find a nebula or an asteroid field or a black hole or something—"

"It will catch us," the Tike said. She spoke so softly that I almost didn't hear her. I'd forgotten she was listening. Her eyes had the faraway look that speaks of old, unpleasant memories. She turned to face me, and I was struck by the intensity of her gaze. "It will catch us, and Simon will have to fight it. Nothing can outrun a shade."

Drake gulped. "But nobody has ever survived a duel with a shade."

"Nobody has ever *won* a duel with a shade," Hawk corrected. "Yet." He looked at me, one eye white and blind, destroyed by an evil that I had set free on the world, one eye bright yellow and filled with a compassion that I had never seen there before. "There is a first time for everything."

Half an hour later I stood in the fighting top, suspended twenty feet above the deck. Hawk was there, too, leaning casually against the rigging that surrounded us. I could see, it seemed, straight into eternity from up here; the lights of the ship were below us, the vast dark of space above, while sparkling nebulae and galaxies floated in the far distance. Hawk was continuing my training, and I was trying to pay attention, though between the glorious view of space, and the crazy back itch I was still dealing with, I was being a poor student.

"Simon?"

"Huh?"

"Are you going to answer my question?"

"Uh...you mean, the one about...uh..."

"Simon, if you don't start listening to me, I swear I will hurl you into space."

"Right. Sorry, Hawk. I'm listening. Ask me again."

"Where does a knight's sword go when he dismisses it?" He held out his hand and immediately a long, slender sword appeared in it. Yellow fire ripped up one side of the blade and down the other, then Hawk let go of the hilt and the sword vanished into thin air. "Where did it go?"

I sighed, thinking of the previous ten times he had given me this lecture. "The mindhold. The knight's blade, when dismissed, moves from this dimension into the primal dimension, joining with the soul-body," I recited.

"Give it a whirl, then," Hawk said.

I unsheathed Kylanthus and held it out with a grimace. This had never worked before. I tried *feeling* my soul-body. *Feeling* my power radiate outward from the "seat of power," burning my imagination into reality. Of course, nothing happened. Nothing ever happened. I never *felt* anything. Honestly, if he said the world *feel* one more time, he was going to *feel* my wrath.

"Easier said than done, eh?" Hawk said. "Can you *feel* your soul-body? Where do you *feel* the center of it to be? Point to it. Show me where your seat of power is."

"BAHHHH!" I shouted, turning on him. I dropped Kylanthus in rage and proceeded to wave my fists in his face. "I'LL SHOW YOU WHERE I *FEEL* IT, YOU OLD WOMBAT!"

Hawk sighed. "No, that's not right. You shouldn't feel it in your fists at all. You should feel it here." Moving faster than sight, he punched me in the gut. Lightly. Just enough to shut me up. "See? Do you feel it now?"

"Yup," I gasped. "But I don't think it's my soul-body. Maybe if you punched me some more?"

Hawk sighed. "The seat of power is deep inside, Simon. It's the same place that falling comes from."

"WHAT?" I demanded. He was talking nonsense again.

"Fall-ing," he said slowly. Then he moved with the speed and dexterity that only a Quick could and shoved me over the side.

"RAAAHHLAAGAAGAA!" I screamed as I plummeted toward the deck. My stomach leapt into my throat as I fell, and I fumbled with the turncoat, searching for B1 (*Leap*) to cushion my fall. But there was no time.

Just before I hit the deck, something grabbed my flailing arms and snatched me out of the air. I soared over the deck and rose slowly upward, and when I looked up I saw Kestra, Hawk's hawk, carrying me. She had been magically enlarged so that she was big enough to support my weight. A second later, she dropped me into the rigging next to the fighting top and then shrunk rapidly to her normal size, landing upon Hawk's shoulder.

"I-I didn't know you could d-do that," I stuttered, clutching the rigging for support. I didn't like heights much. Or falling. Or dangling from magic hawks. "Make her big, I mean."

"Neither did I," he said, and I was surprised to hear his voice sounded strained. He was breathing rapidly, though he clearly hadn't been doing any physical labor. "Not my type of magic. But I do what I have to, to save your life."

"Save me?" I said. "You threw me off!"

"Yes. And where did you feel it? The *falling*."

I grunted as I pulled myself gently onto the floor of the fighting top. "Here." I rubbed my gut, where my stomach had resided before leaping into my throat.

"Yes," he said happily. "Much better. Maybe I haven't been teaching you correctly."

He ignored the sickly green tint of my face and pulled something out of his pocket. A coin.

"You're unlucky today, yes?" he said. "You're heads, Simon. If you win, I will help you mend things with Tessa. If you lose, I will throw you out again. Focus on the seat of power." He flipped the coin high into the air. "Can you feel your luck burgeoning,[103] Simon?" he said, and as I watched the coin spin, I actually did. A little twitch, a flutter of luck in my gut. I knew I would lose the toss, and I did.

"By the surprise on your face," Hawk said wryly, "I'd say our exercise has been successful. That is where you feel from, Simon. Practice feeling there. Keep some of your

---

[103] Growing.

attention on the seat of power at all times, and you may be surprised what you find."

He smiled at me then, and for once I felt like a good student. Just for a second, though. Then I got distracted, and I couldn't feel my seat of power anymore, and that infernal itching between my shoulder blades was back. I wiggled wildly, trying to reach it.

Hawk muttered something under his breath, then said more loudly, "Try to catch yourself this time so that I don't have to save you again."

And with that, he tossed me off the edge once more.

13

REPARATIONS

Mistakes are always forgivable, if one has the
courage to admit them.

—Bruce Lee[104]

Back on deck after lunch, the crew was in a grim mood. To make things worse, the distant shadow that stalked us through space was no longer quite so distant. It was close enough now to be recognized for what it was: a small ship, less than half the size of the *Calliope*, made entirely of what looked like living wisps of gray and black smoke wrapped around each other and writhing like snakes.

"Two days, Cap'n?" Hawk said, stepping up to stand beside Bast.

Captain Bast was looking through a small brass telescope. "Aye. Two days it'll be, if I 'ave a say in the ma'er. He has no' gained as much on us as it do appear."

---

[104] A famous martial artist and movie star. Known the world over for his unparalleled kung fu skills, Bruce Lee was one of the fastest-moving people that have ever lived. To demonstrate his abilities, he would sometimes have a person hold out a coin in the open palm of their hand. He would then take the coin and replace it with another one before the person could close their hand. In short, he was almost as fast as the Tike.

"Aye," Hawk said. He cleared his throat. "Though it may be be'er to let it catch us afore tha' Cap'n, so Simon can fight on a lucky day." He gave the captain a significant look. "Also, if ye don' mind me askin', could I borrow Mortazar for a wee bit? He would be dead useful helping Simon ter train."

Captain Bast jerked the telescope away from his eye and glanced around the deck. "Ye di no' bring tha' boy up 'ere again, did ye?"

"Well, I—" Hawk began, looking around for me. "Swamp me' boats! Where *is* tha' boy?"

Tessa was there. And Drake. And the Tike. But I, very mysteriously, was nowhere to be seen.

"Where'd 'e go, Tike?"

The Tike was searching the deck, looking livid. "I did not see him leave us."

Now, it's hard to slip away from the Tike. Very hard. Almost as hard as writing a scene in a first-person narrative in which the narrator does not appear. Very tricky. But I'm just that good. As it happens, I was, at that moment, busy helping Hobnob clean the galley.

You see, halfway through Hawk's lecture on shades, while I was scratching myself like a madman, it occurred to me *why* I was itching so badly: I had broken my code. I had not helped those in need, nor, I suppose, been my best self. Specifically, I really should have helped Hobnob clean up our mess in the galley earlier. Therefore, while my associates were climbing the staircase to the main deck after lunch, I snuck back down to see if the little goblin needed help cleaning up lunch, and to apologize. When I arrived, I found Hobnob halfway finished with the cleanup. He seemed to be preparing dinner already as well, for there was that zucchini the size of Connecticut on the countertop.

Actually, I wasn't going to tell you about this at all, as it is quite embarrassing for the pretentious boy hero to be caught in such acts of meekness[105] and contrition.[106] My plan was to sneak out of the scene, clean up, and sneak back in before anyone noticed that I was narrating it without being there, but very inconveniently, Hawk *did* notice, and the Tike searched the ship like the bloodhound she is.

She burst through the door like a ten-ton tomato, eyes flashing. "SIMON FAYTER!" she bellowed. "ONE OF THESE TIMES WHEN YOU SNEAK AWAY FROM ME YOU WILL DIE AT THE HANDS OF SOME FOUL CREATURE THAT HAS CRAWLED OUT FROM THE DEMON'S PIT TO FEAST UPON THAT FRAGRANT LITTLE EMACIATED MASS OF INANITY YOU CALL A HIDE!"

I replaced my mop in the bucket and leaned on it. "Tike, you say the sweetest things."

"Hmph." She looked around, taking in the scene. "What are you doing back here anyway?"

Hobnob, by the way, being a creature of some sense, had wisely slipped out of the room during her tirade.

"I'm cleaning up my mess," I admitted.

---

[105] Quiet, gentle, easily imposed on. Submissive.
[106] The state of feeling remorseful or penitent.

She scowled at me. "Does this have something to do with your code?"

"Uh," I said stupidly. "Why would you think that?"

"Because you are not prone to mopping floors," she said, sliding onto a stool at the long counter. "And because I saw you itching earlier. I wondered if you had done something to violate your little wizard's code. No more silliness!" She slapped the giant zucchini for emphasis. "You are my Ardent. I must know of the powers that rule your life. Tell me your code."

I hesitated. She had asked me this before, of course, and I had never really complied. I had learned by sad experience that the Tike watched me very closely. If she knew my code, she'd probably be on me about it all the time.

"I don't know," I said. "It's pretty private."

"Private?" She shook her head, muttering under her breath in her own language. "I forget sometimes how little you know of the Ardentia and the bond we share. You are young, and you are a foreigner to our world, so you are excused of this ignorance. Put out your hand, Simon. Like this." She laid her hand out on the counter, palm down.

I did the same.

In her other hand, she picked up a fork. "Watch." She brought the fork down sharply, stabbing it into the flesh just below her wrist.

"Ack!" I shrieked, waving my hand. "I felt that."

She grimaced, reaching for a cloth to cover the back of her now bleeding hand. "You felt *some* of that," she said.

"Look at your hand."

I did. Unlike hers, the skin on the back of my hand was unbroken, though I could see four faint dots from the fork's prongs.

"Our souls are bonded, Simon. To some degree, what happens to one of us happens to the other. Show me your missing finger."

I held up my left hand, wiggling the stump of my amputated pinky, and she did the same. I saw that while her finger remained attached, there was a thick scar around the base of it, as though she had been cut deeply.

"Tike!" I exclaimed. "You never told me you got hurt when Zie cut my finger off! I mean, you broke free right after that and fought a bunch of minotaurs. You seemed fine!"

She gave a half-smile. "Pain is familiar to one who has lived as long as I have. Also, I do not make it my practice to shriek and dance about in the midst of battle just because I have received a wound."

"Right," I said, remembering my own shriek-dancing. I reflected on what she had said for a moment, and a horrible idea occurred to me. "What happens if I die, Tike?"

"If?" she said. "We *all* die, Simon. It is merely a matter of when... Did you hear that?" She looked around suspiciously, her eyes coming to rest on the suit of armor at the far end of the room.

"Rats live in it," I said.

"Hmm. Well, as I was saying, when you die, I will

experience your death, but whether I go on living afterward depends on much, especially the manner of your death. If you live to an old age and pass peacefully in your sleep, for example, I may survive it. If you were to die in battle, on the other hand, prematurely, in your youth, I would most certainly be overcome."

"That's awful!" I said.

"Is it?" She gave me a wise, ancient smile that made me feel very young and naive.[107] "To be bound to another soul in this manner is the highest honor of my race. To live for another, as I do for you, is to live a life full of meaning and fulfillment. The life lived in isolation is the true tragedy."[108]

She paused for a moment, giving her words time to sink in, then continued. "It will not be the same for you. You will almost certainly survive my death, regardless of how or when it occurs."

"Why?"

She shrugged. "That is the way of the Ardentia. You

---

[107] An impressive feat, considering how mature and brilliant I am…

[108] By the way, this is how books make the world a better place. As Thoreau put it, "the mass of men lead lives of quiet desperation," deprived of the things that would give them meaning and happiness, including (but not limited to) compelling relationships with others and soul-expanding adventure. I learned at a young age that the relationships we have with characters in books—and the things we experience with them—are quite real (on some level), at least to us. Through books, we have friends and adventures that might not otherwise be available to us in our day-to-day life. That is why I became an author. That, and because I felt honor-bound to tell you how awesome I am and set the record straight on exactly how I saved the universe. Did I mention that you owe me BIG TIME? More on that in Book Five.

are my Ardent, not the other way around. Our souls are bound, but mine is bound to yours more tightly than yours is to mine."

"That doesn't seem very fair," I said.

The corners of her mouth quirked in a grin. "As they say, 'fair is where you go to see the pigs.'"[109]

I nodded, feeling somewhat sheepish for taking our bond so lightly up to this point. I reached inside my shirt and pulled out my codex, the bronze medallion upon which my code had been inscribed.

"I will not be an annoying mother to you in this," the Tike said. "If I observe you breaking it, I will not nag you or tease you or tell you what to do. It is enough for me to know and be silent. This is my promise."

I held the codex out to her, and she read aloud:

"I will be my best self
I will honor my word
I will help those I can
I will never give up"

She read it through again to herself and nodded. "Thank you, Simon."

I shrugged. I had been watching the blood-red bird on her neck, aware somehow that it was also watching me.

---

[109] It's true: fairs have pigs. But if you want to see a pig, and your county doesn't have a fair, the good news is there are pigs in other places, too. Farms have pigs. Zoos have pigs. Cartoons have pigs. Fast food restaurants have *lots* and *lots* of pigs…you can interpret that last bit any way you want.

"Tike, can my mom hear us?"

"No," she said, touching the bird gently. "She can only see, and only when she chooses to look."

The bird stretched its neck, looking up at the Tike's face.

"Hawk said he didn't approve of Mom giving you the Rimbakka. What aren't you guys telling me about it?"

The Tike considered me then, but said nothing. I was about to protest, to force answers out of her, but suddenly she picked up the giant zucchini and leaped through the air toward the suit of armor, swinging the three-foot vegetable with frightening power.

It struck the suit of armor's helmet and exploded, coating the partially clean kitchen with goo and sending the helmet flying across the room.

Where the helmet had been, there was now a rather surprised-looking head.

"Aha!" the Tike said triumphantly. "Who are you? Speak or die, spy." For all her talk, she had not drawn her knives, and her posture was relaxed.

The man in the armor was—how can I put this— *gorgeous*. I mean, *I* didn't think so, but all the girls did later (especially Tessa), so you might as well know it up front. How would Tessa describe him? He had hair like fresh-cut straw, eyes like a mountain stream, and a chin that could have been sculpted by an artist. Blah blah, blah, he was handsome.

"I am Lieutenant Larik Montroth of the Holy Wizguard."

"The holy *what*?" I said.

"Wizguard," the Tike said. "And there's nothing holy about it."

Lieutenant Montroth glared at her harshly, but the effect was somewhat ruined by his gorgeousness. "My purpose here lies not with thee, my lady. Yet if you insist on questioning the honor of my order, I will cheerfully defend it." He moved faster than I would have thought possible for someone in armor, snapping a longsword out of the scabbard at his hip and holding it before him as if it were as light as a twig.

"Fine," the Tike said, resting a hand on one of the long knives at her belt. "Defend it. I challenge you to a duel."

"Uhh," I said. "Is that really a good—?"

"Be silent, child," Montroth said. "Thou shalt not dissuade us from the doing of great deeds."

Even his *voice* was gorgeous. Like honey, and deep water, and bright steel. Also, he called me a child.

I hated him.

He backed slowly around the counter, gaining space, and the Tike followed, careful to stay beyond the reach of his sword. She still had not drawn her knives, and she was moving so casually she might have been walking to the mailbox.

"You move as one born to the sword," he said with admiration.

"You move with a skill few humans can match," she said, and I was shocked to hear admiration in her voice as well.

Were they flirting? No…

"I will regret to end the life of one so beautiful," he said, crouching lower and pulling his sword close to his body.

"As will I," the Tike said.

Okay, they were flirting.[110]

He lunged, and his whiplike frame uncoiled with inhuman velocity. His sword thrust and cut but met only empty air. When he stopped moving, his expression was blank, whether from fear or anger or confusion, I couldn't tell.

The Tike was standing an inch away from his face, grinning widely and holding Montroth's sword.

"You are truly marvelous," she said sincerely. "I did not know that such mastery lived among your race." Then she tapped his forehead with the heel of her hand, and he fell unconscious to the floor.

---

[110] But not in a "I want to hold your hand on a rope swing over a moonlit reflecting pond" kind of way. More of a "Wow, I bet you could kill ten giant man-eating killer bunnies with one hand tied behind your back *almost* as fast as I could" kind of way.

14

THE STOWAWAY

To be one's self, and unafraid whether right or wrong, is more admirable than the easy cowardice of surrender to conformity.

—Irving Wallace[111]

Unsurprisingly, Captain Bast was less than pleased to discover that he had a stowaway aboard. So much so that for the moment, he didn't care that I was topside. After he had ordered Montroth tied hand and foot, he began to question him.

"What be yer business aboard me ship?" he demanded.

Montroth didn't answer.

"Wha' 'appened to his nose?" Bast asked, turning to me. "It do be all bruised and greenish. He do not be diseased, do he?"

"The Tike, er...*squashed* it," I said.

"Ahh." He turned back to Montroth and gripped the big man's nose, twisting it. "What be yer business aboard me ship?"

---

[111] A Wisconsinite who served in WWII with Dr. Seuss, and went on to write a bunch of strange books, none of which I have ever read. Incidentally, it's unclear to me whether this quote contains much real wisdom. What do you think?

"I was assigned to find and follow the wizard known as Simon Fayter wherever he should go."

"Why?" I demanded.

"Because the Wizguard has a right to know his doings so that they may better protect him and the people of the universe at large."

The Wizguard, as it turned out, were the intergalactic wizard police, and they had authority almost everywhere. Despite their unfortunate name, they were highly respected and very powerful.

"If yer a member o' the Wizguard," Bast said, "what be yer rank?"

"Lieutenant."

"Aha!" Captain Bast exclaimed, releasing Montroth's nose. "Yer lyin'. Ye be too young to hold such a rank."

Montroth blew a lock of golden hair out of his eyes. "Members of my family are not subject to such laws."

"Ye don' say?" Bast said. "And what family be that?"

"I am Larik Montroth," he said smoothly, "and I belong to the royal house of the Vitarey Kings."

Beside me, Tessa gasped. Then she did something that I will never, ever,

ever, EVER let her forget:

She *curtsied.*

"Your Highness," she said, her voice all flowery and innocent, "I am your loyal subject."

"Tessa," Hawk said, brow furrowed curiously, "do you know this man?"

Tessa nodded. "I didn't recognize him at first, since I've only seen him in person once, but he is who he says. Prince Larik."

Montroth gave her a gracious smile, and Tessa blushed deeply.[112]

"Well, then," Montroth said. "Now that my identity has been verified, I must insist that you remove my restraints so that I may assume command of this vessel."

The dozen or so pirates surrounding us burst into laughter. Captain Bast laughed so hard that he actually

---

[112] Just when I was starting to like her again, too.

cried. When he had control of himself once more, he patted Montroth on the shoulder, jabbed a finger at Tessa, and said, "Ye may be *her* highness, Montroth, but yer not mine. Ye'll stay in yer *restraints* as long as it do please me pudgy pirate pride. After that, ye can swab the deck, scrub the latrines, scrape off barnacloids, and wash the dishes 'til such time as we find a convenient moon upon which to maroon yer sorry self."

"Actually," the Tike said, "if I may impose, Captain, I thought that we might use him as target practice for Simon."

"Hmm," the captain said, stroking his beard. "Target practice, eh? Well, I suppose ye did catch 'im, and I owe yer for that. All right, then. He's yours. But if I's so much as surspect him of uhtempting ter escape, I be throwin' 'im in the brig."

"Oh, he won't do that," the Tike said, eyeing Montroth like she owned him. "Will you, Prince Larik?"

His face tightened. Perhaps he was remembering the ease with which this small woman had disposed of him only minutes before. "No," he conceded. "I will not."

"Good, then," Hawk said. He glanced over his shoulder at the shadowed craft that followed us. It was closer than before.

"Pray tell," Montroth said. "Who is it that pursues us? I cannot see the craft from where I sit."

"It's a shade," I said. "It's coming to kill me and probably destroy the ship."

I was quite pleased to see His Handsomeness go pale

at that, and feeling rather evil, I leaned in so that only he could hear me. "Still glad you came aboard?"

Hawk clapped his hands together briskly. "Come," he said. "Tomorrow is a big day, and we have work to do."

PREPARATIONS

Spectacular achievement is always preceded by
unspectacular preparation.

—Robert H. Schuller[113]

For a minute or two, I actually thought that Hawk and the Tike had rescued Montroth from Captain Bast because they were worried about him being mistreated by the pirates. By the time we made it back to the promenade deck, however, I decided they had done it because they distrusted Montroth so severely, they wanted him as their own private prisoner.

"Surely you can untie me now," he pled when we had walked out to the center of the grassy field.

"No." Hawk looked stern. "Tell me, if we searched you, what would we find?"

"Just what you see," Montroth said.

"I doubt that very much. Shall we search him, Tike?"

"Thoroughly," she said. She proceeded to take off his armor. Then, to my surprise, she unsheathed one of her

---

[113] A famous American Christian televangelist. He preached about God on TV for fifty years and built the largest glass building in the world.

147

knives and began to cut off various articles of his clothing. At this point, Tessa became so embarrassed that she had to excuse herself and wait outside.

"What are you looking for?" I asked.

"A fine question," Montroth said, grunting. "If you are looking for my pride, it abandoned me several moments ago."

"The infiltration of spies," Hawk said, "has been normal practice for the Wizguard for as long as I have been alive. And often, the spy they send in will be bugged."

"Bugged?" I said. "You mean like with a microphone?"

The Tike was now carefully sifting through Montroth's golden hair, as if she were checking him for lice.

Hawk gave me a puzzled look. "Of course not. I mean *bugged*. You know, with a Mujungy nesting spider or a Dervish worm."

"Or an Alatian love beetle," the Tike said, pulling a small, glistening black thing out of Montroth's hair triumphantly.

"Bother," Montroth muttered.

Hawk took the beetle from her carefully. "You see, Simon, the Alatian love beetle mates for life, and it has the rather inexplicable ability to track its mate across any distance. Take one partner away from the other, no matter how far, and whoever has the second beetle can find the first with ease." He inspected the beetle closely and then handed it back to the Tike, who smashed it between her thumb and the flat of her knife blade.

Montroth groaned.

"Yes," Hawk said sympathetically. "I'm afraid you are at our mercy now. No one is coming to rescue you. I'm disappointed, by the way. I asked what we would find on you, and you lied."

"What else are you hiding?" the Tike asked. "Be warned. For every secret I find, I will remove one of your teeth. Slowly."

Drake sneezed.

"Come on, Tike," I said. "You don't really mean that, do you? I'm sure he's just trying to do his job and all that."

"Oh, she means it," Hawk said. "The Wizguard are a treacherous crowd. If he is trying to bring the Wizguard fleet down on our heads to capture Simon, we need to know about it."

"Why would *they* want me?" I asked.

"Who can say for certain?" Hawk said. "But the Wizguard seek, above all things, control. If they have come to realize that the future of the wizarding world turns around your life, they will certainly seek control over you."

"Nothing like that," Montroth said hastily. "I was to simply follow and observe. The Wizguard is interested in what a Fayter will do to the world, given what the last one did. I am even allowed to offer my aid should I choose to do so. You see, you shouldn't think of me as an enemy at all—"

"I hope not," the Tike said. "You overheard sensitive information earlier. If I cannot think of you as a friend by the time our journey ends, I will be forced to remove your tongue, and your thumbs, and return you to the Wizguard with my apologies."

"Wait. Why his thumbs?" I interrupted.

The Tike pressed a finger to Montroth's throat like a threat. "Answer him."

"It is impossible to fight well without thumbs," he told me. Then he sighed and seemed to relent. "Fine. You ask what else I am hiding: There is a miniature thermocharge sewn into the hem of my left sock, and I keep a Jerkish smallsword concealed inside my mouth as a backup weapon, in case I am ever—"

"Captured by pirates and strip-searched?" Hawk finished.

The Tike held out her hand, and Montroth spat a small oval coin into it, no larger than a nickel.

"Beautiful," she said in admiration. "I have not beheld a Jerkish blade for some years." She fiddled with it, and in a mindboggling sequence of mechanical clicks, it unfolded several times in the span of about a half second, until she held the largest sword that I had ever seen. It was so big that she looked like a little child holding her father's longsword.

"What the…" I said.

"You keep that in your *mouth*?" Drake said. "What if you sneezed or something?"

"I never sneeze," Montroth said flatly. His voice was so serious, I did a double take, only to find that he was grinning slightly. "I did accidentally swallow it once in a fit of hiccups—a frightening moment—but in the end it has saved me more times than I can count."

The Tike fiddled with the handle of the humongous sword, and it collapsed in another blur of movements. Then she pocketed it and removed Montroth's socks. She cut open the hems and placed what looked like a tiny metal marble in her pocket as well.

"If that is all," Hawk said, "we can begin now. Montroth, if we discover that you have hidden anything else from us or failed to tell us something you should have or if you harm anyone on this crew or do anything at all that I don't like, the Tike will kill you without further discussion, and I shall feed your eyes to my pet hawk."

"Fair enough," Montroth said.

"Good, then. You will be assisting the Tike in giving Simon here some warm-up practice for tomorrow."

"Might I have some clothes first?" the big man asked nakedly.[114]

"Hmm," Hawk said. "I suppose that's reasonable. Simon, Drake, won't you fetch something for him to wear until he can sew his things back up? The Tike seems to have destroyed them."

We ran and got the best things we could find, which ended up being a set of old coveralls. After Montroth was safely clothed, we told Tessa the coast was clear, and my training began.

Tessa, resourceful as she was, had spent her time outside wisely, rounding up a blanket and a tray of snacks

---

[114] Relax. He wasn't really naked; the Tike left his underwear on. I just enjoy misusing adverbs.

for herself and Drake, as well as several broomsticks to use as practice swords.

"We will attack you in turns," the Tike said, handing a broomstick to Montroth and myself. "Since you will be fighting the shade with a sword, we will practice with these."

Montroth shivered. "A broomstick is a poor substitute for a darksword. If the shade's blade touches you, edge or not, you will be tainted with evil."

"Good to know," I said.

"Did you get that, Simon?" Drake called from the blanket. He and Tessa had hunkered down picnic style and were snacking to their heart's content. "Don't let the bad guy poke you with his sword."

"Yeah, I got it."

"You should experiment with the turncoat," Tessa called. "Try out some new knobs. You'll need all the help you can get tomorrow."

"Right," I said, brandishing my broomstick and undoing the top button of my coat. "Who's first, then?"

"You go first," the Tike said, pushing Montroth forward a step.

He shrugged his massive shoulders, twirling the broomstick experimentally. "I don't want to hurt you, Simon."

Tessa sighed. ("He's *such* a gentleman.")

"Simon has some training," the Tike advised. "And the shade certainly will show him no mercy, so you should not, either."

"Very well," he said, and he leaped at me.

I would like to point out here that a week of hard training had made me a decent swordsman. Not great, but decent. That is why I lasted three whole seconds before he fake-killed me.

"Dead," he said, holding the broomstick against my throat.

"Good footwork," the Tike said as she moved to face me.

When I was ready, she jumped into the air, flipping forward and bringing her broomstick down with a flourish. I ducked it and spun an attack at her sideways, but she parried it easily and smacked me on the forehead with her broomstick.

"Good footwork," she repeated. "Bad bladework."

"Try the turncoat this time," Tessa said.

"Yeah!" Drake called through a mouthful of crackers. "Throw a salmon at him!"

"Way to ruin the element of surprise, Drakus," Hawk said.

"Oh yeah. Sorry, Simon!"

Montroth lunged at me again. I parried once, twice, spun, turned A3 (*Curse*), and slapped the flat of his blade with my open hand. His broomstick exploded into dust, and I touched the tip of my broomstick to his chest. "Dead," I said.

"Simon?" the Tike said. "Why are your eyes closed? You should watch your enemy at all times."

"His broomstick dust got in my eyes," I said. I was

bent double now, blinking rapidly. "Maybe it isn't such a good idea to do this on an unlucky day."

"Nonsense," the Tike said. "In battle, things often do not go as planned. It is good for you to gain experience."

Montroth congratulated me on my victory and retrieved another broomstick. "I heard you had great power," he said. "But I did not realize the extent of your capabilities."

Maybe he was okay after all…

When the Tike faced me again, she stood still, forcing me to attack her first rather than defend. As any fighter knows, this is tricky business.

So I threw some rocks at her. There weren't many, but I had noticed a small pile of them earlier. No doubt some pirate had come to walk the park deck and gathered them for reasons unknown. In any case, she didn't like that. Usually, that would be a good thing; most people are less careful in a fight if they're angry. But then, the Tike isn't most people. She gave me another lump on the head and criticized my bladework again.

When Montroth came at me the third time, I was ready. I turned B1 (*Leap*) and rocketed fifteen feet into the air, flipping around to face him from behind. He recovered more quickly than I anticipated, so I turned C1 (*Chameleon*), and vanished from sight.[115] At this point, I was pleased to see him lose his nerve.

---

[115] Technically. I don't really become invisible, just REALLY well camouflaged, but in certain environments, it's basically the same thing.

"Where did he go?" he said. "I can't see him! His sword hovers in the air as if by magic!"

I darted forward, and to my immense frustration, the blond oaf managed to parry my next three attacks with ease. The Tike clapped in appreciation, and just like that, I hated him again. I turned C2 (*Stink*) and breathed a near-deadly cloud of stink-breath into his face, whereupon he gagged and toppled over backward.

Then *I* gagged, too. And the Tike, and, well, everyone. The noxious stink-breath was filling the whole park like a giant cloud. It was working much more powerfully than usual. Tessa struggled not to throw up, and Drake passed out cold on the grass. In the end, we had to evacuate. It took a full half hour before it was safe to re-enter.

"Still think it's a good idea to do this on an unlucky day?" I asked, but neither Hawk nor the Tike would listen to me.

Back inside, I fought Montroth again. My invisibility had worn off by then, but he still looked much more wary than he had before my stinky-breath bomb.

This time, I attacked him first. I lunged, but not quickly enough, and he nearly caught me with a kick to the knee, forcing me to retreat. I darted in twice more, but he fended me off with ease. The third time I darted, I found one of those rocks that I'd thrown earlier, and something very bad happened.

I stubbed my toe.

Now, this might not *seem* too bad to you, but let me explain: I have a *dragon* living in my boot. It's easy for you to forget this since he doesn't say much, and he doesn't do much. I *never* forget. I mean, do you think I can't feel a dragon living in my boot? Twitching in his sleep, nuzzling my ankle, wrapping his tail around the arch of my foot when he needs to stretch, sharpening his tiny teeth (at least, I hope that's what he's doing) on my toenails? Yeah. I notice. And when I do things like smash my foot into a rock, it tends to tick him off. In this particular instance, he happened to be sharpening his tiny teeth on my big toenail right when I smashed said toenail into said rock, squishing said dragon head between them.

For a second, his tiny dragon body went limp, and I thought I'd killed him. *Ah, rats.* I thought. *The Tike is going to be so mad.*

Then my boot began to rumble. A roar ripped the air with the force of a hurricane, and I fell to the ground. Montroth, who was only feet from me, fell over as well, looking alarmed.

Then, for the first time in days, Leto stuck his orange geckolike head out of my left boot and bared his teeth menacingly. "Simon Fayter," he said in a disproportionately deep voice, "you are a lummox."[116]

Montroth, who had been halfway to his feet again, gasped audibly, pointing a finger at Leto. "D-Dragon," he fumbled. "You have a d-dragon in your b-boot."

"You don't say," I said.

"A lummox!" Leto repeated, pounding me on the shin with a tiny clawed fist. "I have not condescended to

---

[116] A clumsy and/or stupid person.

participate in the menial adventures of your life so that you can ungratefully beat me into a stupor."

"I'm sorry, Leto."

His eyes narrowed suspiciously. "Are you?"

"Sure," I said.

I wasn't really. In fact, ever since Leto—despite, no doubt, having awesome dragon powers—had failed to come to my rescue on numerous occasions (including the time my pinky got chopped off), I had been feeling rather cool toward him. I kept him warm and snug all day. And night (he makes me sleep with my boots on). And what had he done for me? Nothing. Did he swoop in and save the day when my life depended on it? Nope. Did he offer me sage advice while he watched my life unfold? Nope. Did he give me a heads-up when the Tike was about to jump out and hit me from behind? Nope.

Leto seemed to guess my thoughts. "Do you have something *else* you want to say?"

"No," I said coldly.

"Good. Watch your step, then. And Simon, I think you're going to have to start changing your socks twice a day. I have a refined sense of smell, you know."

With that, he nestled back down into my boot and was gone.

"Merciful fates," Montroth whispered, climbing to his feet once more. "If I hadn't seen it, I wouldn't have believed it. A dragon. A real dragon, and it's taken up residence in your boot. Such things have not been heard of since the ancient times. What must it be like to live in such glory?"

"Oh, it's fantastic," I said. "Now, are we going to fight or what?" I lunged forward, hoping to catch Montroth while he was distracted, but he slapped my broomstick away and smacked me on the top of my head with his own, all the while gazing blankly at my boot.

The pain in my head was sharp. That, mingled with the recent dragon-born frustration, made me lose my temper.

"Argh!" I grunted. "That is *it*!" I reached into my coat viciously, turned a new knob, and began dancing the polka.

I tried to stop but found that I could not. It lasted for twenty seconds or so, during which time Montroth followed me around laughing, and Drake began singing a minotaurian drinking song to keep time with my dancing.

When it was over, Montroth lunged at me and I darted away. I turned another knob (D1) and my broomstick sort of...spasmed. A split second later, there were ten broomsticks in my hands instead of one.

"Cool," I said, and started chucking them at Montroth's head. Of course, he dodged them easily. The ones he couldn't dodge, he slapped out of the air like a Jedi. A *sissy* Jedi. ("Wow," Tessa said. "He's *so* talented...")

"I'll show you talented!" I cried, turning another new knob.

A *giant*, indecently loud and juicy-sounding fart noise ripped through the air around me.

Everyone froze.

It was the Tike who spoke first. "Are you all right, Simon?"

"Yeah," I said. "It was just the turncoat." ("*Sure* it was," Tessa said.)

Luckily, there was no smell to go along with it. I supposed the sound alone would have been a useful distraction if I had known it was coming.

Montroth attacked, and I dodged, turning another new knob as I rolled to the side. When I rose to my feet, I found myself holding a vintage rotary telephone.[117] With effort, I threw it at Montroth, and for some strange reason, it actually hit him. Right in the head. Go figure. It hit him so hard, in fact, that it made a single ringing noise, and he stumbled to one knee.

("Oh no, Simon!" Tessa said. "You've killed him!")

I meant to go and see if Montroth was okay. I really did. But instead I accidentally turned another new knob—my hand was still resting on them you see, and I slipped—and started laughing uncontrollably. Big, gut-shaking laughter. The kind that is appropriate during really funny Super Bowl commercials, but slightly impolite when your sparring partner has accidentally been bludgeoned in the head. ("You're such a FREAK, Simon!" Tessa shouted angrily.)[118]

---

[117] If you don't know what I'm talking about, kids, just imagine a giant banana-shaped cell phone attached to a curly, tangled cord attached to a lead brick.

[118] As you can see, I have banished Tessa's dialog parts to the land of the parenthetical (like this space right in here). I have done this partially because her lines don't fit cleanly into the narrative and partially because I just don't like her right now.

I *tried* to stop laughing, but for a solid fifteen seconds, I just couldn't. After that, my laughter cut off suddenly, and I gave a sort of groan while I tried to collect myself. By then, Montroth had recovered from the telephone attack.

"What are you going to do now?" Montroth said. I could tell he was mad. "Are you going to face me like a man, or are you going to disappear again?"

"He can't," Drake called. "Not until tomorrow."

"But I can do *this*!" I said, turning another new knob.

Of course, I didn't know what *this* was yet, but it sounded cool.

I disappeared and instantly reappeared three feet to the left. "Well," I said, "that's lame." I had to roll away to avoid Montroth's attack this time. Halfway through my roll, I turned another new knob.

Nothing happened.

At least, that's what I thought at first.

"Bumbling bumcrackers," Hawk muttered, staring at something to my left.

I turned and saw *myself* standing beside me.

Yeah, it was weird.

On closer inspection, I noticed that this clonelike creature was actually different from me in some important ways. He looked, well, *dumb*. His hair was a bit ruffled, his eyes were glassy and unfocused, and he *slouched*. A lot. On top of all that, he had a bit of drool dangling from the corner of his mouth. In short, he was what I would have been if I were a socially challenged video-game-brain-fried public-school dropout with a partial lobotomy.[119]

After a minute, Dumb Me noticed Smart Me looking at him and gave me a thumbs-up, mouth sagging open in what might have been a smile. ("He looks just like you!" Tessa said.)

Meanwhile, Montroth had decided that Dumb Me wasn't much of a threat. He lunged for me one last time, and one last time I turned a new knob.

The instant it clicked into position, Montroth froze midstep, his sword extended, mouth open in a noiseless cry. I waited for him to move, but he didn't. Then I looked around and found that the rest of the world had frozen as well.

Time had stopped.

"Awesome," I said. Then I stepped forward and placed the end of my broomstick firmly in the center of Montroth's chest, being sure to anchor my back foot against the ground so that when time started back up, I would have enough stability to stop his forward movement.

Then I waited.

And waited.

"Well," I said, addressing my frozen comrades. "This is awkward."

I fought a sudden urge to whistle the *Jeopardy!* theme song.

---

[119] A somewhat antiquated surgical procedure in which the brain is basically cut in half. Needless to say, it's known to have some side effects. I'd also like to mention that in contrast to the above description, I am in fact a socially adept, highly literate, privately tutored genius with a palatial physiognomy.

"OOF!" Montroth grunted. He came to a sudden stop in midair and fell backward to the ground, stumbling away from the butt of my broomstick.

"*Holy* rolly polies!" Hawk said. "Did you just alter space-time?"

"A magician never reveals his secrets," I said smugly.

"Ah," Hawk said, nodding to himself. "You have no idea what happened."

"Which knob was that?" Tessa said, walking up. She had the turncoat chart in her hand. "Actually, which knobs were all of those? Sit down, Simon. I'm not letting you leave until you tell me *exactly* what you did." Tessa, of course, was still taking very detailed notes on the knobs and their apparent uses.

I sighed, resigned to another thirty minutes of grueling explanations, categorizations, guesswork, and planning. In life, you see, whenever you do anything cool, there ends up being paperwork afterward.

16

HOPE

Kindness is giving hope to those who think they
are all alone in this world.

—Anonymous[120]

After my epic defeat of the Montrothity,[121] we had a lengthy discussion on the effects of the knobs and what exactly they might do, during which I stuffed my face with pirate snacks (green olives, saltine crackers, grapes, and goat cheese), and Dumb Me ate some grass and kept trying to snuggle with Montroth. This, by the way, unsettled Montroth considerably. In the end, he beat Dumb Me up, and I decided to push Dumb Me off the next cliff we came to; he was literally making me look bad. Meanwhile, Tessa looked confused and jealous.

By the way, if you are keeping track of the knobs yourself, taking notes on that handy-dandy diagram provided in the front pages of this book, you may wish to know that the knobs I turned were C5, D1, D2, D3, D4, D5, E1, and E2, respectively.

---

[120] Anonymous was a Greek warrior who got hit so hard that his name fell off. He never found it again.

[121] Similar to a monstrosity, but composed of 99% Montroth.

In the end we all agreed that the knobs would require further testing before they could be named or their functions fully understood.[122] I was particularly interested in the one which had apparently made time stop for everyone but me. No one really understood this one, so I pretended not to know what happened, either. What can I say? I wanted time to think. I tried each of the knobs again, but nothing happened. Usually the knobs worked only once per day and then reset at midnight, but some knobs didn't follow that rule.

When we were done, the Tike said that she needed some fresh air, and she took Montroth upstairs. No doubt for another round of threats. Before she left, she gave me the thermocharge and instructed me to take it straight to Captain Bast. Drake and Tessa both wanted to stay and work on the turncoat chart some more. Hawk followed Montroth upstairs, but before he left he took me aside, putting a hand on my shoulder.

"Simon," he said, "I don't know all of what happened a moment ago, but it seemed to me as if you stopped time." He raised an eyebrow, and I felt my cheeks color. "Simon, I must warn you about this. Many of the powers manifested by the turncoat are simply beyond our understanding. Sometimes, when you use them without fully understanding them, you risk your life. That, of course, is a price you are willing to pay. But, Simon, when you alter time, you risk the world...which, admittedly, is kind of

---

[122] Except for D1. That one clearly multiplied the object I held in my hand at the time (the broomstick). Tessa named it *Copy*.

your job." He patted me on the back sympathetically and then walked away, leaving me to contemplate his words.

Five minutes later, I was walking up to the captain's quarters on my own.

As I walked, I couldn't help thinking about the fight that was coming tomorrow. I had done well today. I had learned about some new powers. I had kept my head and beat Montroth a couple of times (sort of). But let's face it: Even the Tike could still beat me nine times out of ten, no matter what I did. How much more powerful was a shade?

I didn't stand a chance.

When I arrived at the captain's quarters, I found him poring over a pile of maps.

"Ah," he said. "Come in. I just be contemplatin' the strange an' 'opeless quest that ye 'ave sent us on."

"Yeah," I said, feeling hopeless myself. "Sorry about all that."

"No, no," he said, gesturing for me to sit. "It do be me utmost pleasure to do whate'er the Circle o' Eight do require, an' ter be honest, me career's been an endless parade o' 'opeless quests. We pirates specialize in 'em."

"It does look pretty hopeless, doesn't it?" I said, glad to finally share my feelings. "On the bright side, if the shade kills me tomorrow, you won't have to worry about finding Dark Haven anymore."

"Aye, there is that," he said. "Care fer some tea?"

He left to make it, passing through a little round chamber with several hallways branching off of it at intervals. On the floor there, in the center of a circle of exquisitely patterned hardwood, was what looked like a large blue diamond. It was easily six inches across, and it pulsated with light in a way that reminded me vaguely of the standby light on my mom's old laptop.

As I waited for him, I tried to find somewhere to sit that wasn't already occupied by maps, papers, strange items, or dirty dishes. The captain's quarters were incredibly spacious; so spacious, in fact, that I wondered how it was possible to fit such a room within the outside dimensions of the ship. The sitting room that I was in consisted of two wall benches in the shape of an L, which surrounded a low worktable.

Above the table hung a huge sword. It was not at all like the graceful sabers that the captain had worn at his waist when I first met him; it was a gigantic warsword—a two-handed affair with a blade as long as I was tall. The leather of the hilt was so old that it was falling off, but beneath that I could see that the steel was as strong as ever. The first foot or so of blade behind the guard was unsharpened, and I knew from my history lessons with Atticus that this was designed so that the bearer could hold the massive blade in one hand and the butt of the hilt with the other, temporarily wielding the sword like a spear.

"Lucky, that sword," Bast said, startling me. "Never let me down in battle."

"Where did you get it?" I said. "It's huge!"

"Aye. A bit too big to wear around, to be sure. Took her from the tomb of Gubolda the Fierce. Big broad, Gubolda was. Bad luck, grave robbin', but not so bad when it's a pirate's grave, and anyways, Gubolda was me great-great-aunt, so I figure she'd ha' wanted me to have it."

I tore my gaze from the sword and pointed at the pulsating blue stone in the circular antechamber. "What does that do?" I asked, accepting my tea.

"Our oscillation stone," he said reverently, sipping his tea. He walked over to the stone and tapped it with the toe of his boot. "This 'ere beauty do be the heart an' soul o' the *Calliope*. If ye 'aven't noticed, there do be some fandangly magic hangin' abou' this ship."

"I have noticed," I said.

"Aye. It do power the gravity sails, an' the lightin' and gravity systems. It also be soakin' up the energy, so ter speak, when we come close ter a star—so we don' burs' inta flames, yer see. Then, if we e'er be in dead space, too far from somethin' with a gravitational pull fer the sails to lock on, we can locomote ourselves usin' the energy stored in the oscillation stone."

"Sounds expensive," I said. "Where I come from, stuff that runs on light always costs you more."

"Aye," he said. "Very expensive, an' very dangerous, too."

"Dangerous?"

"Well, the stone itself be nearly indestructible when

empty, see? But when it be full of energy like now, it becomes…eh…unstabler."

"You mean, *more volatile*," I said.

"Aye. That too. Smash it wit' a hammer, an' it won' do nothin'. But hit it with a blast o' magic, or fire, or an explosion o' some kind—basically anythin' with inordinate amounts o' energy, an'—"

"Boom," I finished.

"Nah," he said, scratching his chin. "More like

BOOM!"

He jumped into the air, splaying his arms wildly and spilling tea all over a picture of a woman holding a small child.

"Ahh, dung doodles," he said under his breath, wiping the portrait clean with the sleeve of his shirt. He whispered softly to the picture then. "I do be sorry, me dear."

"Is that your family?" I asked, instantly regretting it.

Captain Bast stopped moving when I spoke. Then he stepped away from the picture and sat down, clearing his throat. "Wha' brings ye to me humble quarters, Simon Fayter? Tha' stowaway's not botherin' ye no more?"

"No, no, he's been quite helpful, as a matter of fact."

"Huh." Bast looked disappointed.

"Though, he did surrender an item that the Tike wanted you to look after."

I took out the thermocharge, and Bast took it from me, holding it up to the light. "Now what do this be?" he mused. "Galloping guinea fowls! A thermocharge! Do yer know wha' this is, lad?"

"Does it go boom as well?" I guessed.

"Aye. Looks harmless enough, but twist it in half an'..." He gestured widely, making a mushroom shape with his arms. After that, he began to pace around the room as if looking for a place to hide it. At length, he sat down at the low worktable and opened a drawer. He pushed it back in slightly, then opened it another inch, and there was a click. Then the drawer opened an extra six inches, revealing a secret compartment. Bast set the thermocharge down carefully and closed the drawer.

"Best no one finds it," he said. "It do be dangerous on its own in the middle o' a deserted field, or a desert island...but on this ship, why, it be settin' off the oscillator stone like no other, and believe you me, that would be an explosion the likes o' which we ha' ne'er seen. Why, we might even tear a 'ole in space." He looked half horrified, half excited at the prospect, like a man used to keeping others safe but secretly wishing for an unexpected danger at which to throw himself.

"Why don't you just go throw it overboard?" I suggested.

"Aye, I could do that, but would ye leave a bomb floating where anyone might pick it up? Maybe some kid finds it an' don' know what it is."

I didn't think that the middle of uncharted space really counted as a place where "anyone might pick it up," but I didn't want to argue. We talked a while longer about small things—the crew, Drake's skysickness, but eventually our conversation came to an end and he led me to the door.

Before I left, I said, "Sorry, by the way, about the picture. I didn't mean to pry. I've lost people, too."

Bast stiffened. "Lost? What makes you think I lost someone?"

I shrugged.

"Well…" He trailed off, brushing the tip of his nose. "Who'd you lose, then?"

"My dad."

"Hmm," he said. "All right." Then he shut the door in my face.

I stood there awkwardly for a minute, unsure whether I had just offended him, but before I could make up my mind, the door opened again. He looked slightly embarrassed. "Eh…thanks fer, er…bringin' me tha' bomb."

"My pleasure," I said.

Bast nodded as if that settled the matter, then changed the subject. "Do ye think ye can beat that shade?"

I gulped, searching for something manly and brave to say.

He sighed. "That be what I figured. No one e'er beat a shade, they say. Fought an' lived, maybe. Once or twice. But no one e'er *beat* one." He considered me a moment. "I tell ye what, Simon. As far as I know, no one e'er beat a *Fayter*, neither.[123] Me money's on you. No reservation or hesitation, and me crew thinks the same, every last one o' 'em."

---

[123] This seemed like a bad time to point out to him how my namesake was murdered by his own brother.

I nodded, thinking that at least my crew—

"'Cept Mortazar. He thinks ye'll get slaughtered for sure. But the rest o' us believes in ye. So don' stop believin' in yerself, and don't forget: When yer born to do a thing, nothin' an' nobody can stand in yer way. And Simon, ye were born to save the world. I can feel it in me bones." He put a hand to his belly thoughtfully. "I think that's what it be, anyhow. Either that or that blasted goblin's cookin's sittin' wrong with me again. I better go take me vitamins…" He scrunched up his face and closed the door again, leaving me alone.

Alone, of course, is the place where heroes live. At the end of the day they have to do the thing that no one else can do—or *will* do—and usually, no matter how many friends they've made or foes they've faced, at the final moment, when it comes time to face the inescapable ending, the unthinkable fear, the unbeatable foe, they must do it alone. That's just how this hero stuff goes.

Still, right then, with Captain Bast's acclamations ringing in my ears, I felt ready for anything.

Almost anything.

17
THE EVE OF BATTLE

Curiosity killed the cat.

—Unknown[124]

That night, before Drake and I went to bed, we very foolishly decided to go up on deck and check how close the shade had come. The ship was run by a skeleton crew at night, so there were very few people around, and the deck lights were all turned down low, which made it rather creepy to look behind us and see the ghostlike ship, chasing us down like a silent nightmare, only partially emerged from the world of dreams.

"Well," I said, trying to swallow my fear, "this was a bad idea."

"Yeah," Drake said. "Let's go back to our room now."

We did. Back downstairs, I started pulling back the blanket on my bunk.

"You know," Drake said, "I'm pretty glad it's you fighting that shade tomorrow and not me."

"Me, too," I said. "He'll be safer that way."

---

[124] Born 1810. Died 1910. Killed by a cat.

Drake gave a forced laugh, but I could tell he was still concerned.

"You don't think…" he began. "I mean, the turncoat will save you, right? Something super lucky will happen, and you'll be fine, like always."

I searched around for something inspiring to say, but the truth was, I feeling worried again. "Actually, Drake, I'm about 98% sure this will be my last night. Tomorrow, you'll need to find a new best friend."

Okay, okay. I didn't say that, but I was thinking it…

"Sure," I said confidently. "In fact, I have a favor to ask you about tomorrow. Something that will help."

Drake perked up at this. "Really? What?"

"It's about Tessa," I said. "You know how she is. If things start to get hairy, the first thing she'll want to do is jump in and try to help me by beating up the shade herself. I want you to stop her."

Drake paled. "Stop Tessa?" he whispered. "From doing what she wants?"

"She wouldn't be helping me, anyway. She'd only be hurting herself. I want you to promise me, Drake. Don't let her do anything stupid. If I have your promise, then I won't have to worry about it. I can focus on the shade."

"I promise, then," Drake said. "But you have to promise me something in return. Take my body back to my mother. Because Tessa's going to kill me if I stop her from helping you."

We laughed at that, then fell into an awkward silence. I could tell he was still worried.

"Hey," I said, looking for a distraction, "you want to try out a few more turncoat knobs?" I reached for the coat and put it on. I was pleased to see that Drake was now worried about something entirely different.

"What?" he squeaked. "Now? Here? What if something happens? What if something goes wrong and…and—"

"Here we go," I said, and Drake leaped from his bunk to the center of the room. He reached out as if to stop me, but it was too late. I turned E6 (*Travel*).

And vanished.

Okay, so I lied a little bit. Not about turning E6. I did that. But I wasn't testing a new knob. I had turned E6 before. That was the knob that first transported me across the universe from Skelligard to Daru. "So what?" you ask. Well, I had been thinking lately that I wanted to know where that knob would take me next. At the same time, I didn't want to just turn it randomly and be stuck in some other world for, you know, a whole *book* or something.

So I had come up with a plan: I would wait until there were only ten seconds left in the day. When my watch read 11:59:50, then I would turn the knob and travel to wherever it took me. Then I could come back again in ten seconds. If it happened to transport me into the belly of a volcano or the bottom of the ocean, I just had to survive for ten seconds, and then I could return after the knob reset. It was a perfect plan.

I appeared on the edge of a bluff overlooking the most majestic city I'd ever seen. I shielded my eyes from the blazing sun, waiting for them to adjust to the light. The city that stretched beneath me lay in a fertile valley, and at its center was a huge white pyramid. The structure was easily ten city blocks wide at the base and just as high, and it gleamed in the sun like a polished gem.

The city itself was divided into four quadrants, stretching out from the four points of the pyramid: One was filled with simple stone houses, one with graves, one with fields and farmland, and one with a tangled clump of industrial buildings. The city was so large that I couldn't see to the far side, but I could tell that around the outside, like a border, stood a white wall, a hundred feet high.

I glanced at my watch. It was 12:01 *Calliope* time. Drake was probably freaking out by now. It was time to be getting back.

Then I heard something. A soft, familiar noise. I couldn't place it, but it made me feel uneasy. I peered over the bluff, and the noise got louder.

Crying.

Someone was down there. They couldn't be far below me; the sound seemed close.

Carefully, not wanting to be seen by anyone—not wanting to get too involved in this world at all, I lowered myself over the edge and began to descend the cliff face. I had to go quite slowly, as I'm not the best climber in the world, and it took a lot longer than I thought. In a few minutes, I came to another ledge and climbed down onto it. The crying was definitely closer now—it was a gentle, slow sobbing—but I still could not see its source. I glanced at my watch. 12:10 a.m. Geez. This was taking a long time. But I couldn't stop.

I edged along the ledge until I couldn't go any farther, then I got down on my belly and peered over, looking into a small cave that hadn't been visible from above.

A boy sat there, sobbing into his hands. He had blond hair and pointed features. He looked a couple years younger than me—eleven or twelve.

The boy glanced up suddenly, meeting my eye.

My heart skipped a beat, and I froze. Our eyes locked for a moment, and his scared me. They were hard and intelligent. The eyes of someone hiding deep power, or horrible anger, or terrible pain. The eyes of someone who did not appreciate being spied upon in a moment of weakness.

I scrambled back from the edge and turned E6, vanishing once more.

"No, don't," Drake was saying. "It isn't safe."

"What?" Once again, I couldn't see anything. The dim light of our cabin on the *Calliope* was a blotchy swirl of shadows for a second. Then I could make out Drake. He was on his feet, reaching out to me.

"Don't do it," he said, grabbing my shoulder. "If you

really want to test the knobs, let's at least wake Tessa and go down to the promenade."

"What are you talking about?" I said.

"You said you wanted to test some turncoat knobs," Drake said.

"Drake, did you stay in here the whole time? I was gone for over ten…" I glanced down at my watch and stopped talking. It said 12:00 a.m.

"Woah…" I said.

"What?" Drake looked confused.

"I don't know, exactly," I said.

It took a while to bring Drake up to speed. When I had finished, he gave a low whistle.

"Simon," he said. "I don't know who that kid was or why he was crying, but there is only one city that meets that description. The pyramid, the quadrisected[125] city. You went to Tarinea!"

"Tari what?"

"Tarinea," Drake whispered almost reverently. Then his eyes widened, and he punched the air triumphantly. "This is so cool! You have to take me back right now. I want to see it. I want to see it now. Come on, Simon." Drake had crossed the room and was reaching inside my turncoat.

"No way," I said, shoving him off. "It's past midnight. If we go back now, we'll be stuck there for the entire day. Who knows what might happen."

---

[125] Divided into four equal parts.

"Exactly!" Drake said. "Tarinea..." He stared out the porthole, holding his hand out dramatically, as if he could nearly touch it.

"What on earth has gotten into you?" I said.

Drake snapped out of his daydream and looked at me sternly. "Didn't you read the copy of *Tarinea, City of Lights* by Adrogon Grosvl? I gave it to you our first day back!"

"Uh..."

"Simon!"

"The introduction was super boring!" I said. "I think I hid it under Tessa's bed."

"I thought you'd returned it to the archives!" He grumbled something about stubborn Fayters and began to pace back and forth across the floor. "Tarinea was one of the most important cities in wizarding history, Simon. It was the peak of our civilization. The renaissance of magic. Some of the most important discoveries and books and theories and treatises were written, discovered, theorized, and composed in Tarinea! I'd give anything to see that place..."

"Wait a minute," I said. "Did you say it *was* one of the most important cities?"

"Yeah," Drake said glumly. "It was destroyed in an asteroid storm hundreds of years ago."

"You're joking."

"Nope. Wiped from the face of the planet—the planet Sayco, that is. Not even so much as a spoon left for us to study."

"Woah...so I just traveled to the past?"

AUSTIN J. BAILEY

Drake nodded. "Definitely. How long were you there?"

"At least ten minutes," I said.

"Amazing!" Drake said. He closed his eyes and began rubbing his temples with both fingers. "A clean break, just as Balpheas theorized in *Time's Continuities*. And yet you returned…how is that possible?"

"English, Drake," I said.

"What? Oh. No time passed here at all. I didn't even know you had left."

"I don't get it."

"Neither do I," he said slowly. "The theory is that you were living in a time that happened in our past, so to you, time didn't pass at all here. It couldn't, because as soon as you were in my past, my present was in your future."

"Huh?"

Drake rubbed his head in frustration. "Just trust me. You could turn that knob again right now and spend a hundred years in Tarinea and then come back and no time would have passed here at all. Except that you really shouldn't be able to come back…and yet you can."

I reached into my turncoat and shivered. "Dang," I said. "You found me out, Drake. I actually spent fifty years there, and I've learned stuff you couldn't imagine." I gave him my most aged, wise smile, and he paled.

"You didn't…" he said.

"No, I didn't."

"Argh! Don't do that to me. But we *could* do that, Simon. We could go right now! You could take as long as you want, learning to fight, learning to use your power, preparing for your battle tomorrow with the shade. And I could meet all the most important thinkers in history! Think of the books I could write…we could stay as long as we wanted…provided we don't get wiped out by an asteroid storm."

"Hmm," I said. It was a tantalizing idea, but it didn't feel right. "I don't know, Drake. That sounds pretty messed up to me. I think we should finish the adventure we're currently on."

He sat down on his bed, looking defeated. "Okay. But promise me you'll think about it."

"I will." I grinned at him. "Guess what happens now?"

"What?"

"I try another new knob."

"Oh my gosh," Drake said. "You can't be serious."

"Yup. I'm not even tired yet." I turned a new knob, E3, and—

18
FUN WITH DRAKE

I had a little turtle. His name was Tiny Tim.
I put him in the bathtub, to see if he could swim...
—TBA[126]

—Out of nowhere, a new chapter started.

"Nghaaa," Drake moaned, holding his head between his hands. "What happened?"

My head was killing me, too. For a second, it had felt as if my brain had been submerged in ice. Then something hit me, something big and terrible and invisible and mysterious. Like a super-dimensional echo across time... or a duck fart.[127]

"Did you feel that?" I asked. It was a dumb question. Drake had fallen out of his bed and was splayed across the floor, holding his head.

"What was it?" he asked. "What did it do?"

"I'm not sure. Here, I'll try it again."

"No, wait—"

---

[126] This stands for "to be announced." This means that either I don't know who made up this song/poem, or I'm going to tell you later.
[127] In retrospect, I'm pretty sure it wasn't a duck fart. Seriously, though, watch out for those...

19

ARGHHHHHHHH!

*...He drank up all the water, he ate up all the soap,
and now he's sick in bed with a bubble in his throat...*

—TBA

When I regained consciousness, Drake was chewing on my foot. I had to punch him in the nose to get him to release me, and then I had to slap him a few times to get him to stop barking.[128]

"Hey," I said, when he had come to his senses, "it looks like this knob doesn't have to reset at midnight. Cool, eh?"

"Uggh," Drake groaned, holding his head. "Please don't do that again."

After comparing our stories, I determined that the strange effects of E3 were stronger the second time. We had both experienced the same pain as before, the same strange jolt, as if being pinched by the fabric of reality. Then we had each gone into a state of altered consciousness. I blacked out for about three seconds. Drake, meanwhile, experienced a vivid delusion in which he was a dog, and I was a T-bone steak dripping with (get this) chocolate

---

[128] Sorry for all the violence, but what did you expect? We're teenage boys on a pirate ship...

syrup and gypsy wongpongs.[129]

Now, of course, as I write this book, it is clear to me that E3 was creating sudden chapter breaks in my then-future autobiography. Weird. At the time however, all I was thinking was that the effects of the knob seemed to worsen with each progressive turning. Was that right? What would happen if I did it again? Would it be even worse? Of course, there was only one way to find out...

He knew just what I was thinking.

"Wait, Simon. ARGHHHHHHHH—"

---

[129] A minotaurian delicacy that I am too squeamish to describe properly.

THE PENGUIN AND THE PIZZA

*…Bubble bubble bubble, bubble bubble bubble,
bubble bubble bubble bubble, bubble bubble…*

—TBA

Azdark, king of all penguins, ruled the roost with an iron wing. He had faced foes before, and he would face them again, but today he fought the battle of all battles, the foe of all foes: *Slice*, overlord of the demon pizzas.

Slice was the slice of all slices, the pizza of all pizzas. His pepperoni was hotter than hotdogs in Hades. His crust was softer than poodles, his cheese cheesier than the cheesiest noodles.

"Come here, Slice," Azdark said tauntingly. "I was stuffing crusts before you were born. I'm gonna mop you up with your own sauce."

Slice and Azdark stood at the top of a hill, surrounded on all sides by a crowd of penguins—and one random camel—waiting to see their fate decided.

Slice felt his yeast rise and puffed himself up, looking as big as possible. "Thanks for dressing up, Azdark, but that tuxedo won't save you."

"I'm gonna force-feed you your own anchovies,"[130] Azdark whispered.

The tension was too much for the camel to handle, and it collapsed.[131]

SLAP!

Drake and I staggered away from each other. Both of us bore Tessa's pink, pulsating palm print on our cheeks.

"WHAT IN THE NAME OF RELLIK'S LEFT NOSE HOLE ARE YOU TWO DOING?" she yelled.[132] "Have you

---

[130] Anchovies are a type of tiny fish that taste so bad the only way they can get eaten is if they are shipped halfway around the world, hidden in pizza, and fed to unsuspecting American teenagers. On the list of things I wouldn't want to be force-fed, anchovies are near the top. Also on that list is spoiled milk, spoiled meat, spoiled fruit, spoiled children, rutabagas, begging Ruda's, canned beets, beet cans, can-cans, pie pans, pin cushions, seat cushions, diamond-studded cushions, cushion-cut diamonds, pearls, pearl necklaces, Grandma Pearl, Lou Pearlman, headstones, kidney stones, keystones, stone keys, metal keys, pretty much any kind of keys, asteroids, pickled pig's feet, cow feet, cow tongue, pickled cow tongue, wombats, the Eiffel Tower, the Eiffel Valley, the Eiffel Mountains, rubber bands, bouncy balls, Slinkys, boomerangs, bungee cords (these five tend to come back up), Tajikistan, Switzerland, Detroit, day-old McDonald's french fries, dice, lice, mice, uncooked rice, hammers, a vice, a CO_2-gas-pressurized personal flotation device, yak ears, dog ears, dog-eared books, undog-eared books, unbooklearned dogs, frogs, saws, giant blocks of mincemeat, garden shears, lit candles, unlit candles, llama hair, underwear, potpourri, panda bears, pixie sticks, pogo sticks, monkeys, ticks, katydids, baseball caps, baseball bats, letter openers, land mines, and…asparagus. That's right. I don't like asparagus.

[131] Promise fulfilled.

[132] I wanted to point out that "nose holes" are more accurately described as nostrils, but it didn't seem like the right time.

gone completely insane? Simon, why are you waddling like a penguin?"

"I—"

"You were making enough racket to wake the ship!"

"We—"

"I don't care if you're nervous about dying tomorrow. When it's time to sleep, it's time to sleep! And don't THINK I didn't notice that weird headache mumbo jumbo you were doing with your turncoat. Everyone on this ship has been bouncing around like headless chickens because you can't keep your hands out of your pock—"

21

LUCKY

…Pop!

—A Nursery Rhyme

I cannot (for fear of what Tessa would do to me) tell you what happened the fourth time I turned E3. The important thing is that Drake and I recovered before Tessa did. While she was still breakdancing and yodeling in Japanese (whoops, I told you), we shoved her out of the room and locked the door. True, it wasn't the nicest thing we could have done, but the fact of the matter is, when Tessa's really angry, it's better to have a solid oak door between you and her until she calms d—

BAM!

Two Tessa-sized fists burst through the oak panels, grabbed hold of the door, and ripped it off its hinges.

"Come in," I said.

She looked mad enough to breathe fire.

Making the first good decision I'd made since Tessa arrived, I reached into the turncoat and turned B2 (*Silvertongue*). Then I laid a hand gently on her shoulder and said seven words that changed our lives forever:

"Pwease wemove your fist fwom my mouwff."

Realistically, the pronunciation was even worse than that, but she understood me. It was the please that caught her attention.

Anyway, she actually *apologized* for punching me. From there, it was a few short minutes before she had paper and ink out and we were discussing the effects of the latest knob. In the end, we named it "Daze." Then we talked of pleasant things, of the memory of similar nights spent together under the stars, and our youthful dreams of the future.

When they were long asleep, I lay awake in my bunk, brooding. I glanced at my watch, counting the hours until tomorrow. Pretty soon, I would begin the day in which I would meet my end, or send a shade to his.

Yeah. There was no way I was going to sleep. It was after midnight; I was lucky again. So why wait?

I took up my turncoat, slung Kylanthus over my shoulder, and made my way to the upper deck.

From there, I could see the shade's ship clearly. It had gained on us, and now his deck was not a hundred yards off. I saw him emerge from the belly of his craft. He was tall, seven feet or more, and his features were obscured by a cloak darker even than the night—so dark the pale starlight could not find it. From across the space between us, our eyes met—mine shining in the light of the deck lamps, his glinting like coins from the bottom of a well.

I drew Kylanthus out of its scabbard and spoke the

sword's name softly, sending scarlet flames along its edge. I raised the blazing blade into the air in invitation: *Come and get me.*

22
MOTHER'S BLOOD

A mother's love for her child is like nothing else in the world. It knows no law, no pity. It dares all things and crushes down remorselessly all that stands in its path.

—Agatha Christie[133]

When he saw my sword, his beetle-like eyes glinted from beneath his hood. He drew his own sword then, a giant thing—more like a boat anchor than a sword. It shone with a sickly green light. He raised it before him in acceptance of my challenge, and I felt my heart begin to race.

"You should face him now," a voice said from behind me. I jumped and nearly dropped my sword overboard on accident.

"Gah! Tike, stop sneaking up on me like that!"

"You have met him well," she said, ignoring me. "You should fight him now, and wait no longer."

---

[133] Dame (The female equivalent of *sir*, meaning that she was knighted) Agatha Mary Clarissa Christie, Lady Mallowan DBE was a British writer born in 1890. She wrote *And Then There Were None* and about seventy-nine other books, of which she has sold roughly two billion copies. She is the best-selling novelist of all time. She probably never did book signings, though, since it must have taken her an hour or two to sign her name.

I almost laughed. "No, thanks, Tike. I just couldn't sleep, so I thought I'd come and mess with him a bit. Actually, I was thinking you could wear a Simon Fayter mask and fight in my place. What do you say?"

She frowned. "Shades live by a strict code. They always come seeking just one. They will fight only you, and they cannot be tricked, for they can smell your blood and detect imposters."

"Nuts," I said, snapping my fingers. "So much for that plan."

She chuckled darkly. "He cannot be fooled. Though he has power to destroy this whole vessel, he will ignore the rest of us and see only you." She furrowed her brow thoughtfully. "Unless we get in his way."

"It's okay, Tike," I said. "I know you can't defend me this time. You've done the best you can."

"He will be a warrior of immense experience, Simon," she went on, as if by pouring extra advice into my head she could make up for the fact that she would have to sit on the sidelines. "You will not be able to trick him or surprise him. He will try to force you to the edge of the ship, or inside it, some place where you have no room to maneuver."

"Tike," I said, catching her arm as she moved toward the main mast, "can I borrow Montroth's Jerk sword?"

She nodded, handing over the small oval coin. "*Jerkish*," she muttered. "Remember what I said about trying to trick him, Simon. It will not work."

"I have to try something," I said.

She hesitated, then met my eyes with a serious look. "If you fight him with fear in your heart, your blade will not stand against him. You must rid yourself of fear or destroy him with overwhelming force. You will not beat him with skill alone. You must be something more today, more than you have ever been before."

"Right," I said. I thought for a moment. Then I sheathed my sword and ran away.

Kidding. I wanted to, though. Wouldn't you?

I mounted the quarterdeck and found Nub at the helm.

"Stop the ship," I commanded. "And rouse the crew. It do be time for me ter get slaughtered by an all-powerful demon assassin."

"Aye-aye, Captain Simon," Nub said. He turned the ship around sharply and shouted to the men above us, who pulled in the sails. Then he tugged on a small brass lever and the shipwide alarm sounded. Within two minutes, the whole crew was standing above deck. Tessa looked worried, but not nearly as worried as Drake, who was wearing his huge black backpack, ready for anything.

As the shade's ship closed on us, Captain Bast appeared on deck. He was wearing his sabers at his waist again, but he was also holding the huge sword that I had seen in his quarters.

He addressed the crew: "Listen up! The time do be come for Cap'n Simon to figh' the demon from the dark abyss!" The crew cheered for me, though I distinctly heard a couple of them shout things like "Rest in peace!" and "I call dibs on his boots!"

"Ye all know the dangers o' a shade," Bast went on. "If he do at any time attack the *Calliope*, yer orders be ter abandon ship. Do no' fight him, for ye do no' stand a flamingo's chance in a shark tank at winnin'. Ye hear?"

"Aye-aye!" the crew shouted.

Captain Bast looked at the shade, who was now about twenty yards away, and his eyes narrowed, face going slightly white. "Clear the deck! Into the riggin', the lot o' you, and give 'em some room!"

Hawk winked at me and began to climb the main mast, pulling Tessa and Drake behind him. When everyone was up the mast or safely out of the way among the rigging, Captain Bast planted himself firmly at the base of the main mast and rested the sword across his broad shoulders. Between that and the two undrawn swords at his waist, he looked more than ready to protect his crew should the battle go ill.

The Tike dropped out of the rigging then and came to stand beside me. "May I borrow that?" she asked Captain Bast, nodding at the great sword. "I can't help noticing that you have others…"

"Aye," he said, eyeing the big sword lovingly. "I daresay she'll do more good in yer hands than me own." And he tossed it to her.

To my surprise, she caught it with ease, spinning the blade like a quarterstaff so that the unsharpened portion came to rest with a *thump* under her arm.

"Put me in the turncoat, Simon," the Tike said, turning to me. "If, at the end of your need, I can be of assistance, I will."

"But," I objected, "you said a minute ago that no one but me can stand against him!"

She swept my objection aside. "Such things do not matter to you and me," she said and reached into the coat herself. "Fight well."

She turned E8 (*Stash*) and vanished.

As she disappeared, there was a small tap as the prow of the shade's vessel bumped our hull. I turned just in time to see him leap in a high arc, somersaulting in the air. He landed in a crouch, one hand punching the *Calliope*'s deck to steady himself. The impact jarred the whole ship, and several planks cracked beneath him. Then he unfolded himself and stretched to his full height, unsheathing his sickly green blade and raising it before him again in greeting.

"Yikes!" I said, more loudly than I had intended. His sword looked big enough to cleave a giraffe in two. His body was strangely hidden in the shadows of his cloak. I should have been able to see it, but I couldn't.

"Leto!" I hissed, stomping my left boot against the deck. "You don't want to come out here and give me a hand, do you?"

The diminutive dragon peeked one orange eye over the top of my boot, looked the shade up and down, then yawned and snuggled up against my ankle.

It was worth a shot.

"I smell your blood, Simon Fayter," the shade said. Its voice was a deep, raspy monotone. The inhuman sound made the hair on my arms stand up as I raised Kylanthus in return.

I slipped my other hand into my pocket and touched the sorrowstone. Immediately, my fear and doubts vanished. Then, to my surprise, I found my courage once again. I was going to be okay after all. I was *destined* to do stuff like this. I whispered the name of my sword, and it burst into flame once more.

"What do you want with me?" I asked, knowing the answer.

"Battle," the shade rasped, shifting his weight from foot to foot as if filled with latent energy.

Just then, Murphy and Mortazar dropped onto the deck on either side of him. Murphy held a great battle-axe, and Mortazar had two long swords, one in each hand.[134]

"Why don' yeh pick on someone yer own size?" the dugar said, and then both pirates attacked at once.

The shade held up his hand, palm out, and the battle-axe and Mortazar's swords froze in midair. Murphy and Mortazar tugged on their weapons, trying to free them, but the blades seemed to be stuck in invisible concrete.

"This is not your fight," the shade said simply, then swept his hand through the air as if in dismissal. The two pirates flew backward, smashing into various parts of the ship before crumpling to the deck.

---

[134] You gotta hand it to them. They were pretty brave. I suppose they were too brave to watch me fight without trying to help. Poor guys…

I gritted my teeth as the shade swung his head back in my direction. "The great lord has commanded that you be tested."

"Great lord?" I said. "Rone?"

"Hssssss," the shade hissssssed. "Do not speak the Jackal's name."

"Sorry," I said. "Brings back bad memories, huh? Was that your first girlfriend's name or something? She dump you?"

"AGGGHHH!" the shade bellowed. His deep voice hit me like thunder, shaking my bones.

And then he was after me. Soon I was second-guessing my plan to make him attack in anger; I barely dodged his initial thrust. In fact, I couldn't have blocked it if I tried—there was enough force behind that seven-foot sword to skewer an oak tree. His next swing nearly sent my head tumbling into space. As it was, I lost a bit of hair. His third strike was going to kill me for sure, so I turned B1 (*Leap*) and flipped backward onto the forecastle deck.

He didn't jump after me as I had expected. I heard his deep, raspy breathing slow, then there were heavy footsteps on the ladder and his cowled[135] head appeared. It was looking straight forward for a second, then it twitched to the side with insectile precision, and his glinting eyes met mine. "The smell of your blood burns in my nose," he said. "Your death will be a sweet release."

"For me or you?" I panted. My heart was racing. I had become more nervous waiting for him to climb the ladder

---

[135] Hooded.

than if he had leaped after me. No doubt that was a part of his plan. Darn psychological warfare...

He grinned, or at least, I imagined that he did—I still couldn't really see his face. The shadows of his cloak seemed to eat the light. In a dim, lucid corner of my mind, I wondered if that was why they called them shades.

"Your tongue is faster than your sword," he growled.

"Your sword is bigger than your brain," I shot back.

I attacked low, swinging for his heels, then rolled to the side and struck once, twice, three times, my sword licking out like a fly-fishing toad tongue, but he was too fast; my blows glanced off his sword. Then he was pursuing me. His sword fell against mine like an iron mace, forcing me toward the bow of the ship. I had nowhere to go, so I hopped onto the railing. I darted my hand inside the turncoat and turned a whole row of knobs at once (C1, C2, C3, C4, C5). I turned invisible, breathed deadly stink-breath into his face, started dancing an Irish jig,[136] and my head burst into light.

When my headlight hit him, his cloak caught fire at the edges, rolling into nothingness like a withering leaf. His body was almost human in shape, but his chest was twice as broad as any man's, and instead of skin he had a coat of glinting black scales. His nose was broad and flat, with three vertical slits for nostrils, and instead of hair he had what looked like a thin layer of white slime that

---

[136] By the way, if you've been thinking about taking up dancing, I recommend starting now rather than waiting until you're standing on a thin wooden railing suspended in the midst of space, fighting a giant demon warrior. Just saying.

reminded me vaguely of egg whites.

"Ick!" I cried. "You're hideous!"

I had hoped that—you know, being a creature of darkness and all that—shining a light on him might annihilate him Wicked Witch of the West style.[137] But no such luck. It just made him really, really mad, which, as we have already established, wasn't helpful.

Unfortunately, despite his HUGE triple nostrils, the bad breath didn't faze him either. The invisibility didn't do much—I guessed that he could see so well in the dark that a little chameleon effect wasn't as beguiling to him as it was to mere mortals.

He swung his sword in a double-overhand strike, and for some stupid reason, I just stood there and blocked it as if I had the strength for that kind of thing.

Somehow, his sword did NOT pound through mine and split my body in two from head to foot like a block of firewood. Instead, when his sword touched mine, there was no power behind it at all.

For an instant, I was stunned. I wondered briefly if I had suddenly become a superhero. Then, I realized that C3 (*Sponge*) must have absorbed the power of his blow. I didn't realize it worked for physical attacks as well as magical ones.

The shade was even more surprised than I was. His moment of confusion was almost enough to let me get past him, but when I sprang forward, he kicked me reflexively. The heavy boot in my chest sent me flying backward,

---

[137] "I'M MELLLLTINGGGGGG!"

right past the railing and nearly off the ship. I just barely managed to grab the bowsprit before falling into space. I climbed onto it, grateful that my involuntary jig-dancing had now ceased.

Too bad I had already used B1, or I could have super-jumped over his head back onto the relative safety of the deck. As it was, he mounted the bowsprit after me, forcing me to edge out farther, balancing precariously.

Panicking, I turned E1 and pushed my dumb clone at him.

Rather than being thrown off balance or getting confused, the shade simply chopped Dumb Me into two neat pieces and watched them tumble into space.

As I watched my screaming torso fall away, I couldn't help thinking that I was glimpsing the immediate future. I searched my brilliant mind desperately for an escape route. I thought of E2, the knob that had stopped time. I nearly turned it right then. If I stopped time, I thought, I could just waltz up to the shade and defeat him while he stood there, unable to defend himself. Honorable, no. Practical, yes. And yet...

I remembered Hawk's warning from the day before. *When you alter time, you risk the world.* And Rellik's words from the recording in his tomb: *Time is a capricious mistress, Simon.* I didn't know what E2 really did, did I? What if it didn't always stop time? What if it sped up time? What if it took me to some distant future, or some distant past like E6 had done? What if—and this was the thought that truly stopped me in the end—it stopped time for *me* this time, instead of everyone else? I didn't like the thought of myself, frozen in time, getting dissected by a shade. I was willing to try the knob, but not until I had exhausted all other options.[138]

He raised his sword in one hand, holding the other straight out for balance, and then swung.

Out of sheer desperation, I closed my eyes, ducked, and turned E8 (*Stash*). I don't know why I did it. Probably some mixture of habit, instinct, and cowardice; rationally, I knew the Tike couldn't save me. I'd already seen how the shade swept aside those who got in the way of our duel, but I was so accustomed to fighting with her alongside me...

As soon as I turned the knob, the Tike appeared out of thin air, rocketing toward the shade with Bast's huge sword in her hands. She hit him with such force that he stumbled backward onto the forecastle deck, barely deflecting her sword. She hit him again and again, driving him back. She must have been able to see what was going on from inside the turncoat, because she was totally prepared for this moment, hammering him relentlessly, taking complete advantage of her element of surprise.

Eventually my brain reengaged, and I jumped back to the deck myself, looking up just in time to see the shade block her sword and shove her back forcefully. He held up a hand toward her then, palm out.

"STOP!" he commanded. "I am empowered to claim

---

[138] That was a lot of thoughts for me to process in like zero time during a battle sequence, wasn't it? I'm super smart like that.

the blood of Simon Fayter. None may stand in my way."

He must have thought some sort of magic was going to save him, for he completely lowered his guard.

"His blood runs through my veins!" the Tike hissed, crouching like a feral cat preparing to strike. She lifted one hand free of the big sword and drew three fingers across the blood-red bird on her neck, which incidentally now had its wings spread, claws raised threateningly.

"His mother's blood, anyway, and that seems close enough!" Then she leaped forward, and for the first time there was fear in the shade's eyes. He blocked her first attack, but the swiftness of her motion belied a thousand years of training, and her second strike cut off his hand.

He grunted in dismay as it dropped to the deck.

Above us, voices cheered.

I raised my sword and ran up beside her. We were going to win. Together, we forced him to the edge of the deck, and he jumped off onto the lower level. There, however, he stood his ground.

"I admit," he spat. "It has been some time since I have truly felt a challenge." But he smiled with relish, and when we attacked him together, he fought like some nightmarish beast, his movements unpredictable and his power devastating. If his severed hand hurt him, he didn't show it, and he seemed to fight more skillfully now with one hand than he had earlier with two. *He* did not bleed or slow or tire.

Meanwhile, the two of us did. Except bleed, that is. His sword hadn't touched us yet, and I had a mind to keep it that way. There was something sinister about the pale blade, which hinted of poison and despair.

The shade planted his feet suddenly and did not move again. No matter what we did, we couldn't slip past his guard. Eventually, he began to laugh, and it occurred to me that he was toying with us. Testing me, he had said. What would happen when the test ended?

I risked a sideways glance at the Tike and saw that her face was beaded with sweat. "He is beyond my skill," she said. "You were right, Simon. This is *your* fight, truly."

Startled by her honesty and terrified that she was going to give up, I pulled out the last trick up my sleeve in an attempt to catch him off guard. I drew the Jerkish smallsword out of my pocket and flicked it at him, squeezing the oval coin just before I let it go. It winked through the air, transforming into a gleaming blade as large as the shade's, spinning for his face.

Incredibly, he snatched it out of the air.

With his *stump* hand.

It took me a moment to realize how he had done it. By the looks of it, he had performed a series of calculations in the split second it took the sword to tumble through the air, then intentionally let it skewer his arm just above the wrist. Consequentially, he now had two swords, and if he held one of them at an odd angle, stuck through the stump of his arm, he didn't seem to mind.

He pressed us back now, moving with more speed than I would have thought possible. His swords were a blur of gleaming metal, and we were just trying to stay out of the way. He aimed a kick at my head which sent me sprawling, then attacked the Tike in earnest.

I could see now that everything which had come before this was but child's play. He struck her sword with both of his, twisted, and wrenched it out of her hands, throwing it into space. She threw both of her knives in quick succession, and he slapped one of them away, allowing the other to bury itself—apparently without causing much harm—in the back of his shoulder. Luckily, the Tike had the good sense to run away after that, but he caught her in the ankle with the tip of a sword before she could get clear of him, and she hit the deck hard. For a second, I thought she might be all right. Then she reached for her foot, and I saw the blood. Which sword had he hit her with? Which one? It was all a blur.

Before I could see how badly she was hurt, the shade bent over, picked her up, and tossed her into space.

I didn't scream. I didn't run after her. I just stood there, dumbfounded, staring after her retreating form.

Drake slammed onto the deck beside me, buried under the mass of his backpack. Evidentially, he had jumped out of the rigging.

"Don't worry, Simon," he said. "I've got her." Then he dashed away, leapt over the edge of the ship, and dove headfirst into space.[139] As he flew through the darkness,

---

[139] A true friend does not hesitate for a single heartbeat before diving headfirst into unknown darkness to rescue that which is most dear to you. It always seems to be darkness that they must dive into, of course, or something of that sort. An endless, unknowable vacuum from which a normal person might fear they'd not return. But true

he pulled a cord at his shoulder and the pack on his back exploded outward like a rocket-propelled inflatable inner tube. A second later, he was riding a miniature spacesail raft.

Numbly, I lifted my hand, staring at my ward ring. For a moment, I didn't feel anything, but then it was there: the faint, rhythmic pulsing that meant the Tike was still alive. Trusting the Tike to Drake, I turned to face the shade. "I'll kill you for that," I whispered.

"Come and do it, then," he said.

I jumped toward him, turning D5. I disappeared mid-jump and reappeared three feet to the left. I managed to actually hit him with my sword, but just barely. A glancing blow, which irritated him more than it hurt him.

Why didn't my sword cut him like my mom's had?

Then he swung at me with both blades and I ducked, only to have him kick me in the stomach. I retreated and

---

friends aren't like normal people. True friends are as rare as they are powerful, as brave as they are gentle, as selfless as they are stubborn. True friends are like the father who, after purposefully crafting a career which allowed him to spend thrice the normal amount of time participating in the dreams and magic of your childhood, still—though you are now twenty-eight years old with two boys of your own and have moved four hundred miles away—calls you every other day because he knows, deep down, as you do, that he was the first person who truly understood you. True friends are like the wife who, once glimpsed long ago in dreams, now stands beside you fully realized and fairer, purer, surer, stronger than you could have fathomed; who, after knowing you more deeply than any other person in the world—faults, flaws, conceits, regrets, weakness, doubts, and self-delusions all included—shows you every day, in loving eyes, a picture of yourself without them, and offers you with each such look, another hope.

found my back pressed against the door to the captain's quarters. Unbidden, I heard the Tike's words in my head: *He will try to force you to the edge of the ship, or inside it, some place where you have no room to fight, to maneuver.*

I knew what was coming, but before I could move, he kicked me square in the chest. It wasn't a quick, striking kick, meant to snap bones or cripple muscles; it was the deliberate, pushing type, meant to move mountains, and when it hit me, it blew the captain's door clean off its hinges and sent me, the door, and my sword sliding across the floor into a series of small rooms with low ceilings and no exit.

I was trapped.

Okay, let's take a break for a minute. I need to apologize for something, and you probably need to use the bathroom.[140] Here it is: this fight scene is *way* too long. I mean, as a general rule of thumb, I don't like my *chapters* being more than fifteen hundred words, and while I do break that rule all the time, this one is already three thousand nine hundred and twenty-five six seven eight nine words long, and most of it is a swordfight! Wow. I sincerely apologize.[141] I tried to shorten it, but at the end of the day, I just have to tell it like it happened. Also, who doesn't

---

[140] Come to think of it, so do I. Hold on… Okay, I'm back.

[141] What's that, you say? Chapter 2 was over *forty-four* hundred words long? Ahem…uh…look over there! Is that dragon eating your piñata?!

enjoy a good swordfight on a pirate ship?

Maybe what we need is a new chapter. That way you can stop reading this and go back to "real" life. That is, as long as you're okay leaving me nearly dead in an inescapable pirate cabin while an angry shade towers over me with a drawn sword. "Yeah," I hear you saying, "but he's bound to get out of it somehow. He always does. I can just go to bed and see what happens tomorrow."

You're right, of course. I'm bound to get out of it somehow.

Unless I don't…

MAN OR MOUSE

The courage of life is often a less dramatic spectacle than the courage of a final moment, but it is no less a magnificent mixture of triumph and tragedy.
—John F. Kennedy[142]

I'm bound to get out of this somehow, I told myself, scrambling to regain my sword. *I always do.*

But as the shade stepped through the empty doorway, towering over me and nearly filling the space with his long blade, I knew this time might be different.

"He believes that you are truly a Fayter," the shade rumbled. "But I told him you are not. A Fayter holds the balance of the universe in his hands. A Fayter does not scramble away from a fight like a little dog."

I scrambled away from him. If I had had[143] a tail, it

---

[142] Thirty-fifth President of the United States. JFK (as he is often called) was a brilliant politician and an inspiring public speaker. He gave several iconic speeches and is widely regarded as one of the best presidents in history. He served as president for just under three years, and was assassinated on November 22nd, 1963.

[143] Sizzling Scissor-spit! I'm sorry. I've tried very hard to never use the phrase "had had" in any of my books, simply because it's one of those shameful underwear flashes of the English language. And I hate it. And it makes authors look ridiculous. Let's all please say "I *would have* had" or even "*I'd* had" instead, and spare ourselves some

would have been between my legs.

"Come!" he boomed, swinging his massive sword. I ducked, and it destroyed a bookshelf. "Are you a man or a mouse? Stand and fight!"

I rolled to the side, and his sword whizzed through the air above my head, cutting Bast's worktable in two. "Fight me!" he bellowed.

I ducked behind one of the table halves, swinging my sword pointlessly above my head.

I'm such a loser, I thought. I was hoping that he would hit my sword with his, allowing me to roll away in relative safety and regain a standing position, but alas, he stuck his blade through the tabletop (nearly giving *me* a third nostril) and twisted my makeshift shield away.

The desecrated table rolled across the floor, and I caught a flash of silver as something tumbled out of it.

The thermocharge.

Suddenly, in the scant time it took the shade to raise his sword for the final blow, a plan formed. *Three* plans, actually. Plan A probably wouldn't work, but I would try it. Plan B probably wouldn't work either, but I had to try that, too, because Plan C was reckless, selfish, and unthinkably dangerous.

I turned B4 (*Ninja*) and activated five precious seconds of insane fighting skills.

I spun like a tornado.

---

embarrassment. I mean, if you're just talking and it happens to slip out, sure, I see how you could fall into that trap. But if you're typing a book out word. By. Stinking. Word. Then come on! How can you not see that coming?!?! Sigh.

I jabbed with godlike speed.

I flipped and rolled and dodged and twisted.

And I scooped up the thermocharge from where it had landed.

For five whole seconds, I matched the shade blow for blow, and for five whole seconds, I watched him wonder, just a little, if he had been wrong about me.

Then I turned back into a loser.[144]

But now, I was a loser with a *thermocharge*.

Since I had started fighting like an actual hero, the shade had backed off considerably, and since he didn't know that I was a loser again, this gave me the opportunity to dash past him into the little round chamber where the oscillation stone pulsed with blue light from its place in the center of the floor.

"Now," the shade said as he followed me into the tiny space, "you have no place to run."

Without hesitation, I turned E3 (*Daze*) and—

---

[144] Not really. I was still pretty awesome.

24

THE BETTER OF TWO BADS

*There are very few problems that cannot be solved
through a suitable application of high explosives.*

—Scott Adams[145]

—Out of nowhere, a new chapter started.

The sudden, debilitating headache struck me just as hard as it hit the shade, but I was ready for it. That meant that while he was still reeling, I had regained my wits. He stumbled a half step, and I thrust my sword into his belly.

But it just glanced off.

Why could I not harm him like the Tike had? Then I remembered her words: *If you fight him with fear in your heart, your blade will not stand against him. You must rid yourself of fear, or destroy him with overwhelming force.*

Well, I wasn't about to rid myself of fear.[146] I guess

---

[145] Scott Adams is the creator of the Dilbert comic strip and a bunch of other impressive things.

[146] By the way, if you are thinking to yourself: "Oh my gosh, Simon! Pull out your sorrowstone and rid yourself of fear so that you can fight this dude!" Well, that's a really good idea. It might have worked, too. But I didn't think of it at the time. We've talked about this before, remember? Back in book one? How people sometimes don't think very clearly in high-stress situations? Anyway, congratulations, you were smarter than me. Just this once.

it would have to be overwhelming force, then. And yet it seemed irresponsible to resort to that before I had exhausted all options.

I swung my sword at his head, and the blade rang with a metallic clang as it bounced away. He shook his head, still trying to regain his wits, and I shoved my sword tip into his central nostril.

This caused him to stagger backward for a second, but beyond that, he seemed fine. So much for Plan A.

Time for Plan B: I turned E10. Rellik had warned me not to use it unless I wanted to kill, but I'd come to that moment. Of course, nothing happened. I hadn't really expected it to be that easy. This knob had a pocket, after all. No doubt I had to put something in it for it to work properly.

It was just as I had feared: *I* was full of fear, and so he was basically indestructible. There was a reason no one had ever beaten a shade. Escaped, yes. Beaten, no. But where could I escape to out here in the middle of space? There were no two ways about it: This was a simple case of kill or be killed. If I didn't kill him, he would certainly kill me, and if the Fayter died, what did that mean for the world? How many lives were at risk if I was destroyed before I fulfilled my destiny? If I took drastic measures to destroy the shade, if I used "overwhelming force" like the Tike had suggested, I could probably ensure my own survival, but what about the others? How many people on this ship would be harmed?

It was down to me to pick the better of two bad choices,

and in the 1.5 seconds that I had to think it over, I made a decision. Probably the wrong decision, but I had to do something. That's just how life goes sometimes.[147]

Plan C, then: I tugged my sword out of his nose, and he lunged for me, swinging his weapon a little more sluggishly than normal. His mouth sagged open as he righted himself. I twisted the thermocharge, then shoved it down his throat.

He groaned and struck out, but I was already out of reach. I was desperate now, and committed to seeing my plan through, so I turned E2, and time stopped.

Then I turned A3 (*Curse*)[148] and drove the point of my sword into the face of the oscillator stone.

It broke. I glanced up at the shade and saw his neck bulging where I had lodged the thermocharge. How long would it take to go off? Three seconds? Five? Ten? How long would I have to get everyone off the ship? Plan C wasn't exactly foolproof, but there was no going back now.

I burst out of the captain's quarters just as time started flowing again. "ABANDON SHIP!" I screamed. "It's gonna blow! Fire! Death! ABANDON SHIP!"

---

[147] Now, don't get too impressed with my wisdom yet. I face this exact same dilemma (sort of) at the end of this book, and instead of acting responsibly, I totally lose my head and try to run away from my problems. Yeah. I'm human, too.

[148] If you have forgotten, this grants me the power to break the next thing I touch.

That got them moving. Pirates leapt into lifeboats, others swung away on ropes. As for myself, Tessa's hand was on me the second I made it into the open. She steered me toward the railing, and together we jumped into space. I glanced around, searching for Drake, for the Tike, but they were nowhere to be seen.

Then there was a flash of light and a noise so big, so *loud*, I heard it only as silence.

25

AMONG THE STARS

Sic itur ad astra.

—Virgil[149]

The explosion hurled us into space. The heat of it was warm on my back, as if the sun were rising behind me. Then it was hot. Then it was really, *really* hot. The light was beyond compare, as if we had been transported to the center of a star.

I finally pried my eyes open and saw Tessa's face silhouetted against the light. Her lips moved, but I didn't hear the words she spoke—the explosion had rendered me temporarily deaf. We were floating in space now, hand in hand. She gestured earnestly at something behind me, and I turned just in time to get bumped in the face by a black inflatable space raft. Strong hands grabbed my wrists, hauling me aboard.

---

[149] An ancient Roman poet. This quote from *Aeneid* translates as "Thus we go to the stars" or "Thus one journeys to the stars" and speaks to the fact that great deeds (such as living an honorable life) are difficult to do, and that when the going gets tough, the toughness might well be celebrated as evidence that you are going somewhere worthwhile. Because (to quote Virgil again), "There is no easy way from the Earth to the stars."

It was Captain Bast. The Tike was there, too, and Hawk. Drake sat with one hand on the tiller.

"Are you guys all right?" I asked.

"Hawk bumped his head," Drake said, "but it's not too bad."

"Tike!" I said. "Which sword did he cut you with? Which sword?" I lunged for her ankle awkwardly, fearing the worst, but she pushed me away.

"Montroth's sword," she said. "If it had been otherwise, I would be curled up in a ball by now, if not dead."

"Thank goodness," I said, relaxing against the side of the raft.

It was then, as I first took a look around us, that I realized what I had done.

The ship was gone.

Where it had been, there was nothing, just a thin black slit a hundred feet high, as though the explosion had rent a tear in space itself. Around us, there floated a surprisingly small amount of debris. A board here, a windowpane there, half a hank of rope...

"Where is everyone else?" I said, fearing the worst.

"Captain Bast wisely ordered the crew to abandon ship the second the fight moved into his quarters," Hawk said.

"Aye," the captain growled. "I said to meself, Bast, 'e knows where ye hid that thermocharge, and if 'e's 'alf as smart as 'e looks, 'e'll go for it. That couldn' mean anythin' good for the ship, so I figured better safe than sorry."

"So everyone got off?" I said, filling with relief.

"The blast blew the lifeboats far apart," Hawk said,

"but as far as we know, the others are still safe. Not that we have a way to rejoin them."

"They're all safe," I said, reassuring myself.

Bast looked at his boots.

"Who?" I asked.

"Montroth," Hawk said. "Nobody remembers seeing him actually leave the ship."

"But," Tessa added quickly, "things happened so fast. I'm sure he made it."

"And the crew?" I asked, not meeting Tessa's eye.

"Hobnob and Noblob." Bast grunted. "When I gave the order to abandon ship, they ran down to the galley for snacks. I told them not to, but that's goblins fer yeh."

"No," I said, feeling sick to my stomach.

"Don' fret yerself overmuch," he said, thumping me on the back. "A pirate wakes e'ry marnin' ready to die, an' we do no' cling to life as tightly as other folk. When death comes for 'im, tis not so bad. After all, ye killed a shade, and they were a part o' that. 'Ere." He swept the burgundy hat from his head and spat into it. Then he passed it to me.

Not knowing what else to do, I spat in it, too, and passed it on. When we were all done spitting, Bast rose to his feet, placed the hat over his heart, and addressed the wreckage. "Godspeed, me brothers. May yer souls find rest among the stars."

"There," he said, as he sat back down. "That do be the proper pirate sendoff. Now, shall we be off?"

"I suppose," I said, looking around for other lifeboats. I couldn't see them. "Where are the other boats?"

"The crew?" Bast said, surprised. "Why, they be off yonder." He pointed at a distant cluster of stars, and I strained to see but couldn't make anything out. Bast took the spyglass from his inside jacket pocket and extended it, then handed it to me and pointed. "The blast wave carried 'em 'alf a day's journey that-a-way. A 'alf a day's journey in the *Calliope*, that is. Don' know 'ow long it would take us in this 'ere raft."

"What do we do, then?" I said.

"Why," he said, as if it were the most obvious thing in the world, "I assumed ye would be wantin' ter go through the fissure."

"The what?"

"The fissure," he said, jabbing a thumb at the tall black slit in space that I had noticed earlier. "I tol' ye earlier... When somethin' like an oscillation stone explodes in space, it be causin' a tear in space-time. No' a black hole, by any means, jus' a little tear."

"What's inside?" Drake asked.

"Someplace else," Bast said.

"Where?" I asked.

Bast shrugged. "Could be anywhere." He scratched his chin. "But with your luck..." He gave me a meaningful look.

I pushed down a wave of excitement. With my luck, it could be just the place we were looking for. Or it could be a direct portal to the stomach of a killer whale. "Well," I said, "wherever it takes us, it has to be better than wandering around in the middle of nowhere in a raft."

"Aye," Captain Bast said.

And Hawk said, "My sentiments exactly."

Drake nodded and swung the tiller, pointing us at the fissure.

When we got right up to it, it was even larger than I had anticipated. It was just wide enough for our little raft to pass through but taller than a football field is long. I could see a different galaxy through the opening. A large blackish-purple star was circumscribed by what looked like a blue band of sand, like the rings around Saturn. In the band, orbiting the star, was a small, dome-shaped planet.

"Bless me toe-beards," Bast mumbled. "Dark Haven. We found it!"

"This seems too easy," I said as the tip of our raft passed through the opening of the fissure.

"Speak fer yerself," Bast said with one last, longing look at the wreckage of his ship.

"I fear," Hawk said, eyeing the dark star before us, "that there will be nothing easy about this next part."

THE BEASTS THAT ROAM

Beware the Jabberwock, my son!

—Lewis Carroll[150]

Hawk was right. There wasn't anything easy about getting to the island of Yap. I'd like to give you a play-by-play description of the journey, but there just

---

[150] Lewis Carroll was the pen name of Charles Lutwidge Dodgson (good call on using a pen name). He was the genius that wrote *Alice's Adventures in Wonderland* and *Through the Looking Glass*, from which this poem, "Jabberwocky," comes. It's a classic tale about fighting a monster, which is why it serves as the epigraph of this chapter. What's that? You want to hear the whole thing? Very well, here it comes. If you read the book, Humpy Dumpy explains most of the nonsense words in the poem, but I don't have time to do so now. Good luck:

> `Twas brillig, and the slithy toves/Did gyre and gimble in the wabe:/All mimsy were the borogoves,/And the mome raths outgrabe./"Beware the Jabberwock, my son!/The jaws that bite, the claws that catch!/Beware the Jubjub bird, and shun/The frumious Bandersnatch!"/He took his vorpal sword in hand:/Long time the manxome foe he sought --/So rested he by the Tumtum tree,/And stood awhile in thought./And, as in uffish thought he stood,/The Jabberwock, with eyes of flame,/Came whiffling through the tulgey wood,/And burbled as it came!/One, two! One, two!/And through and through/The vorpal blade went snicker-snack!/He left it dead, and with its head/He went galumphing back./"And, has thou slain the Jabberwock?/Come to my arms, my beamish boy!/O frabjous day! Callooh! Callay!"/He chortled in his joy./`Twas brillig, and the slithy toves/Did gyre and gimble in the wabe;/All mimsy were the borogoves,/And the mome raths outgrabe.

isn't time. Suffice it to say, there was a space storm, a shark attack—during which Drake was nearly eaten (yes, space sharks exist)—a plague of raft-eating space beetles, another shark attack—during which Drake was *actually* eaten (I had to jump overboard and cut the shark open to save him. Thankfully, it was big enough to have swallowed him whole, and he was mostly all right.)—another space storm, and finally, a very treacherous crash landing, in which we each grabbed a corner of the beetle-eaten, shark-bitten, storm-thrashed thing that had once been our raft and parachuted at an unsafe velocity into the water near a sandy beach. I'd hate to think of what would have happened to us on an *unlucky* day.

"Are we dead?" I asked, spitting out a mouthful of sand.

"I'm pretty sure I am," Drake said, groaning.

"Where are you?" I asked, getting to my feet. I looked around, but there was no one in sight. The beach was made of a beautiful golden sand, soft underfoot, and the island behind us was lightly forested. From the surface of Yap, Dark Haven gave off a light much like the sun back home.

"Drake," I repeated more loudly. "I don't see you."

"Down here."

I looked down to see Drake's head resting in the sand. "Are you all right? I mean, your body's under there somewhere, right?"

"Yeah," he said. "I think so."

"Good," I said, relaxing. I glanced around for the others again, then, not seeing them, I took a more careful stock of myself, checking for injuries. "Hey," I said. "Where are my pants?"

"They're wrapped around my legs, remember?" Drake said. "You used them to bandage the shark bites."

"Oh, yeah…I really wish you hadn't dropped the first-aid kit during that shark attack. It's a bit chilly without my pants."[151] [152] [153]

"I feel so bad for you," Drake said sarcastically, straining to shake sand out of one ear.

"Right," I said. "Well, I'm going to find the others, then we'll come dig you out."

"No rush," he grumbled.

It took me a while to find them all. We had been scattered across quite a distance when the ocean washed us onto the beach. That said, everyone else had fared better than Drake, except for Captain Bast, who was stuck up a tree with his head wedged uncomfortably between a pair of branches. Eventually we got him down and returned to find Drake, who by now had started to panic.

"You know, I didn't mean 'no rush' literally, right? I thought the tide was going to get me before you got back!"

Tessa and I dug him free while Hawk examined Captain Bast's head and the Tike's ankle, which, it turns out, had been merely grazed by Montroth's sword.

---

[151] Thank goodness I was wearing manly boxers. Otherwise it might have been a bit awkward walking around in my underwear for several chapters.

[152] ~~Whatever, Simon. You were totally wearing tighty-whities that day, lol!!!~~ –Tessa

[153] Tessa, STOP lying to the readers! –Simon

"'Tis no' the tide tha' do be worryin' me," Bast said, eyes shifting from side to side, checking the shoreline. "There do be foul things on this here island, if the legends hold. Mad beasts tha' roam wild. Things tha' can eat ten men fer dinner an' another for dessert."

"Good," Drake said, flopping onto the sand in exhaustion. "I need more danger in my life."

We all gathered around Hawk, who was bathing the Tike's leg in a trough of ocean water that he had dug in the sand. When he had finished ministering to her needs, he checked the bandages on Drake's shark bites and pronounced them fine.

"Shame we don't have some food, though," he said. "The two of you could do with a bit of extra energy."

"I had a whole supply of food and first-aid equipment in the cargo pocket of the pack raft," Drake said bitterly. "But we lost that in the last space storm."

"Don' worry, lad," Bast said, patting him on the back. "Ye did good, all told."

"There's nothing left now but to search the island," Hawk said. "We need food and shelter, and we may as well look for Colm while we're at it." He winked at me.

"We should all go together," I said before anyone could suggest that we split up.[154]

"We could split up," Tessa suggested, "cover more ground that way."

---

[154] When people are about to get attacked by monsters, it always happens after they (very stupidly) decide to split up. I was determined not to make that mistake.

"No," I said firmly. "We're sticking together."

"We should keep the beach in sigh' at all times," Bast said. "So we don' get lost."

"Very well," Hawk said. "Let's be off. It is not midday yet, but who knows how far we'll have to go?"

The Tike limped a bit, as did Drake, with my improvised pants bandage tied around his legs, and it was slow going as our motley crew moved down the bright sandy beach in search of Colm the Insane.

Two hours later, after several miles of hard walking, I was beginning to think that my luck had run out for the day, or that there was simply nothing more to find. But then Bast brought us to a halt.

"Did ye 'ear tha'?" he said softly. "Methinks I heard talkin' up yonder." He pointed to an area just beyond a little rise in the beach.

"I didn't hear anything," I said.

"Shh."

"I heard it, too," the Tike whispered. "Hawk and I will go back into the woods and come out behind where the noise is. The rest of you wait here for two minutes, then approach from the beach."

We waited, and I kept an eye on my watch. It seemed like the longest two minutes of my life.

Finally we continued up the beach and there we found, not a crazy ancient wizard or a terrifying island beast, but two pirate goblins and a lifeboat. They had tipped the boat upside down and were using it as a table for a grand buffet. There was more food than the two of them could have eaten in a week. Once Hawk and the Tike saw them, they came back out of the woods, abandoning their plan to flank them in an attack.

"Hobnob!" Captain Bast cried. "Noblob! Yer alive!"

There followed a lengthy explanation, mostly in Goblin (of which I speak very little even now), of how Hobnob and Noblob, while searching through the refrigerator and securing their desired provisions, were shielded from the blast *by* the refrigerator, thrown toward the fissure during the explosion, and just *happened* to find a spare lifeboat floating past them.

And I thought *I* was lucky.

"Inconceivable!"[155] Bast said when they had finished their tale. "Now, 'ere's what I want ye to do…"

He told them to stash the boat in a safe place out of sight of the beach and sort the remaining provisions for a long journey, guarding them against our return.

"We do be lookin' for Colm the Insane, but if we are no' back by this time tomorrow, we likely died tryin', or we found 'im and 'e killed us," he said, "in which case, yer to save yerselves and sail out o' 'ere straight away. Find yer way to the nearest major tradin' route an' wait fer a freighter to come by. Ye shouldn' 'ave to wait long. If tha' don' work, ye can try to limp it all the way back in the lifeboat, though ye'll likely starve to death."

---

[155] This word doesn't mean what you think it means.

Halfway through Bast's speech, I stuck what looked like a turkey drumstick in my mouth and began eating ravenously. Soon the others were following suit. It had, by the way, been a while since we had eaten. When we finished, the goblins gave a solemn salute, and we continued on.

Three hours later, we had found no other signs of life on the island, and our spirits were beginning to droop. I was about to suggest that we give up searching for Colm and head back when we came to a small creek that emptied into the ocean. It's hard to describe what happened next, except to say that I had the sudden, overpowering urge to splash in it.

"Simon," Tessa said, "what are you doing?"

"Uh...I don't know," I said as I stood in water up to my knees. "I just felt like splashing."

"Hmm," Hawk mused. "Perhaps this is a manifestation of your luck. It could be indicating that this stream is important."

"Perhaps we should follow the stream into the island and see where it goes?" the Tike said.

"About time, too," Bast said. "'Tis gettin' hot out 'ere on the sand."

"Hot?" Drake said. "Just be grateful you aren't covered in fur!"

As we hiked next to the stream, everyone seemed to cheer up a bit. It was cooler under the shade of the trees, and after a while Bast and the Tike started a competition as we walked, to see who could throw river rocks with the most accuracy. In the end, the Tike won, but surprisingly, only by a small margin.

The farther inland we went, the denser the underbrush became, until after a while we had to walk quite close to the stream in order to avoid having to hack our way through the bushes and vines.

After traveling another hour like this, Drake, who had been bringing up the rear, gave a shout. "You guys, look at this!" Then he stepped through a canopy of vines and disappeared from view.

"Wait, Drakus!" Hawk snapped, hurrying through the vines in pursuit. "Do not just go off on your—Oh, hazelnuts…"

The rest of us followed.

The other side of the vines was not, as we had assumed, a stretch of dense forest like the one we had been walking through, but a wide green valley with a picturesque pond in the center of it. The grass was dotted here and there with patches of purple wildflowers and two or three dozen bunny rabbits. The rabbits were incredibly large—most over three feet tall—and were grazing on the flowers and sunning themselves in the pond. Near to where we stood was a tall barnlike structure made of dark wood, and at the far end of the valley there stood an expansive, derelict castle of black stone.

"Hey," Drake said. "A castle. What do you want to bet Colm's in there?"

"Ooh," Tessa said. "Bunnies! Aren't they cute?"

"Shh!" Hawk hissed. He continued in a frantic

whisper, "Everyone step back slowly. If we can just make it back through the vines without—"

Tessa, who was either too far away to hear Hawk's whispers or just being a half-baked zonderkite[156] right then (I'll let you decide which), waved one hand aloft and called loudly, "Here, bunny bunnies!"

Everyone froze.

Except Tessa, who continued to dance and wave.[157]

"Do we run?" the Tike said.

"No," Hawk said. "They'll only chase us, and we won't have room to maneuver in the trees."

"Uh, guys," I said. "What's going on?" As far as I could tell, the only thing that had happened was that one of the bunnies had looked up from its flower patch and twitched an ear in our direction.

"Yoohoo! Bunnies!" Tessa called.

"Stop her!" Hawk commanded, and I tackled Tessa to the ground. After all, I'd been feeling like attacking her for a while now.

"Ow! Simon!"

"Shh! You're doing something stupid!"

"What?"

"I don't know!"

"Yap rabbits," Bast was mumbling. "I was hopin' they was jest a myth."

"They appear to be quite real," Hawk said. "On your

---

[156] A Victorian word meaning *idiot*.

[157] We didn't know this back then, but Tessa has an unnatural fondness for bunny rabbits. It's her fatal flaw...

feet, you two. We may be able to retreat if we move very slowly. They haven't attacked us yet."

"What are you talking about?" Tessa said, shoving me off and getting to her feet. "They're just bunnies."

"The wild Yap rabbit," Hawk said quietly, edging back toward the wall of vines through which we had passed earlier, "is said to be one of the most vicious, bloodthirsty creatures in existence."

"They don't look bloodthirsty," Tessa said, folding her arms stubbornly.

Actually, I had to agree with her. Six or seven bunnies were approaching us now, and if anything, they looked rather timid. Every now and then they would stop and sit back on their haunches, noses twitching curiously, as if unsure whether they should approach us or run away.

"Things are not always as they appear to be," Hawk said, motioning us to follow him through the vines.

"They've not transformed yet," Bast murmured, backing up slowly. "But mark me words, if they perceive danger, they'll be on us like flies on a yakpie. Don' talk no more. Any sudden moves or sounds, and it may be th' end of us."

Drake's eyes had gone suddenly wide in fear. He had one foot through the vines, but was turning to look back at the Yap rabbits, terror plain on his face.

"Drake," I whispered. "Don't. *Please* don't."

But it was too late. Drake was already afraid, and the instant you tell someone not to do something, the only thing they can think about is doing that thing.

With one last look of horror, Drake threw back his head and sneezed.

THE GATEKEEPER

According to the calculations of some naturalists, one of these animals, only six feet long, would have tentacles twenty-seven feet long. That would suffice to make a formidable monster.

—Jules Verne[158]

A t first I thought nothing was going to happen.

Then the Yap rabbits nearest us all twitched their heads to one side at exactly the same time. Their eyes turned red, their teeth grew into six-inch-long fangs, and the hair on their backs stood up from the tops of their heads to the tips of their fluffy tails. If that wasn't bad enough, the other bunnies followed suit, until the meadow was full of giant killer rabbits, eyeing us as if we were lunch.

"To the castle! Split up![159] Confuse them!" Hawk cried. "RUN!"

---

[158] A French novelist born in 1828. He is considered by some to be the father of the science fiction. This quote is from one of his more famous works, *Twenty Thousand Leagues Under the Sea*, and refers to a giant squid. The monsters in *my* story are, of course, giant *bunnies*, so they don't have twenty-seven-foot tentacles. However, I think you'll see that they are still formidable monsters.

[159] Here we go again with the splitting up. I guess it's not *always* a bad idea, especially if the danger has already struck.

Before he had taken two steps, Hawk made a gesture with his right hand, like he was throwing a ball, and touched the ward ring on his middle finger. A silver hawk burst out of the air before him with such speed that when it struck the nearest Yap rabbit in the head with its razor-sharp beak, the beast fell to the ground and never moved again.

Several of us dashed off, but when I spun around to face the castle, I stopped short. One of the Yap rabbits had already singled me out; it stood before me, blocking my way.

So there I was, in my underwear, face-to-face with a man-sized killer bunny.[160] I drew Kylanthus and spun to the side, changing direction as my blade caught fire. My plan was to keep moving and hope that my incredible speed and intimidating flaming sword would deter the Yap rabbit from attacking me. But in one bound, it leaped over my head and stood before me once more.

My backup plan had been for the Tike to swoop in and save the day, but at that moment she was several yards away, fighting three Yap rabbits at once. Tessa was way ahead of me, thumping rabbits right and left with her cudgel, and Drake was following on her heels, pelting them with bullets from his sling. Evidently they thought I was still with them.

I was on my own.

The Yap rabbit roared like a lion, then it crouched low and leapt for my face, fangs bared.

---

[160] Okay, so it wasn't man-sized, but when it stood up on its haunches it was nearly *me*-sized, and that was big enough.

I reacted on instinct, dropping to the ground and swinging for its legs. To my delight, I not only avoided being eaten, I also managed to lop off my first lucky rabbit's foot. I was almost done congratulating myself when my bunny—which had been writhing on the ground—suddenly popped back up and doubled in size. *Now* it was as tall as a man.

"WHATE'ER YE DO," Bast called from somewhere across the meadow, "DON' WOUND 'EM. IT ONLY MAKES 'EM STRONGER. IT BE KILL OR NOTHIN'!"

"THAT WOULD HAVE BEEN NICE TO KNOW A COUPLE SECONDS AGO," I shouted back, staring down my now larger (and madder) Yap rabbit. Just then, three "normal-sized" bunnies bounded up to flank the larger one, and I turned B4 (*Ninja*).

Nothing happened.

Duh. My fight with the shade had been earlier that same day, so none of the knobs that I had used then had reset yet.

The bunnies pounced, and I spun and jumped and sliced and rolled. Four seconds later I had another rabbit's foot, two ears, and a fluffy tail to my name, and I was facing four super-sized bunnies. One of which was now taller than a school bus. As if that weren't enough, four more bunnies came up from behind me.

I was surrounded.

I turned D6 (*Lightning*) and bathed the bunnies in a shower of blue bolts. One of them dropped backward, dead, its fluffy tail smoking. I managed to stab a second bunny through the heart while it was frozen in place, being electrocuted.[161]

The other six doubled in size again. They were big enough now that as they surrounded me, their bodies touched each other, forming a closed circle.

I turned A2 (*Whisper*), which was my last hope because it lets me talk to animals.

"I want the head," the biggest bunny was saying.

"I want a drumstick," someone else called.

"The middle bits are mine!"

"Hi there, fellas," I said. "Any chance we can call this party off? Let's just talk for a minute. I know a song about a little bunny named Foo Foo that I think you really need to hear…"

The largest Yap rabbit swatted at me, and I jumped over his paw, only to be plucked out of the air by a second pair of paws.

"He's mine!" my captor said.

"No!" a third bunny cried, smacking me free of the second's grasp. "I just want his feet. You can have the rest of him when I'm done."

Speaking of my feet, I managed to get them under me just in time to dodge two more bunny swipes. I racked my brain for a way out. I clearly wasn't going to be rescued. I reviewed the knobs that I had left: I didn't want to forecast the weather, and I certainly didn't want to take a nap. I had

---

[161] By the way, if you ever find yourself in a situation where you want to stick a two-and-a-half-foot-long *metal* sword into something that is currently being struck by lightning, don't. It really hurts.

no use for poetry or a beard, and I didn't want anything multiplying; a second sword wouldn't do me much good since I wasn't skilled enough to use two at once, and there were more than enough Yap rabbits to be going around.

The only other knob I had previously tested was the one that had seemed to transport Ioden from one end of the hall to the other. Thinking that there might be some merit in moving the bunnies around and perhaps confusing them, I turned A6.

Ioden appeared beside me. He had apparently just gotten out of the tub, for he was wearing nothing but a lavender bathrobe, and he was midway through brushing his teeth.

The Yap rabbits paused, glancing back and forth between me and Ioden as if unsure which of us to attack. Then Ioden spat out a gob of toothpaste and screamed, pointing at the humongous rabbits with his toothbrush.

The rabbits pounced on him, and I jumped sideways and rolled away from the scuffle. I darted off, only to stop and look around at the sound of a massive explosion behind me. Ioden was running flat out in the opposite direction, bathrobe streaming behind him in the wind, with all six rabbits in hot pursuit. He had red fireballs in each hand and was lobbing them over his shoulders as he ran. Of course, this just made the bunnies bigger.

Wishing him the best, I sprinted toward the castle, pleased to find my path now clear. As I passed beneath an archway and entered the outer courtyard, I found my friends in front of the closed castle gate, fighting a dozen rabbits of varying sizes. Bast, Hawk, and the Tike fought back to back in a twirling triangle of blades, and for the moment, their whirling death trap seemed to be keeping the bunnies at bay. I leaped past the line of rabbits and rolled beneath the swirl of swords to join Drake and Tessa at the gate.

"Simon!" Hawk said brightly. "Rude to be late to a party. What kept you?"

"Why are we just standing here?" I demanded, pounding the gate with my fist.

"It won't open, genius," Tessa said.

Drake sneezed, then, his sling forgotten, he took the glob of kulrakalakia out of his pants pocket and licked it several times, keeping his eyes on the Yap rabbits all the while.

Nothing happened.

"Have you tried knocking?" I asked.

"Of course we've tried knocking," Tessa said.

"No, I mean with that." I bent over to pick up a giant rust-covered hammer from where it leaned against the wall, but I couldn't budge it.

"Move over, sissy britches," Tessa said, shoving me aside. She picked up the massive hammer and smashed it against the gate, producing a deep thud.

"Yes?" a voice said from somewhere above us. The voice sounded cracked and awkward and put me in mind of a toothless old man.

"Let us in!" Drake cried. "In Scayla's name, *please* let us in! They're going to eat us!"

"Certainly."

A second later, a strange new sound reached me. It was like a rain stick, or a sprinkler—or like someone shaking a can of dry rice. I turned, looking for the source of it, and saw that the Yap rabbits had stopped their attack. They were swaying back and forth to the rhythm of the sound. A second later, they began to shrink down to their usual size. The sound stopped, and the rabbits blinked at us, twitching their noses curiously before wandering off.

I noticed Hawk looking at something above me and stepped away from the gate just in time to see an elderly man jump down from the ramparts above. He fell fifteen feet and landed spryly on the stones below, twirling a long staff with what looked like a big wooden baby rattle lashed to one end with dried flowers and vines. As he spun it, the soothing sound came again, and a Yap rabbit that had perked up at the sight of him relaxed and walked away.

"Hello," he said, squinting at the sun. "Nice day. What do you want?"

He was a short, wiry man, barely taller than me, and extremely old. He wore a simple brown tunic that reached past his knees like a dress, and there was curly white chest hair spilling out of the neck. His head was bald, but his beard was huge and strangely shaped. It reminded me of a white dandelion, strands sticking straight out in all directions, as though he lived in a constant state of static charge.

I cleared my throat. "We're looking for Colm the Ins— uh…" I stopped myself.

"Ahh," the old man said wisely, wrinkled face twisting

into a grin. "Yes. Rude to call someone insane right to their face, isn't it? First impressions. But you're in luck. I am not Colm. Just his doorman."

"Doorman?" Bast said incredulously. "'E 'as a doorman? Out 'ere?"

"Obviously," the old man said sternly. He waved a hand above his head. "Lord Colm is far too busy and important to sit by, twiddling his thumbs and waiting for the odd guest to drop in."

"Of course," Hawk said, taking control of the conversation. "Sir, we have important matters to discuss with him. Might we go inside?"

"Hmm," the man said, scratching his beard thoughtfully. "You really shouldn't have roused the Yap rabbits. Colm doesn't like rabbit rousers."

"*Roused*?" I began, but Hawk shot me a withering look and I bit my tongue. "I mean, yes. Sorry about that."

"Killed nine of them," he said, folding his arms. "Colm will not be pleased."

"We didn't mean to…er…*rouse* them," Tessa offered. "Really, it was an accident."

"Accident, yes…" he mused, then he poked Drake with his staff. "This one sneezed." He sighed. "But, I suppose you can't be blamed. You're allergic to Yap rabbits, I take it? Terribly inconvenient…"

Drake looked confused, then nodded several times. "Yeah. Allergic. Sorry."

"Well, then," the old man said, puffing himself up grandly, "who calls upon Lord Colm this day?"

"Uh…Simon Fayter," I said. "And company," I added lamely.

"Excellent! He's been expecting you. I shall indeed admit you to the castle, assuming you brought the required offering?"

"Uhh," I said. "Yeah. I mean—of course we did. Could you just remind me which offering he wanted?"

The old man looked at me suspiciously. "Colm values knowledge, young man. Knowledge! No doubt you wish to ask knowledge of him—everyone does. So as a peace offering, to win an audience with him, one must bring a piece of knowledge as yet unknown to him. A fact of which he is not aware of. What knowledge do you bring?"

"Uh," I said. Tessa elbowed me in the ribs. "Ouch! What type of knowledge?"

"Anything he does not know. Yet I warn you, he knows much. If you answer wrong…"

"We don't get to see him?" I guessed.

The man laughed. "Of course not. That would be silly. If you answer with a fact he already knows, you don't get to leave here alive."

I swallowed hard. I turned to face the others. "Any ideas?" I said.

Hawk held up his hands, and the Tike stared at the ground.

"Come on," I urged them.

Bast folded his arms. "It's not us who Rellik sent here, lad. It's you. I don' doubt we'd come up with the wrong answer."

I grunted and turned back to the old man.

"You got this, Simon," Drake said, patting me on the back.

"Don't screw up," Tessa hissed.

I cleared my throat. "I offer Colm," I said grandly, "not a fact, but a mystery. How many licks does it take to reach the center of a Tootsie Pop? No one knows. Several studies have been done at top universities from Harvard to Cambridge. Licking machines have been constructed. Focus groups have been assembled. But the answers range widely. One study says three hundred and sixty-four. Another says two thousand two hundred and fifty-five. According to my own research, and depending on the force of the lick, the temperature of the tongue, the acidity and solubility of the licker's saliva, it takes an average of two hundred and seventy. And yet, the answer remains elusive. This is the knowledge I offer."

The old man blinked several times, then shrugged. "Sounds good to me." He struck the heel of his staff three times upon the ground, and the gate swung open.

28
COLM THE INSANE

There are times when the mind is dealt such a blow it hides itself in insanity. While this may not seem beneficial, it is. There are times when reality is nothing but pain, and to escape that pain the mind must leave reality behind.

—Patrick Rothfuss[162]

The old man motioned for us to enter, and we passed through the gate onto a cracked stone landing which led to a long, steep set of stairs. From the outside, the castle wall had looked fairly well kept, but on the inside, everything was falling apart. The place was obviously a few thousand years old, and the roof and interior walls had crumbled away in large sections, leaving gaping holes that cast everything with strange shadows.

At a gesture from the old man, we headed up the stairs, leaving him behind. Strangely, we found him waiting for us at the top.

"Hey," I said, "how'd you get up here so fast?"

"And you changed your clothes!" Tessa said.

Indeed, the old man now wore a richly embroidered

---

[162] An author. He has a big beard, and writes *big* books. He writes them very slowly, but who am I to complain? They're some of my favorite fiction books in the world.

velvet coat and silk pants. He held a shining brass bugle in his hand—the only thing I had seen so far that was not in a state of dereliction.[163]

"Excuse me," he said in a tone of importance. "But to whom are you referring?"

"I mean," I said. "We just saw you down there, and now you're up here, and you've changed clothes."

"I beg your pardon, young sir," the man said, sounding affronted. "The man you would have met below is but the gatekeeper. *I* am the herald. Now, with whom do I have the pleasure of speaking? What name shall I announce to the hall?"

I sighed. "Simon Fayter."

"And company," Tessa added.

"Ah!" A look of sudden recognition lit his face. "Yes. I *do* seem to remember meeting you once before…Most excellent! Lord Colm has been expecting you. If you would follow me…"

He turned grandly, threw open a set of double doors, and raised the bugle to his lips, pipping a little melody. "SIMON FAYTER…and company," he announced, then stepped back and ushered us inside.

We stepped into a small antechamber that sat beside what looked to be a grand dining hall, and the doors closed behind us. As soon as they did, we found another man standing before us. That is to say, the same man, but now dressed like a soldier.

"Agh," Bast huffed. "No' another one."

---

[163] That means falling apart, usually due to extreme age or disuse.

The man shot him a dark look. He had a longsword at his waist and a pair of daggers strapped to his thighs. He held himself with an air of command. "I cannot let you go before Lord Colm armed as you are," he said. "Leave your weapons on the rack." He indicated a series of shelves and pegs beside him.

Bast widened his stance, resting a hand on the hilt of his saber. "Is tha' so?" he said.

"That is so," the man replied.

"We could just force our way in," Bast said stubbornly. "There be six o' us, an' jus' one o' you."

The man raised an eyebrow. "You could try. In the off chance you get past me, Colm himself will be waiting for you, and he would not be pleased."

Bast made to continue his argument, but I held up a hand. "We have to talk to Colm. If he says we go unarmed, we go unarmed."

Bast grumbled but handed over his sword. The Tike and I followed suit.

"You, too, wizard," the man said, nodding at Hawk.

"There is no lock here that could hold my blade," Hawk said, "should I have need of it."

"There's this," the old man said, kicking open a rusty iron trunk.

Hawk bent over it curiously. "Hmm," he mumbled to himself. "A Saldari warding vault...most impressive." Then he flicked his wrist, summoning his sword out of thin air, and placed it in the trunk. The man closed the lid with a loud snap.

"There," he said. "You may go in now. He is waiting for you."

The great hall was a long oval room surrounded on all sides by broken stone pillars. The roof was completely gone, and the wooden tabletop that had once capped the granite blocks in the center of the room had long since disintegrated.

Loose rocks, rusted nails, bird droppings, and other debris coated the floor between a series of carved stone seats, which somehow had remained mostly intact. At the far end of what had once been the table sat the man whom we had met three times already. He now wore a long cotton shirt, faded with age so that its original color was undetectable, and stained down the front with sweat and blood, and whatever Colm had been eating for all this time.

"Welcome, guests," Colm said, leaning forward onto at stone pillar that had once supported the tabletop. "Simon, come here and sit with me. The rest of you can stay where you are." His voice had a weariness to it that the other Colms had not, but the same excitement was there, and a hint of something else... Desperation?

"If you don't mind," I said politely, taking a stone chair some feet from him, "I'd like for my friends to join us."

"They are nothing," he said dismissively. "You and *I* must speak. Come closer, Simon. I'm an old man. Eyes and ears are not what they once were."

I moved one seat nearer to him but kept a couple empty ones between us; he was creeping me out pretty bad by then. Was that red stuff on his shirt really blood?

"Ah," he said, following my gaze. "Yes. I've been meaning to change this shirt for several years now...I keep forgetting..." He glanced to the side as if thinking, and his eyes stayed there, staring into space.

I cleared my throat, and his eyes snapped back to me. "Ah!" he gasped, rising halfway to his feet. "Simon! You've come at last." He furrowed his brow as if struggling to remember. "Have you, eh...been here long?"

"No. I just arrived."

"Oh, good. It's just that sometimes..." He glanced to the side again, looking for a word, but before he could glaze over again I cleared my throat.

"I have some things to ask you," I said.

"Yes, yes," he said eagerly. "But first tell me...what brought you here?"

"Rellik told me to find you," I said.

"Did he?" Colm's face broke into a mischievous grin, and he slapped his thigh with a laugh. "Sent you himself, eh? The old devil. How is he these days?" As soon as the words were out of his mouth, Colm frowned at them. He dug a knuckle into his forehead and grumbled to himself. "No, no. Dead, isn't he...? Long dead now...with the rest of them. He left you some sort of a message, I suppose."

"Sir," I said hesitantly, "what I've really come to talk

with you about are the bloodstones. Rellik said you would know where Ro—"

"AAAHHHH!" Colm cried, drawing the sound out as if my words had pained him. One hand went to the side of his head. "Not yet. Not yet! Do not speak of it yet. Sit a while. Talk. It's been such a long time since I've had a real conversation."

I folded my arms, feeling uneasy. The thought of idle chitchat with a madman hardly seemed like a good idea.

"I have the knowledge that you seek," Colm assured me, pointing to his head. "Right in here. Talk with me a while, and I will give it to you." He glanced up at the open sky above us, and his face went blank again.

I cleared my throat, and he started. "Fine," I said. If I had to play some stupid game to get the answers I needed, I could do it.

"Ahh," he said, relaxing. "Good. Now, what shall we talk about?"

As it turns out, we talked about pretty much everything. That is, I talked, and he listened. The more I talked, the saner Colm seemed to become. After a while his attention no longer wandered. He no longer forgot what was going on. After two hours, the crazed look left his eyes, and his mouth relaxed into a calm smile. From time to time he would ask me a question, but if I ever tried to press him for information about Rone, he became distraught again, so I stopped trying. I told him of my childhood instead, of discovering that I was a wizard, and the Fayter. I told him about Daru and the Tike, and my friends and teachers at Skelligard.

As I talked, day turned into night, and soon the stars were visible above our heads, shining through the broken roof. At dawn, when the birds began to warn of an impending sunrise, we switched to jokes and riddles. He told me many that I did not understand, and in the end I got him laughing with some Chuck Norris jokes (after I had explained who Chuck Norris was, of course).

"Giraffes were invented when Chuck Norris uppercutted a horse," I said, after explaining what giraffes were. The morning was moving on toward midday, and still we had not discussed what I had come for. On the other end of the room, Drake and Tessa were huddled against the wall, sleeping. Bast was sitting erect, as if attentive, but his head hung down, and he had been drooling for over an hour. Only Hawk and the Tike were still watching us. Hawk sat at the other end of the table, fingering his ward ring. The Tike stood with her arms folded behind her back, in the exact place where I had left her hours before.

Colm was laughing so hard that his eyes began to water, and he dabbed at them with the corner of his shirt.

"Ah, satire," he said. "Simon, it has been a hundred years or more since I laughed." He closed his eyes and breathed the morning air deeply, as if trying to memorize the moment. "Thank you for that." Then he straightened in his chair. "Very well. I have kept you long enough— and for reasons you cannot yet understand. I will answer your questions now. It is inevitable, I suppose, and better for both of us to have it over with. Rellik was right to send you to me. I knew him well, and I know his brother better. I will tell you all that you wish to know about the bloodstones and…" He hesitated. "And about…*Rone.*"

When he spoke the name, his voice changed, dropping a whole octave and splitting into several voices, like ten men speaking at once. His fists clenched before him. A small gold medallion swung free from where it had been hidden in his shirt, and the weight of it seemed to bend him over. His eyes rolled up into his head, and when he opened them again, they were pure white and shining with an eerie glare. "Simon," he said in the voice that was many voices, "I have been waiting for you."

I leaped to my feet. Across the room, Hawk snapped upright, and the Tike sprang toward me, but neither were fast enough. With a swift motion, Colm brought a small metal sphere out from beneath his shirt and smashed it on the stone before him. The sphere collapsed and exploded.

Rather, it *seemed* like an explosion. In truth, it released a magical energy field—a translucent yellow dome that spread outward from the broken sphere until it covered Colm and myself. It stopped before it reached the Tike, and she bounced off the outside edge of it like a fly off a windowpane. She beat at it with her fists and was about to charge it again before Hawk grabbed her from behind.

"Stop," he said. "It is impenetrable."

Inside the energy field, Colm slumped to the floor.

Slowly, he struggled to his feet, then eased himself back into his chair. His eyes were normal once more, and his voice was his own.

"I'm terribly sorry about that, Simon. The name was the trigger, you see. It is Rone, of course, who has imprisoned me here for so long, forcing me to live beyond my years, unable to die. He possesses me, you see." He spat the last words out with utter contempt, fingering the medallion. Then, looking up to find my face, he softened. "It was all a trap, Simon. A trap in which to snare you, and now it has sprung."

He glanced down, indicating the metal sphere. The golden field flowed out of it, wrapping around the sphere itself before spreading upward like a mushroom cloud and descending again to the floor in front of the others. "This is a Gothgal siphon. A *soultrap*, some call it." He spoke the word with distaste. "It is an evil thing. A dark magic from long ago." He looked away, avoiding the sight of it. "I have been forced to carry it these long years, waiting for the day that you should come. He always knew you would come. I don't know how."

"How do I get out of it?" I said, eyeing the glimmering yellow dome.

"You don't," he said. "As you see, the generator is now encased inside the shield." He indicated the sphere. "The shield itself is powered by the most potent of all energies, and it has no weakness. Nothing can breach it, and it will never die. A soultrap is a Frathanoid object, just like a codex, and it can be altered or destroyed only by the person who created it."

"Rone," I said.

He nodded sadly.

I walked to the edge of the dome thoughtfully. I could see right through it to freedom. It was so close. I positioned myself sideways, then reached inside the turncoat and flipped D5 (*Sidestep*).

Rather than vanishing and reappearing on the other side of the dome, as I had hoped, I vanished and reappeared in almost exactly the same spot. I groaned, rubbing the back of my head; it felt as if I had run headlong into a brick wall.

"Ahh," Colm sighed. "This is, of course, not how I would have liked things to turn out, but as you will soon see, I had little choice."

"How long do we have?" Hawk said. His voice came through the soultrap clearly.

"Before Rone gets here?" Colm said. "An hour. Maybe two. He can travel quickly when he needs to."

I lifted my watch, pressed a couple buttons, and started a stopwatch. "Okay, then," I said. "If he is going to kill me, I might as well get what I came for first. I need to know what Rellik wanted me to know. Tell me about Rone."

A TALE OF TWO BROTHERS

Those who cannot remember the past are
condemned to repeat it.

—George Santayana[164]

F irst let me put your mind to rest on one matter," Colm said. "Rone is not going to kill you. Not yet, anyway. He needs you alive."

"Why?"

Colm sighed, rising to his feet. "It is a long story," he said. "One that is now remembered by none but Rone himself—and me, I suppose." He paced around the edge of the dome as he talked.

"Our story begins before the power of wizards was broken, in the time when wizards used all six branches of magic. This is not now remembered by the world, but it is true. There was a wizard in those days named Rok, and he was a man of peculiar skill and daring. His only son, Ronan, died, leaving him two young grandsons to raise—Rellik and Rone. But I am getting ahead of myself. Our story begins before they were born…

---

[164] A Spanish-born American writer who is remembered mostly for clever sayings like this one.

"When Rok was young and wild, he roamed the universe, looking for adventure. His travels took him to places few people ever find; among them, the planet Zoharadon. Do you know it?"

I nodded. "The home of the Zohar."

"Yes. The Zohar are not, as some believe, gods. Yet their power far outstrips that held by wizards, and their relationship with magic goes beyond our comprehension. They are one of the high races, the other two being the Ginn—which are now extinct—and the Atar, or dragons, which are nearly so."

I shifted. He didn't know it, but I had one of those nearly extinct dragons living in my boot.

"When Rok visited the Zohar, he had an adventure most strange—and fortunate—in which he ended up saving one of the Zohar king's own children from a fate worse than death. That, I am afraid, is a tale of which I do not know enough about to tell properly. Suffice it to say, the Zohar king was indebted to Rok. Never before had he seen such wisdom and kindness among wizardkind, and never before had he felt such hope for our race. So it was that the king of the Zohar gave Rok a mighty gift—a stone like clear glass, the color of blood. 'With this stone,' the king said, 'you may touch the fabric of life itself. You may see the inner workings of magic and bend them to your will. You may change the past, alter the present, or craft the future to your liking. This we bestow upon you, for it has long been our desire to lay great power upon one of your race and watch him change the fate of wizardkind.'"

Colm paused, scratching his beard. "You see, back then the Zohar were very concerned about us. When we used all six branches of magic, we were far more powerful than we are today, and with that power we did…strange things. Horrible things, sometimes. Wizards were not all wise and well behaved, and the Zohar foresaw our eventual self-destruction. Upon meeting a special member of our race, I suppose they wanted to make a savior out of him." He smiled weakly, as if at a joke that no one else understood. "Ah, well. Even the best laid plans go awry."

"What did Rok do with the stone?" I said. "And did you say there was just one of them? One bloodstone?"

"Oh, yes," Colm said. "When the Zohar gave it to him, the bloodstone was in one piece. Rok knew exactly what he wanted to do the moment he received it. He channeled the six magics through the stone and saw into eternity. He stood in the midst of all truth. He saw the flows of the six branches of wizarding magic, and he reached out and rewove them."

Colm reached his own hand out, grabbing the air and looking far off. "Thereafter, all wizarding power flowed through the Zohar, and what access we had to it was predicated upon our obedience to the moral codes that we submit to them. Rok wanted to bind our power so that it flowed only for the righteous. You're familiar with this idea, of course."

I nodded. "The story I heard was much less complicated, though."

Colm laughed. "Indeed. None now remember the true

story of Rok. The origins of wizarding relations with the Zohar have passed into legend." He grunted, rubbing his head. "Where was I? Ah, yes…"

"For a while, all was well. Wizardkind prospered under their newfound moral integrity, and if it was forced upon them, well, they needed it. Rok told no one about the bloodstone. He kept its existence secret, maintaining that the Zohar had wrought this mighty change upon the wizards themselves, and he was just the messenger. He feared—quite wisely—that if others learned the truth, they would seek to use the stone for evil. The first people to learn of its existence were his two grandsons. And that, I'm afraid, was the undoing of our race."

Colm finished pacing and returned to his seat. He seemed to be pondering how best to tell the rest of the story.

"Rok's grandsons were powerful wizards. More powerful than the world has seen before or since—until you, I mean. Rellik, the elder, had a gentle disposition. He cared for people, and his talents lay in healing and in harnessing the powers of nature. Rone, the younger child, had a mind of surpassing brilliance. His talents lay in great mental feats: the moving of objects with his mind, mind-to-mind communication across great distances, the fabrication of grand mental delusions in the minds of others, and even the control and domination of another's mind. He was filled with ambition, and no accomplishment could satisfy him.

"When Rok had grown old enough to face death,

he gathered his grandsons to his side, showed them the bloodstone, and told them of what he had done to the wizarding race. Immediately Rone saw in the bloodstone an answer to his insatiable lust for power—an opportunity to influence all mankind at once, and he took it.[165]

"Rone did not know how to use the bloodstone himself, but he used his formidable power to infiltrate his grandfather's mind. There, on his deathbed, Rok became a slave to his own grandson. He was forced to activate the bloodstone. Then Rone, sharing in the flow of power and knowledge that his grandfather experienced, forced Rok to break the magical abilities of wizards everywhere. He laid on them a curse, so that when they came of age and the six branches of magic began to flow through them, they would go mad and come under his control,[166] or, with the assistance of other wizards—such as with the use of celestial lamben or Thorlak poison—they would break, giving up their true power and retaining access to only *one* of the six branches of magic.

---

[165] I know what you're thinking…If Rok knew what a bad egg Rone was, why did he tell him about the bloodstone in the first place? Good question. I suppose the first answer is that Rok, like any man faced with the end of life, may have been possessed with the common human pride which seeks to be understood. It may have been important for him to let his grandsons know who he truly was and what he had done, regardless of the consequences of sharing that information. The other answer is that people are often stupid about their kids. Better said, in incredible displays of optimism unique to their kind, parents will overlook flaws in their children which are obvious to others and afford them opportunities and privileges which no one else would. Alternatively, Rok might have been an imbecilic wacky-loon.

[166] He's talking about shades, of course.

"Rone sought to break all wizards everywhere, leaving only himself with the ability to touch all six branches of magic. In this way, he thought, he would finally be more powerful than everyone, and he would be free to rule the world as he saw fit. But in a last, small act of rebellion, Rok broke Rone's hold over his mind at the last moment, changing the spell: He made *Rone's* power break along with everyone else, and left only Rellik able to touch the six branches.

"Then, fearing that his younger grandson would manipulate Rellik as he himself had been manipulated, Rok broke the bloodstone and scattered the pieces to the farthest corners of the universe. That act of defiance saved the world, but it killed Rok…" Colm stared at his withered hands, rolling them over in the light.

"It is a terrible thing to be possessed by Rone, to be controlled by him. I should know. He is always at least peripherally aware of your thoughts, and when he wishes, he can make you do whatever he pleases. He can make you lie to your friends or lose your mind slowly in a deserted castle. To defy him like Rok did takes power well beyond the reach of most. I, who have been under Rone's power now for the better part of an age, have never so much as managed a single private thought. How Rok achieved what he did, I cannot fathom.

"After that, of course, Rellik and Rone spent the rest of their lives searching for the bloodstones. Rone sought to reunite them. When he broke, he became what we now call a Bright, and he retained the bulk of his strongest magical abilities, including remarkable powers of illusion and his capacity to possess and control the minds of others. He sought the bloodstones in the hopes that when he reunited them, he could force his brother to restore him to his full power. Rellik sought them simply to ensure that his brother could not succeed. He became famous among the people. A *Fayter* they called him, because he alone could wield the six branches of magic, and in him some had hope for the future, hope that through him, their fate could be changed."

Colm paused, looking beyond me. I turned and saw the others all gathered at the edge of the soultrap, listening intently. Colm frowned. "I did not intend to reveal so much to so many at once. Though I suppose I have now outlived my usefulness to Rone, which will make one less in this world who knows these things. Perhaps it's better this way…"

"Please," I said. "What happened after that? Did Rellik find the bloodstones like the history books say?"

Colm nodded grimly. "He did."

"Then why isn't everything better?" I said. "Why are wizards still broken? Why is Rone still alive? How did Rone ever get the better of Rellik if Rellik could still use all six branches of magic?"

Colm smiled weakly, raising his hands. "I don't know. I do not fully understand what Rellik saw when he activated the bloodstones, but for whatever reason, he was unable to reverse the previous actions of his brother. He could not fix the past—or if he could, he was not willing to. He told me once, long after, that he was unwilling to pay the price.

"At any rate, when he looked into the future, he saw only that Rone would eventually succeed in controlling him and gaining the power of the bloodstones. So, rather than allowing Rone to manipulate him, Rellik used the power of the bloodstones to break himself, thereby cutting off Rone's only access to them—for only a wizard touching all six branches of magic could activate the bloodstone—but before he did, he erased from the minds of all wizards the memory of their former power. He spared only himself, and Rone, and the other members of the Circle of Eight, including myself, of course.

"Thereafter, wizardkind, which had been suffering under the pain of loss and the terrible memory of their former glory, became blissfully ignorant. They had the sudden feeling of being healed, spared from some great horror—the Great Plague, they called it afterward, though they did not remember what it truly was. They said that Rellik had healed them and taken away even the memory of their pain, and in a way, they were right; he had spared them their pain, but at a terrible price: ignorance of their true nature."

Colm stopped his story again and looked up at me, studying my face for a long moment. "Of course," he said, "I have not told you of the last thing he saw when he held the bloodstone. He looked into the future and saw the birth of another who would be able to wield it. One who, be it by the blessing of the Zohar, or because of some heritage even more powerful, would be born with the capacity to touch all six branches of magic. Another Fayter—a wizard who, living amid a world of broken wizards, remains himself, *unbroken.*

"He saw *you*, Simon. He hid some of the bloodstones in places only you could find." He glanced up at me then, his face pale with fear. In his eyes, an ancient weariness gave way to a glimmer of new hope. "He saw that you would unite the bloodstones and do what he could not. He saw that you would stop Rone, once and for all, and heal the wizard race."[167]

---

[167] No pressure.

THE TOMB OF RONE

Faith, like a jackal, feeds among the tombs, and even from these dead doubts she gathers her most vital hope.
—Herman Melville[168]

S imon?"

"Simon?" the Tike called. "Are you okay?"

"I think he passed out," Tessa said, worried.

"I did *not* pass out," I lied, picking my head up gingerly from the table. "I was just resting."

"I imagine it is a lot to take in," Colm said, his voice gentle. He turned to the others. "You should leave now, while you still can. Simon and I may be stuck here, but you can get away before Rone arrives."

"We will not leave him," the Tike said.

"Aye," Captain Bast said. "We would no' get very far anyway."

"There is a ship," Colm said. "The very ship that I arrived here on, so many years ago. It sits in the wooden

---

[168] A rather brilliant American writer whose work didn't catch on until after he died. Poor guy. These days nearly everyone knows who he is, or has at least heard of his most famous book. You know…that one about the white whale?

barn just outside. You must have seen it on your way in. It has been of little use to me, but you should be able to use it without a problem."

Captain Bast looked questioningly at the others.

"Take the ship, Bast," Hawk said. "Take Drake and Tessa to safety. I must remain here with Simon, and I expect the Tike will not be moved."

"Hey, wait just a second," Drake stammered. "I won't be moved, either! I'm staying."

"Everyone just calm down," I said, glancing at my watch. Colm had been talking for nearly thirty minutes, but that meant we still had a little time. As Colm had been talking, I had been racking my brain for a way out (whilst listening carefully, of course). "Don't leave just yet. I might have a way out."

"What?" Hawk said. "How?"

"What are you talking about, Simon?" Tessa demanded.

"Hold your horses," I said, returning my attention to Colm. "I still haven't asked you the question I came to ask you. It's about the location of one of those bloodstones Rellik hid for me to find."

"Oh?" Colm said, surprised. "What do you want to know?"

"What is the last place that Rone would think to look?" I asked.

"I beg your pardon?"

"That's what Rellik told me to ask you. The last place Rone would ever think to look."

"Well," he said, scratching his beard, "that's not much to go on, is it?" He closed his eyes. "Let me think on it a moment."

We were all silent, watching him impatiently.

"Take yer time," Bast mumbled, but Colm seemed not to hear him.

Finally, Colm opened his eyes. "Once, during the years when he and Rellik were hunting the bloodstones, Rone faked his own death in an attempt to fool his brother into lowering his guard. He went so far as to throw a fake funeral for himself and seal an empty tomb. That is when history marks the death of Rone and the birth of the Jackal. Though, of course, he lived on, and they are one and the same. If I were to pick one place that Rone would never look for a bloodstone—other than under his own pillow—it would be inside that tomb. After all, Rone built it himself, and he knew it was empty. Rone takes great pride in his deceptions and would not expect one to be turned against him."

I nodded. "That's where I'll look, then. Where is this tomb?"

"On Cathagorous, of course. The burial planet. It's not far from here, actually."

"How can ye possibly know tha'?" Bast demanded. "Dark Haven ne'er be appearin' in the same place twice."

"Ah," Colm held up a finger. "To one seeking it, Dark Haven can never be found in the same place twice, but whenever one departs from it, one finds themselves traveling through the Aladna system, in the third seal."

"Yer kiddin'!" Bast said. "But then, Cathagorous be right 'round the corner, if tha' ship o' yours can move with any speed at all."

"Then you had better be going," Colm said. "Rone will be aware of all that I have told you, including my guess about the location of the bloodstone. He will no doubt go to his tomb as soon as he has come here."

"Oh, I think he'll be going to his tomb first," I said. "When he realizes that I'm not trapped here anymore."

I turned D1 (*Copy*), then reached out and touched the soultrap. As soon as I touched it, the metal sphere became three metal spheres, sitting about six inches apart from one another. The now *three* domes of invincible energy crackled and sparked at several points of intersection, and as I had hoped, the intersecting fields began to tear themselves apart.[169] Then, with a great whooshing sound, they vanished.

"I don't believe it," Colm said.

"Wahoo!" Drake cried. "You're a genius!"

"Brilliant, Simon," Hawk proclaimed, clapping me on the back happily.

"Well," I said, brushing some imaginary dirt off my sleeve casually, "I'm not a magic *expert*, but I get lucky now and then."

"Now get out of here!" Colm said. "All of you! Run, and do not look back!"

The others did not need telling twice. The three adults

---

[169] Basic hero principle: when fighting an invincible force, simply turn it upon itself.

ran to retrieve their weapons, and Drake and Tessa were right behind them. Still, I lingered, watching the tattered old man who had already suffered a worse fate than I could have imagined. Knowing what he had been through, how Rone had imprisoned him in his own mind and forced him to do his will, I could hardly blame him for luring me into a trap. After all, he didn't have a choice.

"Will he kill you?" I asked.

Colm scratched his beard thoughtfully. "If I am lucky."

He smiled at my look of confusion. "I have lived a long time against my will. To me, death would be a great mercy, and Rone is not in the business of dealing out mercy."

"If he keeps you trapped here," I said, "I'll come back and free you somehow."

"That's a very kind offer," Colm said. He gave me a long, measuring look. "Now, run."

Before I could follow his advice, something scratched my leg and I looked down to see Leto scampering up it. He climbed onto my shoulder so that he was eye to eye with Colm, and the old man let out a silent breath. "Good gracious," he whispered hoarsely. "Your Eminence, it is an honor to—"

"Hush, my friend," Leto said gently, and Colm froze. "Pay no heed to guilt or regret. Yours was the worst part to play, but you have endured it well. Your journey is almost over."

Leto leaned out then and wiped a bit of something out of Colm's beard. Food, maybe, or drool. Colm held the tiny dragon's gaze for a long moment, then seemed to relax, the last of his worries slipping free of his clear eyes. When he turned away from us and walked back the way he had come, there was, I thought, a little bounce in the old man's[170] step.

Leaving the island was far easier than arriving had been. We found Colm's rattle-staff by the front gate, and I twirled it as we ran past the Yap rabbits. We arrived at the tall wooden structure we'd passed on our way in, but the doors were rusted shut. Tessa broke them down in a

---

[170] Provided we live long enough, we all eventually grow old. Our backs bow and our skin sags and wrinkles and heals less and less quickly. Our eyes dim and our ears grow ever larger. Our hair turns white, perhaps, or falls out. Our bendy parts cease to bend, and our unbendy parts begin to. We can no longer reach our toenails, so they grow and grow, and we watch them, powerless. When we grow old, we often become much like we were when we were very young: We talk to ourselves. We laugh or cry more often than others and feel a sense of wonder toward life. We pass gas in public loudly and without apology. The people who care for us, who pick us up and lay us down, feel...what? Love? Fear? Happiness? Disgust? And who are they? Are they our own kin, playing out life's last great legacy in returning to us what we once gave to them, or are they strangers? Do they do it because it is their job, their career? We take care of our children, and hopefully someday, should we need it, they will take care of us. Hopefully we will not end up like Colm, imprisoned on an island, forgotten by the world, alone with the varied creatures of an abandoned mind. Hopefully when we meet the Colms of the world, we will visit their islands and sit with them and bring a sense of fellowship to the lingering hours, and wipe the drool from their chins, and listen to their gibberish with a patient ear and a ready smile, as they once, long ago, listened to ours.

hurry. Sometimes it's really nice to have a strong woman in your life.

As Colm had said, the ship was still in working order, and since it was powered by light and gravity as most spacesail ships are, it was ready to go the minute we pulled it out of the barn and scared away all the rats and bugs that had taken up residence in it.

"All aboard," Bast said, and soon we were in the air. It was a bit cramped—I may or may not have had to sit on Drake's lap. Tessa, of course, had to have her own spot, but no one seemed to mind much. We sailed over the beach that we had spent all of yesterday walking across and attempted to locate the goblins.

They were nowhere to be found.

"Don' worry, lad," Bast said. "I told Hobnob an' Noblob ter get off the island if we weren't back in a day, remember? They likely left two or three hours hence. They'll be fine, mind you. There do be major trade routes nearby, an' those goblins be knowin' how ter handle a ship. Why, they're probably already on their way back to Skelligard."

"Well," Hawk said, peering over the side of the ship as we rose into the sky, "I guess that just leaves Ioden."

"Ack!" I said. "I forgot about him. Hawk, I didn't know you saw him arrive."

"What are you talking about?" Drake asked.

"Ioden is down there somewhere," Hawk said. "Simon somehow summoned him here earlier, straight out of his bathroom and into a pack of angry Yap rabbits."

Drake burst out laughing and Hawk stifled a grin.

"Poor soul," Bast said, scanning the ground for signs of life. "Where should we be lookin' fer 'im?"

"Oh, I doubt we could find him even if we tried," Hawk said genially. "If I know Ioden, he'll be hiding from those Yap rabbits for days. No matter. We can always send someone to collect him later. Onward and upward! I, for one, would prefer to arrive at Cathagorous before Rone does."

It didn't take long to get there, which was good, not only because we were racing against the clock to plunder an evil wizard's tomb before he had time to arrive and murder us all, but also because I was getting really hungry.[171]

The burial planet, as Colm had called it, was just what it sounds like—a large, dour-looking planet with no live residents. The whole face of the gray world was covered with hills and valleys full of tombs, crypts, monuments, mausoleums, catacombs, sepulchers, tombstones, headstones, and every other thing you've ever seen in a graveyard. Except grass...nothing grew naturally in the

---

[171] Think about it. When is the last time you remember me eating? That's right, on the beach. But how long ago was that? A day? And just think of all the running, river frolicking, bunny fighting, etc. that I've done since then. This is a common problem in books. Some of the more successful authors provide between-the-scenes snack breaks for their characters. But, this being an autobiography and all, we don't get those kind of benefits.

place except for a seaweed-green groundcover called space moss. At first, as we neared the planet's surface and Bast began to soar over the endless rows of graves, it felt, well, *grave*. After a while, though, I detected a certain peace about the place—a peace which was enhanced by the presence of millions of flowers, wreaths, pictures, and tiny, ever-burning flames.

My stomach growled loudly. "Are we almost there?" I said.

"Almost," Hawk said. "It's been a long time, but I think it's just up ahead. Though, I doubt there will be a breakfast buffet..."

"Do you want some Yap rabbit fur?" Drake asked, pulling a wad out of his pocket and munching on it. "It's pretty good."[172]

"Pass," I said. "But if you don't need those bandages on your legs anymore, I'd like my pants back now."

"You don't want to wear your man bloomers while we go grave robbing?" Tessa said.

"They're called *boxers*," I snapped. "And no. Bushwacking, rabbit-fighting, and nighttime riddles with Colm were bad enough, but I definitely draw the line at graverobbery[173] in my underwear."

"You sure you want them?" Drake said, unwrapping his legs. "They're kind of dirty."

In fact, my jeans were covered in Yap rabbit fur, sand,

---

[172] Drake looked for all the world like a kid trying cotton candy for the first time. Minotaurs...

[173] Not a word.

space-shark saliva, and a good amount of Drake's blood. Worse, they were torn in half right up the you-know-what. I grimaced. "It's still better than nothing. Plus, I have an idea about how to put them back together. Tike, lend me one of your knives."

In under a minute, I was in business. Connecting the front of the pants wasn't a problem; thankfully they tore apart at the zipper, so I just had to zip them back together. The, er, *bum* area posed more of a challenge, but I used the Tike's knife to cut several thin horizontal ribbons into the rear pockets. Then I put them on and tied the ribbons together in the back. Or at least, I tried to.

"Do you want some help with that, champ?" Tessa said, reaching for my backside as I fumbled awkwardly with my bumties. Her voice dripped with evilgirlishness.[174]

"Don't touch me!" I said. "I can do it myself. Uh… Drake, can you help a fella out?"

When I had finally donned my pants, Hawk declared that the tomb of Rone was in sight. "I see it!" Drake declared, stepping on tiptoes to get a better view. The ship spun around and landed smoothly, and we disembarked.

The tomb of Rone was a low, simplistic structure of white marble. His name was etched boldly into the top face, while the front was covered in a carving of the man himself, pictured as an elderly figure with a bald head and a long, flowing beard that fanned out beneath him gracefully. The whole thing was overgrown with space moss; it had clearly been here a long time.

---

[174] Not a word, but definitely a real thing.

"How do we open it?" I said lamely.

"I think the lid just lifts off," Tessa replied, throwing her weight against one corner. It budged. "You guys get that side."

Hawk, Bast, the Tike, and I all lifted one side while Tessa got the other. Tessa's side lifted slightly, but ours wouldn't budge.

"Hey, Drake," I said. "You look awesome, standing there doing nothing, but could you give us a hand?"

"Right," he said. He gave his kulrakalakia a lick for luck and then joined us, and we just managed to lift the lid free of the bottom and slide it off. Tessa gave a little show-offy heave right at the end, and the lid tipped unexpectedly. It landed with a deep thump on the ground.

"AHHHHHH, ME TOES!" Bast screamed, hopping on one foot.

"Oh my goodness," Tessa said. "I'm so sorry, Captain Bast!"

"Ha! Only jokin'."

"Quiet, you two," the Tike said. "This is no time for jokes."

"Sorry," Bast said. "Just tryin' ter lighten the mood. Blimey. Goes down an awful long ways, don' it..."

Inside the tomb was a set of very narrow, very steep steps that led almost straight down.

"After you," Tessa told me, smiling politely.

"Ladies first," I said.

"I'll go," the Tike said, and she vaulted over the side of the tomb to land lightly on the steps.

"Oy!" Bast said. "Careful there. Fall now an' we'd have ter carry ye back up in a bucket..."

"Here," Hawk said, and summoned out of thin air what looked like a handful of fire jelly. It gave off a surprising amount of light and was apparently cool to the touch. He laid it in her palm, and she thanked him.

"Hey," I said, "I want some."

"Come on, Simon," the Tike chided, and she began to descend.

I followed the Tike, and the others came after, with Bast bringing up the rear. As we descended, I could hear him grumbling about railings, heights, and other "land problems best lef' alone by sailors."

When we reached the bottom, Hawk made more fire jelly and handed some to each of us. The space before us was surprisingly vast and—unsurprisingly—empty. The air was cold and stale. The floor was dirt, as was the ceiling, which stretched far above our heads in the middle of the room and curved down toward the edges.

"I can't see the end of the room," Bast said.

"Fan out," I said. "See what you can find."

It wasn't long before there were nervous calls coming from several corners of the room.

"Ahh, no!"

"What the?"

"Hawk, there are bloodhound statues over here. Stacks of them." That was the Tike.

"Here, too," Drake called. "Rows and rows."

"There must be hundreds!" Bast said. "Thousands!"

I ran in Drake's direction and saw what they were talking about. Around the edges of the room, lining the low outer walls, were row upon row of miniature bloodhound statues like the one that was sent to me at Skelligard, all stacked together neatly.

"We should go," Drake said. "This is beginning to feel like a trap."

"Agreed," Hawk said.

"What about the bloodstone?" I objected. "We haven't searched everywhere yet."

"Guys!" Tessa's voice issued excitedly from somewhere near the center of the room. "I've got something."

We converged on her in seconds, and I saw that she was holding a metal box; it was the approximate size and shape of a shoebox. My name was scratched into the top of it.

"That's it!" I said. "Let me see it." I tugged on the lid, but it didn't move. "It's stuck!"

"Let me see it," Hawk said. He ran his fingers over the edges of it gently, and I got the feeling he was doing something more than looking for secret buttons. In the end, he shrugged. "It appears to be just what it looks like. The lid must be rusted shut. Here, Tessa, rip it open if you can."

Tessa took it back from him with relish, dug her fingers under the lid, and pulled. The metal peeled back slowly, tearing the sides apart as it came.

"It's empty," she said.

"What? Let me see it." She was right.

Drake's shoulders drooped. "He's already been her—"

Hawk clamped a hand over Drake's mouth. "Shh. Did you hear that?"

"Hear what?" I said uneasily.

Then I *did* hear it: a low rolling noise coming out of the shadows at the far end of the room. Someone was chuckling.

"Run!" I cried, but it was too late. Something round and silver flew out of the shadows, and before it hit the ground at our feet, I knew what it was going to be.

A soultrap.

It broke on the ground between us and the pale golden shield erupted out of it, arcing in all directions before slamming back into the ground, trapping us inside.

"Not this again," Bast groaned.

The near edges of the room were visible now, illuminated by the dull light of the soultrap. All around us, the little bloodhound statues glinted red. But I had eyes only for the end of the room. There, a light shone through the darkness, an oval of gold. No, *face* of gold—a golden mask.

Rone started toward us, and the bright jackal-head mask came into clear focus. He stepped out of the shadows like a nightmare being born.

"Simon Fayter," he said, pronouncing each word carefully, "...and company."

He spread his arms wide in greeting. "Welcome."

31
THE HERO'S CHOICE

*Great heroes need great sorrows and burdens, or half their
greatness goes unnoticed. It is all part of the fairy tale.*

—Peter S. Beagle[175]

Rone's voice was soft but resonant. "Do not look so
surprised to find me in my own tomb. Do I not belong
here?"

No one spoke. Beside me, the Tike's hands tightened
on her long knives, but she did not draw them.

"Oh, that's right," he said. "I never died, did I? In that
case, did you think that I would not know you would be
coming? But I waste words..."

Rone took something small and red from the inside
pocket of his robes and held it up to show me. It was the
bloodstone. He had found it, then. He must have arrived
before we did, found the stone, and set this trap for us.

And I had led my friends right into it.

He swept around the room with an almost catlike
grace until he was face-to-face with me, the invisible

---

[175] One of the best fantasy authors of all time. He wrote *The Last
Unicorn*, from which the quote comes. Fun fact: *The Last Unicorn* is
the favorite book of *my* favorite fantasy writer.

shield between us. "Simon," he said. "It has been a long time." He cocked his head. "You look just the same as I remember. Exactly the same, in fact. Down to your socks. I don't suppose you remember me? No. You wouldn't yet."

He retreated slightly into the shadows and seemed to take in the scene before him, the six of us, beaten and weary, trapped within his tomb.

Remember him? I thought. What was he talking about?

"I was surprised, Simon, when you defeated my shade. Surprised, and yet *not* surprised. That is when I knew for sure that it was really you. Of course, I've seen you fight monsters before, though as I said, you don't remember yet. Do you know, Simon," he went on, "it was *you* that gave me the idea for this little trap. You described it to me once, long ago."

Rone raised his right hand, and it glowed red. Instantly, the miniature bloodhounds began to glow, too. A second later, they were growing. The beasts began to move, to stretch, to change from stone into flesh, and then the room was filled with bloodhounds, hundreds of them, so crowded for space that in some places they stood one atop the next, clawing their way toward us, growling, baying, biting at the shield.

"You see it now, don't you, Simon?" Rone said, his voice rising over the commotion. "The task that I have set for you? It is not your death that I desire, but your *pain*. I need you alive, of course. I need you to find the lost bloodstones for me... So I cannot have your death, but

I can have your *anguish*. I can feast on your despair, and one day, I can own your soul."

He paused and seemed to gather himself, as if, in his fervor, he had said more than he intended. "I will be leaving in a moment, Simon. When I am gone, the shield will fall. Then, I'm afraid, you will be in a great deal of danger." As if reacting to his words, a bloodhound leaped past him and thrashed at the shield between us. Its movements were frenzied, its eyes empty pits, like tiny windows into death itself. I felt sure that this one hound alone was enough to finish me off, and yet there were hundreds. More and more seemed to be pressing in on the crowd, so that now whole walls of dogs were rising up the sides of the domed shield, rolling against one another, clawing at each other in a frenzied attempt to reach us.

Rone bent down and grabbed the bloodhound that had come between us, throwing it roughly to the side. "But then," he said, "your life isn't really the one in danger here, is it, Simon? You can escape any time you please. You can reach inside your turncoat and flip your little switch and be gone. Gone to someplace safe—safer than this, anyway."

He crept back to the edge of the shield, leaning in so close I could almost make out dim shapes within the black pits of the mask's eyes.

"But how many of your little friends can you take with you?" he whispered, then he threw back his head and laughed. "Four! Yes, I know the number. Do not be surprised. Five including yourself, but that means four friends. *Four* you can save, yet five surround you."

I spun to face my friends, counting them again, though I knew already that he was right.

"Which one?" Rone sang.

"Which one?" he whispered.

"Which one will you leave to die?"

He laughed then—a strange, twisted sound that built and rose and echoed around us like a demented song. Then he backed slowly toward the stairs and was gone.

I spun around, grabbing the Tike's shoulders, shaking her. On her neck, the red bird, the Rimbakka, flew in tight, frantic circles. "Can we fight them?" I demanded. "Can we beat them?" I didn't wait for a response. Hawk was next. I seized the hem of his robe, pulling his face down to meet mine. "Can we defeat the bloodhounds?"

But I could see the answer in their faces. Six was no match for hundreds.

"They will overwhelm us," Hawk said.

"It will not take long," the Tike added, almost peacefully. "A few seconds, and it will be over."

Captain Bast began to laugh. Not as Rone had done; it was the dark, bitter laughter of a man who was seeing his own grave. "Leave me, lad," he said, meeting my eye. "I've lived me life. Me ship do be gone, me crew disbanded, me family—" He choked off, eyes brimming with tears.

"No," Hawk said. "You must leave *me*, Simon. I am your teacher. It is my right. You must listen to me in this."

"You already have my life," the Tike said, pushing Hawk aside. "Keep your teacher and let me keep my oaths."

"Stop!" Tessa cried, clutching at my arm. "Don't make him choose! That's what Rone wants. We can beat them, Simon. We can fight!"

I looked at Drake. His face was pale and drawn, but his eyes held the truth that I had already sensed.

We couldn't fight.

I had to choose.

"No," I said. "I won't do it."

Hawk gripped my shoulder. "You must."

"Quickly, Simon!" the Tike said. The roof of the dome cracked, and a small hole opened at the center. A bloodhound scrambled through it and fell toward us, shrieking in triumph. Bast caught it in the chest with his saber, spinning it to the ground. It should have been dead, but still it writhed and fought.

"Now, Simon," Hawk said sternly. He grabbed my arms, forcing my hand inside my jacket. Then he pushed me away roughly. "Leave me and be gone with them. I may make it yet."

The shield opened wider, and two more bloodhounds dropped through. Hawk flicked his wrist, and Kestra burst out of the air, striking the closest hound like an arrow. The other landed on its feet and began to circle us.

"It's okay, Simon," Tessa said. She was crying now. "Come on. Let's go."

"No," I said, shaking her off. I stepped back from my friends. "I can't do it. I won't. I need…I need more time."

I looked at my watch. It read 11:59:45. In fifteen seconds, the turncoat powers would reset. Fifteen seconds.

Fifteen seconds in *this* time. Time. I needed more *time*.

I reached inside the turncoat.

"What are you doing?" Tessa cried.

"I'll be back," I said. "When I have a way to save you all, I'll be back."

"NO!" Drake cried. He grabbed Tessa's arm and lunged for me, reaching out. In fact, his fingers just managed to brush the sleeve of the turncoat. But before he could take hold of me, I turned E6 (*Travel*) and was gone.

I imagine that was not the ending you predicted. Perhaps you expected us to fight the bloodhounds. Perhaps you expected me to let Hawk die, or Bast, or the Tike.[177]

But the truth was, I wasn't ready to make that decision. I was young still, and I thought I could run away from hard things. I didn't yet understand that when you run, it only gets worse.

I suppose that if I hadn't had a way out, I would have come to a decision then and there. But I *did* have a way out. I had a whole other world. No doubt, a whole other *mission* to fulfill. Not only that, because of my experiment with Drake, I was certain that I could spend as much time in the past as I needed, working out my problem, coming to a choice. Then, when I was good and ready, I could

---

[176] The epilogue is much like its cousins, the EpiPen and the epiglottis, in that while nobody likes looking at it, its existence is often imperative.

[177] It's a shame Montroth wasn't with us instead. I think I could have brought myself to sacrifice him to a thousand bloodthirsty demon-dogs. It would have been hard(ish), but for the greater good, I could have done it.

return to Rone's tomb, grab the ones I was going to save, wait five seconds for the turncoat to reset, then turn E6 again and take them to safety.

All in all, it was a perfect plan. Except for one thing: I was doing it alone.

If I had been smarter, I would have realized that Rone was wrong. I wasn't alone in making my decision. I could have taken all but one of my companions with me to Tarinea, and they could have helped me there. Then, when I was good and ready, I would have had to come back, of course. I might still have had to make the choice in the end, but at least I could have worked through the next chapter of my adventure with some support.

But I wasn't smarter.

I was a scared kid, trying to run away from his problems, and I made a mistake.

If only I had not gone alone.

If only I had taken just one of them with me, things might have been different...

AUTHOR'S APOLOGY

In the world of writing, it is extremely bad form to end a book with a cliffhanger. Scenes can end with cliffhangers, chapters can end with cliffhangers, but books should end with closure. Or, as the French would say, *denouement.*[178]

Setting aside the fact that we probably shouldn't listen to the French, the fact still stands that at the end of a book, there should be a sense of closure, of satisfaction, and yes, in the case of a series, a healthy twinge of apprehension about the future to keep you coming back for more. Novels should NOT end with all the supporting characters stuck in a deadly trap while the hero conveniently disappears to who-knows-where. (Though, if you read the book carefully you *do* know where.) That would not only subvert the whole climax of the story and destroy the main character's most important moment to grow, it also would be a sinister, and quite frankly *lazy* thing for a fiction writer to do.

---

[178] Pronounced *day-new-MAW.* The closing sequence of a narrative, in which the plot comes together and everything is resolved neatly.

I, however, am *not* a fiction writer, and this is not a novel. As I've told you many times, this is my autobiography, and these things really happened. Therefore, I need no excuses. You can't complain about history. I *did* run away right then. If you had been clever enough to find the way out, I expect you would have done the same thing.

Accepting that you cannot be mad at me over how this story ended, you may believe that you can still be angry at me for *where* it ended. After all, if I had gone on, say, for just a bit, we could have stopped at a happier, more resolved spot.

Again, you are wrong. I know my own history, and I can assure you there is no good stopping place for a long, long while. If I had continued, this book would have been six hundred pages long instead of three hundred, and you would be mad at me for writing such a long book. You'd say, "Mom, it won't fit in my backpack," and things like that. See? There's just no pleasing you.

If, against all odds, you're *still* mad at me right now, I recommend that you simply start the next book. It picks up right where this one ended. As always, you can find my books at your local library. Or if not, you can find them at your *un*local library. As a last resort, you can surely find them on the internet. Or, if vampires have finally attacked and the world as we know it has deteriorated into post-apocalyptic chaos, then you can find them wherever good books aren't sold. I would check secondhand stores, school libraries, or museums. If that doesn't work, go straight to the dump. Or the junkyard. I once saw a whole stack of my books at Al's Auto Yard, propping up half a Geo Metro.

Lastly, if you have the misfortune of reading this book just after it is released, in which case the next book isn't out yet, I suppose you'll just have to hold your horses. Don't worry—you won't have to hold them for more than a month or two, as the next one is nearly finished already.

Yours truly,

~~Simon Fayter~~ **Austin J. Bailey**

P.S. Since I titled this section "Author's Apology," my editor has pointed out that I should really apologize somewhere in here. So here goes nothing:

I'm sorry.[179]

---

[179] Not really.

THE UBER-AWESOME, SUPREMELY COOL, INCONCEIVABLY IMPLAUSIBLE[180] EMAIL CONTEST

A little nonsense now and then
Is cherished by the wisest men.

—Roald Dahl[181]

I have been accused from time to time—not often, mind you—of writing books that are, to use a naughty word,

[180] I think inconceivably implausible might be a double negative. Let's not think about that.

[181] An RAF (Royal Air Force) pilot who went on to become one of the most beloved children's authors of all time. He wrote *Matilda*, *James and the Giant Peach*, *The BFG*, *Charlie and the Chocolate Factory*, and (my personal favorite) *Danny the Champion of the World*.

boring. Obviously this accusation is preposterous.[182] Take this book for example: magic, mayhem, traps, wizards, pirates, giant man-eating bunnies... I rest my case.

However, to prove once and for all that my books are NOT boring, I have inserted this chapter as bonus content, and set up a little contest for you. I bet you didn't see *that* coming. Anyway, to win, you must solve the following equation using only this book, your parents, the internet, and anything else you want, to help you:

The Equation

Bilbo Baggins's birthday (expressed as a four-digit number—MMDD, including the zeros), MINUS Frodo Baggins's birthday (expressed as a four-digit number), PLUS Harry Potter's birthday (expressed as a six-digit number—MMDDYY), PLUS my birthday (Expressed as a six-digit number), MINUS the licks to the center of a Tootsie Pop (Expressed as a three-digit number), PLUS the answer to the meaning of life, the universe, and everything (expressed as a two-digit number), PLUS James Bond's secret-agent number backward (expressed as a three-digit number) MULTIPLIED[183] by pi to eleven decimal places (expressed as a twelve-digit number, with

---

[182] The *Preposterous* is a large, flightless bird native to South Africa.
[183] Remember, add and subtract before you multiply.

the decimal point to the right of the first digit from the left).[184]

The answer should be expressed as a seventeen-digit number, with the decimal point to the right of the sixth digit from the left, like so:

XXX,XXX.XXXXXXXXXXX

The Instructions

To win, simply be the first person to email this number to the following address: simonfayter[at]gmail[dot]com. In order to qualify, you must include in the email body the following items:

The correct answer to the equation given above.

Your favorite joke or riddle.

Your favorite part of this book (mostly to appease my ego, but also so I know you actually read something and aren't just looking for prizes).

The Prizes

The FIRST person to answer correctly will win a private jet, a castle in the south of France, and a fleet of street-legal giraffes.

---

[184] For those of you who struggle with the order of operations, math at large, or instructions in general, your equation should look like this before you solve it. In this example, X represents a number between 0 and 9 inclusive: (XXXX-XXXX+XXXXXX+XXXXXX-XXX+XX+XXX)X.XXXXXXXXXX

I'm kidding! Who do you think I am?

The FIRST person to answer correctly will win (for real now) a signed copy of this book and one hundred dollars in whatever form of legal U.S. tender I see fit to pay them in.

The SECOND person to answer correctly will win a signed copy of this book and a lifetime supply of Tootsie Pops.

The THIRD person to answer correctly will win a signed copy of this book and a gently used crayon in my favorite color.

All SUBSQUENT winners (that means all you slowpokes out there) will receive a *hand-typed* email response containing my favorite joke, written by me personally, or—in the event that I am too busy saving the world to check my email—by Austin J. Bailey.

The Conditions

To win, you must (a) be 18 years of age or older, or (b) have parental permission to enter this contest and use email. You must (3) have the ability to do basic math, find a calculator that will compute to eleven decimal places, and send an email. You must also (j) have a mailing address within the continental United States. I'm sorry, but I simply cannot afford to ship a lifetime supply of Tootsie Pops to Timbuktu. Editors, beta readers, proofreaders, family members (*my* family members), and *Xena: Warrior Princess* fans are not eligible to win.

ACKNOWLEDGEMENTS

Thank you to…

…My beta readers: Spencer Bowen, Bryonna Bowen, Spencer Bagshaw, Cameron Moore, Anjali Mathias, and Hailey Walton.

…To God.

…And to my launch team, upon whom I depend:

Patti Anderson	Riche Boyce
April Angel	Shelley Brade
Sonia Arroyos	John Chasteen
Terri Arturi	Suzanne Christensen
Candice Aucamp	Rachel Church
Katie Babbit	Amanda Comrie
Angel Barraza	Emma Curtis
Lydia Barron	Brandy Dalton
Karen Bennett	Janice David
Melanie Bessas	Bryan Deal
Jeanine Bevacqua	Brandy Emmert
John Bigelow	Charlie Evans
Bry Boler	Roger Fauble
Melissa Bonaparte	Jennifer Firestone
Rachel Bonnichsen	Sarah Flint
Randall Booth	Shannon Forslund
Alisha Bowen	Danielle Foster

Jamie Francke
Sierra Furrow
Jennifer Fury
Bradley Gartin
Kisara Gibbons
Carmen Gomez
Daniel Grala
Mike Grant
Charlene Greene
Phil Gulbrandsen
Elva Guzman
Linda Hansen
Ondreya Harper
Bruce Hastie
Sarah Heinisch
Zoe Henricksen
Christine Holmes
Shirley Holten
Claudia Howard
Jody Huffman
Geeta Indar-De Bourg
Sara Ingles
Krista Jasper
Bonnie Keck
Richard Kellerman
Manie Kilian
Barb Kubiak
Jennifer Lapachian
Tiffany Lawrence

Kenneth Loiacano
Melissa Long
Georganne Lynch
Khyla Malone
JoLynn Marcusen
Arisleny Martinez
Kimberly Matthiensen
John Maxim
Marilee McQuarrie
Julie McWilliams
Veronica Meidus-Heilpern
Joyce Michelmore
Candace Miller
Michael Minkove
Becky Modderman
Mary Moffatt
James Morrow
Cathy Mulcahey
Sarah Nicholes
Shirlee Nicol
Anna-Lena Nielsen
Debbie Nix
Krysten Noel
Anna Olsen
Daria Peterson
Eva Pontious
Isaac Reyes
Isaac Reynolds
Nicky Robinson

Angela Ross   Karen
Kari Schick
Britton Schwartz
Shelly Sessions
Crystal Shapiro
Michelle Shelton
Eileen Smith
Leena Smith
Lauren Smith
Matthew Thornton
David Thorp
Aiden Tombuelt
Cheryl Torricer
Chelsea Tracy
Lana Turner
Corinne Vizer
Chelle Wakeley
Alex Weise
Maria Wetherbee
Deidre Williams
Kelly Williams
Liz Wilson
Ron
Rebekah
Jeanine
Shari
Anna
Tanya
Robin